GIVE ME THE WEEKEND

WESTON PARKER

BRIXBAXTER PUBLISHING

Give Me The Weekend

Copyright © 2020 by Weston Parker

The novel is a work of fiction. Names, characters, places and plot are all either products of the author's imagination or used fictitiously. Any resemblance to actual events, locales, or persons – living or dead – is purely coincidental.

First Edition.

Editor: Eric Martinez
Cover Designer: Ryn Katryn Digital Art

FIND WESTON PARKER

www.westonparkerbooks.com

DEDICATION

To all of my amazing readers and especially any of you that have felt like the black sheep of the family! I think we're a special breed from time to time. Funny enough, my family has never felt that way about me. Or they're brilliant at hiding it. I hope you love this book and that you & yours are doing well during this COVID time. I'm thinking of you and grateful for you picking up a copy of my book.

Weston

CHAPTER 1

ELSIE

Pale afternoon sunlight filtered in through the only window in my small office. It picked up specks of dust that glittered in the air between me and the tweenager glaring at me from across the desk.

"What would you like to talk about on this fine Monday, Claire?" I asked as I sat back on my threadbare, standard-issued chair.

Her stringy, dirty-blonde hair shifted when she lifted one of her shoulders to shrug. "I don't want to talk to you. I don't even know you."

"We met last week," I said, the corners of my mouth lifting to give her a smile. "I'm Elsie, remember? The new temporary guidance counselor while Mrs. Carr is on maternity leave."

Claire rolled her hazel eyes at me. "I know who you are. I just don't know you."

"Okay, what would you like to know?" Placing my arms on the plastic armrests on either side of me, I kept my gaze on her. "You can ask me anything. I want you to feel comfortable with me, and to do that, you and I need to build up some trust."

For a beat, she just stared at me. Since her eyes weren't narrow anymore, I took it as something of a win. I'd known when I'd taken on this job that I was going to be met with some resistance from the grade-schoolers who regularly saw Elena Carr.

"You don't look very old," Claire said eventually, studying me with her red-rimmed eyes.

It was obvious she'd been crying. Her lids were puffy and her eyes still had that glassy sheen to them.

She was putting up a good front, though. At first glance, I'd pegged her as being a little ball of anger, but by now, I'd picked up on the small tells that betrayed her.

Claire wasn't angry. She was sad. It was right there in the downturn of her mouth, the slump of her narrow shoulders, and the lack of any kind of spark in her eyes.

I'd met with her for the first time about a week ago, and it was remarkable to see how much more defeated she seemed after only a few days. I had to get through to her today, even if it was only a small breakthrough.

"I don't look very old because I'm not," I said. "I'm twenty-eight but that's not much younger than Mrs. Carr."

Claire didn't react for a long second as her eyes searched mine. When she finally replied, her voice was soft. "Do you know how she is? Mrs. Carr?"

A smile spread on my lips. "She's doing so well. The baby was born a couple days ago and they're adjusting at home."

She returned my smile—reluctantly—but it was still something. "That's good. I'm happy for her."

"So am I." Shifting in my seat, I folded my hands in my lap and decided to wait her out.

It was becoming clear that somewhere deep inside, Claire was a sweet girl. She obviously cared about Elena and the baby, and I got the feeling that she *did* want to speak to me. She just needed to figure out how.

Her eyes dropped to the pockmarked wooden desk between us before flitting to the bright yellow flowers growing in the pot in the corner. The office might not be mine for good, but I figured I'd add some personal touches in the time I was here.

Aside from the flowers, I also had a couple of framed pictures on my desk, a small oil painting on the wall, and a mess of my own stationery surrounding me. Brightly colored pens and sticky notes, a spiral notebook, and a handful of highlighters lay within easy reach. *My happy place.*

Claire took it all in before bringing her eyes back to mine. "Twenty-eight is old enough to have finished school, right?"

"Yes." I smiled as I motioned to the framed certificates on the floor beneath the stand that held the plant. "I haven't put those up yet, but I have a Bachelor's and a Master's degree in Psychology. I'm working on my Doctorate at the moment."

Claire's eyes widened before she lifted herself out of her chair and walked to where the certificates lay. She bent over to swipe them up off the floor and carried them back to the desk while she examined them.

When she set them down, it was gently and with a certain kind of reverence I hadn't seen in many twelve-year-olds. "I want to study psychology one day."

"Yeah? That's great. You should do it." A tingle of anticipation ran through me. I was getting through to her. I felt it. Waiting her out was working. I just needed to be patient.

Claire fell silent again as she fidgeted with her hands in her lap, her eyes glued to my certificates. After a minute, I was just starting to wonder if she needed a small nudge when she finally started speaking.

"I don't have a Dad," she said suddenly. Her chin dropped and a tremble moved her shoulders. "My mother is raising me by herself. She's all I have, but she hasn't been around much lately. I guess I'm just… lonely and worried about her."

My head tilted, but I kept my expression neutral. "Where has she been?"

"At work." Claire's lips parted on a deep sigh, and when she looked up, I saw tears welling up in her eyes. "She had to pick up extra shifts, and now it's like she's gone all the time."

"That's why you're having trouble at school?" I asked, my voice soft.

3

Empathy and understanding radiated through me, warming me up on the inside and bringing with it the urge to hug this poor girl.

She nodded and bit her lip. "Yeah. Mom used to help me with my homework and stuff, but now she doesn't have time. All the other girls…" Her voice got strangled and she trailed off, taking a few deep gulps of air before she regained her composure. "Everyone else is starting to wear makeup. Their hair looks nice."

She chewed on her lip and she closed her eyes when a tear escaped. "There's all this girly stuff happening and I don't know what to do."

My heart burned for her. I couldn't take it anymore, so I stood up and walked around my desk to take the chair beside hers. Offering her my hands, I squeezed her much smaller ones and waited for her to meet my eyes.

"Being a girl is never easy, but it's really hard being twelve. There are so many changes happening with your body and they can be really scary and confusing."

She nodded but withdrew her hands and clasped them in her lap. "I just don't understand why my Mom can't be around anymore. I need her."

"I know," I said. "But if she's working more, it's because she's trying to make a better life for you. Being a single mother is tough. Sometimes, they have to sacrifice time they'd rather spend with their kids so they can make ends meet."

"You don't understand," she burst out, her little hands balling into fists and her spine shooting straight. "No one does. I'm all alone now."

Breathing in through my nose, I watched as she sucked air into her lungs and glared daggers at me. Once she'd calmed down a little and didn't look like she was about to spit a ball of fire at me anymore, I shook my head.

"That's where you're wrong, Claire. I do understand. Perhaps a lot better than you might think." I reached for one of the photos on my desk and turned it around, running my finger fondly along the face of the woman on it before showing it to Claire. "This is my mother. She raised me by herself, so I do know what you're going through."

"Really?" she whispered as she took the photograph from me, eyes dancing across the frame. "She's pretty."

"She is." I smiled as I brought my gaze to my mother's heart-shaped face. "To this day, she's my best friend. I don't know what I would have done without her growing up and I still don't know what I would do without her."

"Did she work a lot?" Claire asked as she handed the picture back.

I set it down again but kept it facing us. Even through the picture, her kind, smiling eyes encouraged me. "She did. She's a lecturer in psychology at a college not too far away from here. In between her classes, she has consultation hours, grading papers, counseling sessions, and she volunteers at a few places."

"Were you lonely growing up?" she asked before sucking her lower lip between her teeth again.

I nodded. "Sometimes, but once I figured out that she was doing what she needed to do to keep us going, to support me as much as possible, and to stay true to herself all at the same time, it got better."

"Is that why you also studied psychology?" She glanced at the photo again. "To follow in her footsteps?"

"Yeah, it is. She's my best friend and I've learned so much from her." I rolled my lips into my mouth as I tried to decide how much of my past to share with Claire. I could see she needed me to be honest, though. "I went through some rough times when I was about your age. I was bullied quite badly, and if it wasn't for my mom, I don't know how I would have gotten through it. I did get through it, though. With her help. Once I had, I just knew that I wanted to help other people like she had helped me."

Claire blinked at me, a bushy eyebrow lifting. "You were bullied?"

I nodded and got to my feet, opening my desk drawer once I sat down behind it again. While I answered her, I pulled out a few sheets of paper. "Like I said, I know that being a girl can be hard at your age. I have personal experience with just how hard it can be."

Claire frowned at the papers as I pushed them across my desk and placed a pen down on top of them. "What's that?"

"It's enrollment forms for an after-school program for girls nearby.

My mother used to volunteer at the center, and I do sometimes too. When I have time. If you're willing to give it a shot, I think you could be happy there."

Cocking her head, she pulled the forms closer and studied them. "What do they do there?"

I shrugged. "A little of this and a little of that. Basically, it's a safe place for you to go after school. It's free and the women who work there are kindred spirits, as well as the other girls. They're pretty awesome. You won't be alone there and there are plenty of people who will support you with what you're going through."

She paused before lifting her gaze to mine, worry clouding her eyes. "Do you think they'll like me?"

"I know they will." I offered Claire a smile and talked her through some of the activities offered by the center. Then I walked her out of my office.

"I think I'll go check it out," she said just as the bell rang. She joined the throngs of kids out in the corridor and was swallowed up by the crowd in no time.

Exhilaration traveled through me as I breathed a sigh of relief. The program was going to be good for Claire.

My thoughts were interrupted by a buzzing sound coming from underneath my notebook. A frown flickered across my forehead before I remembered I'd taken my phone out of my purse just before Claire's session had started.

An unfamiliar number lit up my screen and my stomach grew strangely cold as I slid my finger across the green bar. "Hello?"

"Hi, is this Elsie Landrum?" a clipped voice asked.

The cold feeling spread. "Speaking."

"Ms. Landrum, this is Dr. Jennings over at Dallas General Hospital. You're listed as the emergency contact for a Catherine Landrum. She's your mother, correct?"

"Yeah—yes," I stammered, my heartbeat kicking into a much higher gear as it raced like it was trying to break out of my chest. "Is she okay?"

"I'm afraid your mother has had a heart attack. We need you to come down here right away."

The icy fingers of dread crept through me, wrapping around all my vital organs as my knees went weak. "Of course. I'll be right there."

Without bothering to pack up my things, I grabbed only my purse and ran at a full sprint to my car. My mind felt hazy, but my body moved on autopilot. All the way to the hospital, I sent up prayers to every deity who might listen that my mommy would be okay.

It hadn't escaped my notice that the doctor hadn't answered me when I'd asked him that question. Hot tears burned my eyes and spilled down my cheeks as my heart kept pounding in my chest.

After arriving at the hospital, I nearly slammed into another car as I made a sharp left into a parking spot. I ran inside without a backward glance. I didn't even know if I'd locked the vehicle or not, but it hardly seemed to matter.

All that mattered was getting to my mother. People swarmed everywhere around me, but it was like I had tunnel vision. Announcements came over a system, but I couldn't make out what was being said.

I managed to get myself together enough to ask a harried-looking woman at the front desk where to go. Then I raced off in the direction she pointed me in. A tall man with graying hair stood at the nurses' station when I made it to the right floor, and as if he'd sensed me coming, he turned just as I threw open the door into the ward.

"Ms. Landrum?" he asked, stepping forward. "I'm Dr. Jennings. We spoke a little while ago."

"Yes," I said, my eyes wide as they darted from the doctor to the rows of doors in the hallway behind him. "Where is she? Where is my mother?"

His mouth formed a straight line and his eyes were kind as he gave his head a slight shake, saying the words that sent my world crashing down all around me.

"I'm sorry, Ms. Landrum. I'm afraid she didn't make it."

CHAPTER 2

TAYDOM

"There's a woman here from the Dallas Times to interview you, Mr. Gaines," my secretary said when I picked up the receiver of my office phone. "She's a few minutes early. I can ask her to wait."

"No, I'm ready for her." I wanted to get the interview over and done with. "Send her in."

I exhaled through my nostrils and closed my eyes, praying for some semblance of patience. *Why the fuck had I agreed to do this interview again?*

Oh, yes. Andrew, my supposed best friend, had set it up. Apparently, the reporter was hot and she'd agreed to go out with him if he got her a sit down with me. *Typical.*

For some reason, though, I loved the asshole, so I buttoned up my jacket and stood as I waited for this hot reporter to come in.

When she did, I was underwhelmed. Red hair tumbled past her shoulders and her lips matched the color. Dramatic makeup on her eyes made them seem smaller and almost beady.

I sighed internally. *Seriously, Drew?*

"Mr. Gaines," she said as she stepped onto the laminate flooring that covered the expanse that was my corner office. "It's nice to meet you."

I wish I could say the same. "Have a seat. Ms. Maxwell, was it?"

"Yes." She flashed me a toothy smile that was way too flirtatious for a woman who'd agreed to a date with another man to get this interview. "Call me Hannah please."

"Hannah." I gestured toward the chair on the other side of my glass-topped desk.

She teetered over to me in heels she seemed to be struggling to walk in, pausing before she sat down to sweep her gaze across the floor-to-ceiling windows that made up two walls of my office. "This is quite a view you have here."

"Yes. Nothing like downtown to keep the motivation levels up." I sat down and wheeled my chair in before inclining my head. "Shall we get started?"

Her eyes widened in surprise, allowing me to see that they were a shade of brown that might have been relatively alluring if it hadn't been overpowered by all that paint on her face.

A frisson of exasperation tightened my gut at her expression. "Did you want something to drink before we get into it?"

She beamed at me as she set her satchel down and finally lowered her skinny ass into the chair I'd offered her. "Water would be great. Thank you."

"Sure." I put in a quick call to my secretary and straightened my arms in front of me to adjust my jacket before folding them on the desk. "I'm sure my secretary told you, but I only have twenty minutes for this, so you might want to get started."

"Of course." She cleared her throat as a pink flush spread on her cheeks. She hid her face behind a curtain of hair as she looked down to extract a tablet from the satchel.

Holding a button to power up the sleek device, she seemed to have pulled herself together by the time her gaze met mine again. "Do you mind if I record the interview? Purely for the purposes of making sure I can refer back to your answers while I write my article."

I ground my teeth but nodded. "If that's what you need to do."

"I would also like to take a few pictures of you once we're done. We need one for the feature."

For fuck's sake. "I'll have my secretary send you a few options from a recent photoshoot we did for use on occasions such as this."

I glanced down at the thick charcoal-colored hunk of metal on my wrist and, more specifically, the broad face of the watch it secured there. "You have seventeen minutes remaining, Ms. Maxwell. I assure you, the twenty-minute slot you have really is only twenty minutes long. It wasn't an estimation or a guideline about how much time I have for you this morning."

God, my mother would shove a pineapple up my ass if she heard me speaking to a woman this way. Thankfully, Mommy Dearest was all the way in Woodstock, Illinois and never came out here, so the chances of her finding out were slim.

Also, this fucking reporter was getting on my nerves.

At least she had the decency to look a little flustered. At least the rude words seemed to kick that bony butt into gear. She cleared her throat again and looked down at the lit screen of the tablet before setting her jaw, annoyance flashing in her eyes when they met mine.

"Of course, Mr. Gaines." She'd obviously picked up on the fact that I was sticking to being formal and she was following my lead. Usually, I wasn't a stickler for formality, but this woman wasn't my friend and she never would be.

Until I saw the article she wrote, I wasn't even sure what her real goal with it was. The publication had claimed it was for an industry feature when I'd had my secretary call them, but I wouldn't know for sure until it was published.

The last one was also supposed to have been a professional profile but it had turned out more like a dating profile than anything else. *Fucking reporters.*

"The Times is currently running a series of articles on the most influential and successful men and women in the city," she said, seemingly having found her professionalism somewhere deep down inside. "We're trying to include people from a variety of professions and industries, and you have been chosen for real estate."

"Go me," I muttered under my breath.

If she'd heard my sarcastic remark, she chose to ignore it. "There's surprisingly little known about you for a man of your stature. It's like one day your firm just popped up out of nowhere and now you're the biggest name in commercial real estate in Texas. How did that happen?"

"The firm didn't pop up out of nowhere. I can assure you of that much." My lips curved into a smirk. "I started this company and it took me years to build it up from nothing into what it is today."

"Okay, but that's still a vague answer." Her tone had changed and was now as sharp as the edge of a blade. "How did you do it?"

So, she has some spunk after all? This was more like a woman I could imagine Andrew going out with, even if it wouldn't last. The man was allergic to commitment, but it wasn't like I was one to talk.

I shrugged as I relaxed back into my padded chair. "Blood, sweat, and tears, Ms. Maxwell. It's the only way to make something of yourself, wouldn't you agree?"

She gave me a smirk of her own. "I would, which is why I'm not letting you get away with your vagueness. I had to run to make it here on time, so I've had my fair share of sweat for today. How about you give me something to make it worthwhile?"

"Fair enough." I cracked a smile, but I knew it didn't reach my eyes. Andrew called it a serial-killer smile, cold and cruel. "After I moved here, I got my real estate license and I worked every day to become, as you called me, the biggest name in commercial real estate in Texas."

Hannah rolled her eyes, and I wondered if her makeup would crack from the action. Sadly, it didn't. "Okay, let's change it up a little. You're rumored to be worth billions. Is that true?"

"I've closed some pretty large deals in my time and I was careful with my money. I invested well and wisely. Now I'm reaping the fruits of making smart decisions."

A soft snort came from her. "Would you care to tell me more about those decisions?"

"No, I'm not a financial adviser and I don't pretend to be. If you want my advice, find someone who really knows what they're doing to look after your money for you."

"Thanks," she said curtly, sarcasm thickening her voice. "What about other kinds of investments? Is there a woman in your life you're investing time in right now?"

"No, but that was a clever way of working that question in there."

"Interviewing you is like pulling teeth. Do you know that? I've heard you have such a charismatic personality that you could sell ice to the Inuit, but you're not being particularly forthcoming."

"On the contrary, I'm an open book, Ms. Maxwell. Being charismatic is not the same thing as being forthcoming. Two different qualities, one of which I've been told I have, and the other? Well, I can be forthcoming. You're just not asking the right questions. Everything you've asked me is out there already."

She sat back and lifted her tablet, barely sparing it a glance before putting it down on the desk again. I knew she was still using it to record, but it appeared she was changing direction and leaving her pre-determined set of questions behind.

"What are the right questions?"

"You want me to write the article for you?" I arched a brow. "That's not quite how it works. What I will tell you is this. You don't make the amount of money I have without sacrifice, risk, and balls. Am I a billionaire? Yes. Several times over. Did I have any family money backing me when I started out? No. Do I give back to the community? Every fucking day. Is there anything else on your generic list of questions, or have I covered it all?"

Her head dropped to one side. "What about your family?"

"What about them?" Over the years, I'd worked on not showing any outward signs of how much it irked me when I was asked about my family. Whenever a reporter had seen it back before I'd learned how to hide it, it basically guaranteed they would cling to that topic. I practically felt my blood pressure rise, but my expression remained stoic.

"Where are they?" she asked.

"Illinois. It's a matter of public record." No one knew anything more than that about where I came from and I planned on keeping it that way. I liked to keep my personal life private, and so far, I'd done a pretty fucking good job of it.

"You mentioned you give back to the community, but what about your family?"

"I don't believe that's any of your business if you're doing an article on me as a success story for the real-estate industry."

She pursed her lips. "It helps to know where you come from to showcase how successful you've become."

"My success has nothing to do with my family." Technically, that wasn't true. My momma had certainly helped turn me into the man I was today, but she had nothing to do with my business or real estate.

"What about your childhood?" she asked. "What was that like? Did you play a lot of Monopoly to stoke your interest in your chosen profession?"

I snorted out loud. There hadn't been time for anything as mundane as board games on our farm. My father's motto was that if you weren't working, you should be.

"Again, Ms. Maxwell, I don't see how that's relevant to an article about my firm or the success we've achieved. If that's all—"

"It's not." Her eyes drifted away from mine to the bright, cloudless blue sky beyond the window before she looked back at me. "Why don't you want to talk about anything personal?"

"I prefer to focus on the future. Isn't that what your readers would like to know as well? Where Gaines Inc. is going and how we plan on getting there?"

A soft sigh escaped her, but she nodded. "Sure. What are your plans going forward?"

The rest of the interview passed quickly as I outlined a few of the projects we had going and what our vision was for the next five years. All of it was information that was already available on our website and had been crafted by a strategic team within the firm, but Hannah seemed satisfied with getting it from the proverbial horse's mouth.

After she left my office, I heard a familiar voice on the other side of the door she'd left ajar. She giggled and I rolled my eyes at whatever shit my best friend was pulling outside.

A few minutes later, Andrew strode into my office like he owned the place and dropped into one of the leather couches against the far wall. He put his feet up on the armrest and crossed his ankles before propping his hands behind his blond head.

"Thanks for doing that. What did you think?"

"I think you should get your fucking feet off my couch." I got up and went to join him in the lounge area, shoving his feet off the armrest when he made no move to do it himself. "I also think you could probably have some fun with her. She'll certainly challenge you more than some of your conquests in the past."

"I know." His blue eyes filled with mischief and humor when he moved them over to where I sat down on the couch across from him. Sitting up, he rubbed his hands together and chuckled. "I'm glad you agree, though. I've been getting bored, but it's time for the games to begin."

"Don't you have something more productive to do with your time?"

"Like what?"

"I don't know, like maybe consider doing your job as an agent for my firm?" I suggested with a shake of my head.

Andrew pouted, but he couldn't completely hide the grin trying to kick the corners of his mouth up. "Yeah, I guess I could do that. I'm supposed to be out looking for houses for clients right now, but I'd rather go get drunk. Interested in coming with me?"

I opened my mouth to say no, but then I changed my mind. Doing interviews pissed me off every time and a drink would help take the edge off.

Plus, what was the point of being the big boss around here if I didn't get to blow off steam when I needed to? For years, I'd kept my nose to the grindstone and my head down.

Once I'd gotten my firm on the map, I vowed to be the kind of boss people actually wanted to work their asses off for. I needed them to, and in return, I didn't micro-manage them. If Andrew wanted to get drunk on this fine Friday afternoon, I knew he'd either already put in the work necessary for this week or would be getting it done over the weekend.

The same could be said for my other employees. This wasn't the nineteen-fucking-eighties. Workplace habits and dynamics had changed, and I was trying to keep up with the times.

Andrew pushed to his feet. "Well?"

"Why the fuck not?" I shrugged and walked back to my desk to tell my secretary to reschedule the rest of my meetings. "Let's get out of here. I need a drink after all those fucking questions."

CHAPTER 3

ELSIE

The tinny ringing of the school bell made my head jerk up. A groan fell from my lips as my neck protested the sudden movement after being bent down, poring over feedback reports to Mrs. Carr all morning.

Reaching up to massage the sore muscles, I heard noise starting up outside my door. Children laughed and whooped, their excited chattering causing a pang in my hollow chest.

Mom had been gone for a little over a month now, and sometimes, I still felt so removed from the world that it was difficult to hear normal life carrying on when it felt like mine had ended. Nothing had been normal since that fateful day, and I struggled to accept the fact that it was because this was my new normal.

I felt empty, numb, but I knew that I had to keep putting one foot in front of the other. Mom wouldn't have wanted me to perish in my misery, so I kept going.

Realizing that it was lunch time when my stomach grumbled and the noise outside intensified, I kicked my shoes back on and picked up my purse. Beth's food truck had been parked nearby all month, just in case I needed her during the day. My best friend's hotdogs did well around here anyway, but I appreciated her moving the truck to stick close to me.

She'd been an absolute godsend since that day, and honestly, I didn't know if the whole putting one foot in front of the other thing would have been possible if it hadn't been for her support. When she'd first asked me what she could do to help, I hadn't had a clue. Somehow, she'd figured out exactly what I needed from her anyway—even without any help from me.

Her shoulder was always there and ready to be cried on. Her door was always open and that was only on the days when she wasn't already in front of mine with coffee and breakfast by the time I woke up in the mornings. Since I couldn't face large plates of food, she'd made sure to bring bites we could have on the go, and at night, she always had a chilled bottle of wine ready in both of our fridges.

She'd laughed with me, reminisced with me, and cried with me. When I'd had no strength of my own, she'd wrapped me up in hers until I had enough to face the world again.

In that blurry awful patch of darkness before the funeral, Beth had taken charge where my administration skills had failed me and had dutifully stuck close to my side before, during, and after the service.

I'd always known she was my ride-or-die girlfriend, but she'd proven to be so much more than that. She was also my sit-and-cry girlfriend, the one who was strong enough to face my grief with me without flinching. And my wonder-why girlfriend and the one who reminded me that one day, I'd be able to feel happiness again. Every girl needed a friend like her and I thanked my guardian angel for making sure I had her.

As I locked my office door on my way out for lunch, I heard a voice saying my name. "Ms. Landrum, have you got a minute?"

I turned around to find Claire standing behind me. I'd seen her once or twice in the last month, but that had only been in passing. She hadn't come for another session, but I'd been keeping an eye out for her.

The transformation she'd undergone since our session was visible. Her previously stringy hair now shone like spun gold, clean and braided in an intricate plait that hung over one shoulder. There was a sparkle in her eyes and only a hint of lip gloss on her mouth.

The clothes she wore were similar to the outfit she'd had on before, but she filled them out better. Like she was back to being the size she had been when they'd been bought.

Despite the painful memories seeing her brought back of what had happened after our last session, I smiled at her. "Hey, Claire. Of course I've got a minute. What's up?"

"I just wanted to thank you," she said, even her voice sounding better now. Stronger. "I've been attending that after-school program and you were right. I love it there."

"Yeah? I'm glad. I can see the difference in you. You're looking great, kiddo."

"Thanks," she said shyly. "They've been showing me how to apply just a little bit of natural makeup and how to do my hair."

"That's not what I meant about you looking great, but I did notice they've helped you in that department as well."

"Yes. Brandy, my group leader, says girls my age are beautiful enough without makeup or fancy hairdos, but she also says if we want to, to keep it natural."

"I totally agree. Have you made some friends?"

She nodded enthusiastically and gripped the strap of her backpack to adjust it. "Yes. I'm actually meeting them for lunch, but I wanted to come by to see you first."

"I'm happy that you did. Come back if there's anything I can help you with, okay?"

"Okay." She smiled and walked backward, giving me a wave before turning around and getting swept up by the crowds once again.

Beth's food truck was parked only about a block away from the school, and as soon as she saw me, she flipped a sign that said *out to lunch*. She closed up the hatch and locked her door, then came over to give me a big hug.

Her familiar vanilla scent enveloped me as I buried my head in her soft brunette curls. I breathed in deeply, trying not to feel like a creep while at the same time needing the comfort enough to not really care.

Beth's shoulders shook as she chuckled before releasing me. "I'm happy to see you too, friend, but I've got to tell you right now that I don't swing that way."

Stepping out of her embrace, I laughed and shook my head. "Seriously? How are you only telling me this now?"

Her soft blue eyes shone with amusement. "I'm sorry. I thought you knew I was into those ugly but oh-so-functional bits that guys have."

I winked, but I couldn't quite hold on to the levity of the moment. "It's your loss. They make plastic stuff that's just as functional, you know? And a lot more reliably effective."

"True that." She nodded at a bench across the street. "Want to take a seat? I'll grab us some food and meet you there in a minute."

"Sure."

She dashed back into her truck and I made my way to the bench.

It was made of concrete that was cool when I sat down. It occurred to me to be grateful that it was in the shade of a giant tree because I hadn't bothered to test the temperature before sitting down.

"You're lucky you don't have a scorched ass right now," Beth said, echoing my thoughts as she came over carrying two paper plates with hotdogs on them. "Chicago style for you and traditional Texan for me. Let me know if you get over the insanity of eating it that way and are ready for the real deal."

"How is it the real deal if it doesn't even have a bun?" I asked, mindlessly rehashing the same argument we'd had many times before. "Mine is iconic. It's got yellow mustard, chopped onions, a pickle spear, tomato wedges, sport peppers, and relish with celery salt all on a poppy seed bun. Yours is a deep-fried sausage."

She gasped, pressing her hand to her chest in fake outrage. "How dare you? It's so much more than just a deep-fried sausage. It's America's favorite snack."

"Keep telling yourself that." I patted her thigh and took a big bite of my lunch.

Beth didn't do the same, the humor fading from her expression as she watched me. "How are you holding up?"

I appreciated that she never asked me how I was doing. It wasn't like anyone was really ever fine such a short period of time after losing someone important to them. "I'm okay, I think. I'm getting along, but it hasn't been easy. You know how much she meant to me."

Beth hummed her agreement. "Have you made any decisions yet?"

"About the money?"

She nodded. "The lawyer called me again. Apparently, you're still dodging her calls."

"Sorry about that." Since Beth had been with me all the time at the beginning, the lawyer my mother had hired to handle her estate had taken her number as well.

Because yes, my mother, who had single-handedly raised me and paid for everything for me except for the tuition I'd gotten scholarships for, had also somehow managed to amass a noteworthy estate.

It was pure insanity, but I guessed she'd been trying to get caught up on saving for her retirement over the last few years that I'd been working and studying on a scholarship. It killed me to know that she would never get to enjoy the benefits of having worked and saved so hard.

Unbeknownst to me, she'd also recently put her house, the home I'd grown up in, on the market. Apparently, she'd wanted to scale down and had signed the contracts with a buyer just a few days before her death.

The sale had gone through, adding a hefty amount to her savings. I hadn't touched the money and my revulsion toward it extended to speaking to the lawyer. I didn't want to discuss what my mother had left behind with anyone because it was hers. Not mine.

"There are steps that need to be taken, hon," Beth said quietly. "Avoiding the lawyer isn't going to bring her back."

I let out a sigh but nodded. "I know. I've been realizing that and I think I'm coming to terms with it."

Beth had been telling me for weeks now that regardless of whether I felt like the money was mine or not, it had been left to me and I needed to step up and manage it.

"You've decided then?" she asked, curiosity and sympathy mingling to darken the light blue of her eyes.

I lifted my hand and dipped it from side to side. "Sort of. I still don't really want to make too much of a dent in it, but I'm thinking about moving closer to school and really focusing on getting my doctorate done."

My best friend's lips spread into a wide smile. "That's a great idea."

I shrugged. "I think I need some time away from work anyway. I don't know how I'm going to help the kids if I'm having trouble helping myself."

"I can see how that might be a problem," she said. "Besides, this is only a temporary job, right?"

"Right, but the agency already had something else lined up for me. It's a permanent position on the staff of a high school somewhere in the city, but I turned them down."

"It's for the best." She nudged my arm with her elbow. "Want me to help you shop for a place to move into? I love going to open houses."

Despite the melancholy of the moment, I chuckled. "I think I should be fine. For some reason, I think that it's important to try to do this alone. Can I let you know if I change my mind?"

"Of course," she said, slinging her arm over my shoulders to give me a side hug. "Whatever you need, girl. Just remember that I'm here if you need me."

"I know." I smiled at her as she released me, watching as she finally tucked into her own lunch. "Thanks for everything you do for me. I think they'd have locked me away in one of the very institutions I might end up working at if it wasn't for you."

It was true too.

Little by little and day by day, I was trying to reconstruct the world that had come crashing down around me when the doctor had given me the news. It looked a lot different from what my world used to look like, but at least it was starting to look familiar again.

A bit battered, a bit skewed on its axis, but familiar nonetheless. What I needed now was a new place to live, a place where I could bask in the familiarity of the things I could while not being caught up in memories of a past I could never get back.

CHAPTER 4

TAYDOM

"You should've fucking been there, my man. It was epic." Andrew spread his arms open wide and grinned. "I don't know how you can keep passing up the opportunity to come out with me. I'm a good time."

"You are, but if I keep coming out with you, I'm going to develop liver failure or catch something that's going to make my dick fall off."

A couple of ladies eating lunch at the table beside ours on the patio at the country club gave me the stink eye. I flashed them my most charming smile and pulled my aviators off my face.

"I'm so sorry. Please excuse my language. Let me buy you all a drink to apologize for my lapse in judgment. My mother would never forgive me if I didn't."

Crow's feet deepened as all three of the older women gave me smiles in return. They wore wide-rimmed sun hats, even underneath the broad umbrella over their table, but at least they didn't seem to be as uppity as it made them appear.

"We'll have a bottle of bubbly, son," one of the old birds said. "The good stuff, or we're getting your mother's number out of you and calling her ourselves." She winked at me before exchanging a look with her friends. "Also, I'll have you know that no appendages have been lost as a result of any one of us."

Andrew choked on his craft gin with some kind of flavored tonic, and I nearly did the same on nothing but spit, but I managed to catch myself just in time. "I'll get you a bottle of the finest Champagne the club has to offer."

When I turned back to Andrew, I mouthed, *What the fuck?*

He lifted his big shoulders in response, then shot me a smirk. "I swear you could get a wall to drop its pants for you."

"Too bad walls don't wear pants."

He rolled his eyes. "You know what I mean, and it's exactly why you should've come out with me last night, dude. The women were fine, and they lose their panties when they even hear your name."

I risked a glance at the ladies, but they seemed to be too absorbed in their own whispered conversation to have heard him. Since Andrew had lowered his voice some, it didn't look like they'd even been able to hear him.

"Please tell me you didn't test that theory." I kept my volume at the same level his had been, and since I didn't hear any snickering and no one had threatened to call my mother again, I figured we were in the clear.

Andrew's chest swelled with pride and his smirk became a smug grin. "I did actually. I used your name to get a girl to come home with me. She was extremely disappointed when she found out I wasn't the billionaire of the hour. Did you know that since Hannah's article came out, you've got this whole mystery-man thing going on that chicks apparently dig?"

"What?" I scoffed. "That's ridiculous."

I'd been sent a copy of her article, but I'd only scanned through it, and even that had been weeks ago. Andrew swallowed the sip of his drink that he'd taken, then nodded. "I know, but apparently, you're the billionaire bachelor of choice around these parts now. Every girl wants to be the one who gets to, and I quote, 'break through the hand-some yet ice-capped exterior' that you apparently portray to the world."

I laughed and pointed at him with my beer bottle. "You know, you could be a billionaire yourself if you'd only work."

"I'm fine with being a regular old millionaire, thank you very much. You know I don't have your drive. I just want to live in a nice house, drink whenever and whatever I want, and fuck pretty things, all of which I can do without a bank balance the size of an island."

"Your ambition astonishes me," I said dryly, but if I was being honest, I kind of envied Andrew's approach to life. He was a laidback guy who never took anything, including himself, too seriously.

He was one hell of an agent and one of the best I had, but he had no intention of progressing any further than he was now. Being able to live off the commission he earned and doing it well was more than enough for him.

"My ambition is to have as much fun as I possibly can while I can still enjoy it." He wagged his eyebrows at me. "What were you doing last night that could be better than that?"

"I was looking over some properties on the housing market that will be good for us to sell. Get us the right kind of exposure in the right neighborhoods to remind people we don't only deal in commercial property."

"I don't know why you're still messing around with residential properties. We make more money on one commercial deal than we do on ten houses in some of the neighborhoods around here."

"It's about the people." I took a sip of my beer. "Meeting people that buy the kinds of houses I was looking at can lead to bigger sales later. Besides, I enjoy dabbling in the residential market. It's relaxing."

"You know what else is relaxing?" he asked, and I knew from the tone of his voice that I was going to have to order two bottles of bubbly once the waiter came back our way. "Drinking, dancing, and then ending the night with a good ol' fuck before passing out."

Sure enough, I heard a prim throat clearing behind me. I twisted in my seat to face the old birds again before pressing in the corners of my mouth and shrugging. "Sorry. How about two bottles? Will that do the trick?"

"Just order them already," one of them grumbled before they stuck their heads together and started clucking again.

I motioned to the waiter and asked him to bring our check after adding the champagne to it. Andrew and I nodded goodbye to the ladies, then made our way through the club and waited at the valet station for our cars to be brought around.

"I'll be back at the office in about an hour," he said when he was handed the keys to his brand-new low-slung Italian sports car.

"Where are you going?" I narrowed my eyes then laughed and shook my head when I saw his lids lower. "Never mind. I don't want to know. Enjoy your afternoon delight or whatever the fuck it's called these days."

"I'm planning on it." He tossed me a wave before getting into the shiny black beast he'd had imported. With the rev of his engine, he tore out of the lot while the valet stared after him with longing in his eyes.

"Might want to wipe the drool off your chin, buddy," I said, laughing as I gave the guy a tip for bringing my car out after Andrew's. "Thanks for not getting a scratch on either of them. He would have bawled like a baby if anything had happened to that thing, and I just don't have the time to take mine to the shop."

The valet looked surprised that I was talking to him at all. Then he nodded and hurried away. I sighed as I climbed into my own vehicle, an equally ostentatious but, in my opinion, far more sexy Mercedes Geländewagen.

I had hardly settled in behind the wheel when my phone started ringing. I smiled when I saw who was calling, a genuine smile that only one woman in the world elicited.

"Hey, Mom."

"Taytay," her warm voice said through my speakers. "How's my baby boy doing?"

"Thirty-two and at the helm of a massively successful company, but she still calls me her baby boy," I teased.

She tutted, laughing softly. "You'll always be my baby boy. I don't care what in the world you achieve or how old you get. One day, you'll have kids of your own and then you'll get it. Now answer my question. How are you?"

My mother still liked to believe that I was going to get married and make her some pretty grandbabies someday. I'd tried to shatter the delusion countless times, but she clung to it like an addict to their next hit.

"I'm good, Momma. How about you?" I laid my head back against the sinfully soft leather of the seat.

"Everything is going well here. You know how it is on the farm, always busy."

"True." I closed my eyes. "How's Dad?"

"He's doing well. He asks about you."

She was lying, but I loved her for trying to make my father look as if he cared. "Yeah? Tell him I said hi."

"I'll do that. Listen, sweetheart. I don't want to keep you. I have to go soon anyway. I just wanted to check in to say hi and make sure you're still breathing. You really ought to remember that a phone works both ways."

"Sure, Mom. I will."

She sighed. "You know what else works both ways? An airplane and a car. You should come visit us sometime soon. It's been too long since I've hugged my baby."

For a good fucking reason. "I'm sorry, Mom. Things are crazy around here right now, but maybe soon, okay?"

When she brought it up again in another month or two, I'd have another excuse ready. I always did.

My mother didn't question me, though. She knew better than that. "Okay, sweetheart. I'll look forward to it. I love you."

"I love you, too." I really did.

If there was one thing I wished for that all the money in the world couldn't buy, it was to be able to spend more time with my mother. It really was too bad that she was married to my father, and there wasn't enough money in the world to convince me to go to the home she shared with him.

CHAPTER 5

ELSIE

Using two fingers on my dresser to balance, I stood on one leg and pulled on my shoe as I cradled my phone between my cheek and my shoulder. "I'm actually on my way to an open house right now."

Beth squealed into the receiver. "Really? Wow. You're not wasting any time. Here I was, calling to find out if you wanted to drink wine and shop for a place online later just to get a feel for where you want to be, but you're way ahead of me."

After pulling the strap of my kitten heel through the loop, I straightened out. "That's the thing. I haven't been in the Bishop's Hollow area for years, so I do want to go to get a feel for the place."

"Bishop's Hollow?" she asked after a beat. "That's expensive. Can you really afford something there?"

"If it's small." I chuckled as I smoothed out my turquoise shirt dress and grabbed a brown leather belt from the rail in my closet. "There are a couple of open houses in the area and there's one property with a few smaller places on it that I'm particularly interested in."

"Okay, but why there?" I heard the surprise in her voice. It didn't come as a shock to me that she would be surprised. I had been surprised myself when I'd first started opening links to look at properties in that area.

The more I thought about it, though, the more it made sense. If I was going to buy a property, it would have to be somewhere I could live long term, and Bishop's Hollow checked all my boxes.

"It's close enough to school for me for now and there are good opportunities for a career around there once I finish. Some of the best schools in the city fall within that district, and since I'd like to keep working with children, that's something I need to consider."

"I hear you, but I'm still not sure I follow. Why not just rent a place close to school for now and take it from there?"

"I don't want to waste any money, and buying property is an investment. If I find a nice place to rent, I'd consider it, but the price would have to be right." After cinching the belt around my waist, I applied another sticky layer of gloss and smacked my lips at myself in the mirror. "Anyway, I have to go. I want to get there with enough time to take a walk around before the open houses start."

"Okay." She still sounded uncertain. "Good luck. Let me know if you want me to join you later."

"Thanks, Beth." I smiled, said my goodbyes, and hung up the phone a minute later.

Dragging in a deep breath, I studied my reflection. I thought I looked nice, or at least as nice as a girl could look when she was carrying more than a few extra pounds, but I didn't know if I looked nice enough to be taken seriously as a potential home buyer.

Whatever. It doesn't matter. You know what you can afford.

Nerves rattled around in my belly. I'd never done anything like this before. The apartment I lived in now was the same one I'd moved into after leaving home. Mom had chosen it based purely on the safety of the building and its proximity to her place, and I'd agreed.

Deciding that I looked as good as it was going to get, I slung my purse over my shoulder and headed out. The drive to Bishop's Hollow was an easy one, the traffic light and flowing well for a Friday afternoon.

I sang along to pop songs on the radio and drummed my fingers on my steering wheel to distract myself from the nerves. Before I knew it, I was cruising down wide, clean lanes with trees towering over the sidewalks.

It's like another world over here. It felt like I'd somehow driven through a time barrier and had gotten transported back three or four decades.

There was none of the hustle and bustle I was used to here. I slowed the car and rolled down my window, taking in the quiet streets, open green spaces, and parks with brightly colored playgrounds in them.

The main street into the neighborhood ended at a large square with quaint shops around it. The square itself was covered with neatly trimmed green grass with a multitude of trees offering shady patches beneath their canopies.

All the shops were open, but there weren't many people around. There was a small greengrocer, a laundromat, a candy shop that claimed to make the best fudge in the county, and a bookstore.

Bright green awnings stretched from the stone walls of the shops over the sidewalks in front of them and only ended when they hit the outer edge of the square. As I marveled at the fact that this cutesy neighborhood, reminiscent of small-town charm, could be my new home, I found a public parking lot on the far side of the square and decided to go on foot from there.

I walked down the paved sidewalks and followed several signs for open houses leading away from the main square. The few people I passed seemed friendly. They smiled and peered at me curiously, as if this was the kind of place where everyone knew one another and they could tell I was an outsider.

I felt a bit out of place as I clutched the strap of my purse and made my way down the tree-lined streets. Shoving the feeling down when I reached the flags on a front lawn that indicated I'd arrived at the first open house, I took a deep breath and went inside.

It was one of the places I'd seen online, the one with the smaller units on the property as well, but I soon realized two things. One, it was much bigger and better than I'd seen online, and two, the smaller places were part and parcel of the main residence.

For some reason, I'd thought I might be able to purchase the adorable cottage at the back end of the property separately, but it seemed I'd misunderstood the ad. Which meant this place was way out of my budget and far too much for me anyway.

The sprawling bottom story of the house contained the most gorgeous, modern kitchen I'd ever seen. What made it even better was that one entire wall of it opened up to the entertainment area and a sparkling swimming pool beyond it.

There were more people milling around the house than I'd seen all the way from my car to here, and everyone looked suitably impressed. I heard snippets of their discussions as I moved farther inside and decided to give myself a tour of the house, even if there was no way I was going to buy it.

I was already there and it really was hard to resist taking a look around one of the most opulent, luxurious homes I'd ever been in. *So what if it makes me feel just a smidge like a Peeping Tom?*

The funniest little thrill traveled through me as I walked from room to room. I felt like a naughty kid who was going to get caught doing something they really shouldn't be doing, but that only made me want to do it so much more.

When I'd thoroughly explored every nook and cranny of the six-bedroom house, I was almost giddy and I totally understood why Beth had said she loved open houses so much. I had a feeling touring them was going to become a problem for me, like a secret addiction or something.

Back in the kitchen, I noticed that fancy ice buckets had been set out and bottles of champagne were chilling in them. *Oooh, this is only getting better.*

I snagged a glass of salmon-pink bubbly and cocked a hip against the wall in the kitchen as I watched the people around me. I wondered how many of them had families big enough to justify a house this size.

Several of them seemed genuinely interested in the place, though I still thought it was crazy to think a place like this could be a home.

It was fascinating, but just as I started to wonder if I had previously undiscovered voyeuristic tendencies due to how much I was enjoying my people watching, all my attention was stolen by a man moving toward me.

Holy hotness, you gorgeous motherfluffer.

The other people in the big open-plan room parted for him like he was a warm knife and they were butter, simply flowing to the sides without him having to say a word. Or maybe that was just because my vision seemed to have narrowed in on him like my life had suddenly turned into a men's fragrance or underwear commercial.

This man would have been able to star in both if it wasn't for this innate ruggedness he radiated. Something about him suggested that underneath the bespoke light gray suit lay a man who wasn't quite as polished as he appeared to be at first glance.

Moving with grace I wouldn't have expected from a man who had to be at least six and a half feet tall, he carried his leanly muscled frame over to me. At least, I was guessing that was the kind of frame he had.

He definitely looked built, solid and broad, but not in an obnoxious roid-ridden monster way. There was no giant bulk of muscle. It was far more subtle than that. *Just the way I like it.*

It had been a long time since my blood had made a visit south of the border, but it was certainly flowing there now. It was easy to imagine tangling my fingers into his thick, dark brown hair and stare into his golden-flecked milk-chocolate—

Hang on. How did I know about the golden flecks if he's halfway across the room?

As I blinked myself out of the trance I'd gotten flung into, I realized I knew about the golden flecks because he wasn't halfway across the room anymore. He was standing right in front of me, an amused yet cool smile gracing his full lips.

"Great place, huh?" His voice was rich and smooth, but there was a rough quality to it that mirrored that feeling I'd gotten about there being some ruggedness underneath all that polish.

He was like a beautiful contradiction that I wanted to explore, but as I was having all these thoughts, I realized his eyes were still on me and that he was still waiting for an answer.

Crap. Why do I always have to be the awkward duckling?

"Yeah. Yep." I bobbed my head up and down with far too much enthusiasm. "It's beautiful."

Jerking my gaze away from those golden hues in his, I swept an arm out. "Can you imagine cooking in this kitchen?"

"It's crazy, right?" A low, rumbling chuckle came from him.

The sound was so much more carefree than I'd have expected from a guy who owned a suit like that. I was tempted to poke him just to hear it again.

I didn't, of course. I wasn't *that* awkward.

"It's like you read my mind. I was just thinking earlier how crazy it would be to call a place like this home."

"Yeah, I'm only sticking around for the free snacks." He winked one of those alluring light brown eyes at me, and somehow, it didn't make him look like a total dickhead. "Have you had some of the prosciutto and mozzarella balls? They're divine."

I lifted my glass. "No, I haven't yet, but I will. To be honest, I only saw the champagne."

"Understandable." He flashed me an easy smile that revealed perfectly straight, perfectly white teeth. "I tried some earlier and they definitely splurged on the good stuff."

"Yeah, well, the real-estate agent is probably going to add double what the cost was for all the fancy snacks and drinks to their commission at the end of the day. It's daylight robbery, but that's just what agents do, I guess. I'm Elsie, by the way."

"Taydom." He extended his hand, a smirk tugging at the corner of his lips and amusement dancing behind those eyes. "I'm the real-estate agent, by the way."

Oh, God. I groaned, feeling my face turn beet red. *Just move on, folks.*

Nothing to see here, just Elsie being the most awkward duckling of them all. Again. Urg.

Foot meet mouth. Then again, the two were old friends by now. Unlike me and the gorgeous man in front of me. We would never be friends or anything else.

In fact, I was pretty sure I was about to get escorted off the property.

CHAPTER 6

TAYDOM

"Don't feel bad about talking shit about me," I said as I tried not to laugh at the horrified girl in front of me.

I'd spotted her the second I'd come back downstairs after giving yet another tour of the mansion, and I'd instantly known she wasn't the buyer I'd been hoping this open day would attract. But that hadn't stopped me from approaching her because *hot damn*, she was sexy.

It had been another long week and I figured I deserved a little treat. Since the options around here were limited, I'd decided to reward myself with a few minutes in the company of a beautiful woman. Then I'd go play agent again.

What had made me decide on this particular beautiful woman out of a room filled with them was simple. She was the only one who had curves like an old Bentley, which automatically made her the sexiest girl in there.

The long shiny black hair piled into a messy ponytail behind her head and the striking, emerald-green eyes were simply cherries on top. As were her plump lips and the little upward flick of the tip of her nose.

Unlike a lot of men who claimed to like curves because it gave them something to hold on to or whatever other crude reasons there were, I liked curves because I genuinely loved the female form.

Those bony chicks Andrew tended to like did nothing for me. Fucking them, to me, was like cutting a hole in an ironing board, attaching a fleshlight to the back of it, and sticking your dick in there.

I had to suppress the shudder the thought brought to mind. *No, thank you.*

"I wasn't talking shit about you," her sweet voice said, yanking me out of the nightmare that was imagining fucking an ironing board.

Turning my attention back to Elsie, I lifted my eyebrows. "Oh really? Because I'm pretty sure you just said the real-estate agent was going to rob these people blind, and I happen to be that agent."

"I didn't say that." More pink spread across the apples of her cheeks.

Sexy and cute. I like it. "It was what you meant, though, am I right?" I asked, cocking my head as I waited for her answer.

"Yeah, I guess so." She sighed and took a long sip of her champagne, wincing as the bubbles burned their way down her throat. "I'm sorry, but the champagne and the fancy snacks and everything? It's all just a little bit too much, don't you think?"

"I *do* think." I moved to stand beside her and leaned down so she'd be able to hear me even if I kept my voice low. "To be honest, it would be pointless to try robbing these people, considering that they're selling because they couldn't afford the place anymore."

She let her head drop back against the wall as she laughed. Then she stopped abruptly. "Wait, are you serious?"

"Yes and no." I chuckled. "I was joking about it being pointless to rob them obviously. I mean, there's still a ton of valuable shit in here. Like that painting and the—"

She jabbed me in the side with her finger, which cut me off and surprised the ever-loving fuck out of me. I hadn't had anyone do that to me in years, and certainly not a woman I'd just met. Like I was her best friend or something.

"What was that for?"

She shrugged, but her mouth tilted up at the corners. "I needed you to stop. You can't go pointing out all the valuables to me. What if I'm really the one planning on robbing them?"

"Oh, I don't know. I trust you." I grinned as I nudged her with my elbow. *What? Two can play that game.* "Want to know where the safe is?"

Elsie let out a soft laugh and shook her head. "You're the worst real-estate agent I've ever met. Remind me to never hire you if I have a house to sell. I wouldn't have anything left to furnish my next house if this is the way you conduct your open houses."

"I'm legitimately the best real-estate agent in the city actually." I smirked, unable to help it. Then I tapped the side of my nose. "But let me assure you, I'd never point your valuables out to anyone."

She laughed again. "Thanks, that's very kind of you."

We lapsed into a comfortable silence for a minute as we surveyed the others who had come to look at the house. I couldn't keep my attention on them, though. Out of the corner of my eye, I kept looking at Elsie.

She sipped her champagne and held the glass to her chest when it wasn't against her lips. A thin silver ring encircled her index finger, but otherwise, she wasn't wearing any jewelry.

Her shiny lips were parted ever so slightly and her eyes flicked to mine. "Shouldn't you be working the room or something?"

"Nah. I've already shown most of these people around. The ones who are serious anyway. The rest of them are just here to check out the house because they're curious." I tilted my head. "Which brings me to you. Why are you here if you're not interested in the house?"

"I thought I was interested in it, but then I realized it wasn't for me."

"So you really are house hunting? Just not for this house?"

She nodded. "This is way too big for me. I thought I might like the cottage, but it turns out I can't buy only the cottage."

Reaching into the inner pocket of my jacket, I pulled out one of my business cards and held it out between two fingers. "I don't do residential real estate much anymore, but give me a call sometime. I'd love to help you find your first house."

"I'm not sure whether I want to rent or buy yet," she said with a glance up at me. "You might not want to waste your time on someone like me."

"It could never be a waste of my time to find the perfect place for a client." Okay, so maybe helping her find an apartment to rent wouldn't be the most productive use of my time, but there was something about her that made me want to do it anyway. "Why are you conflicted between the two?"

She shrugged, twisting the ring around her finger with her thumb as she took another sip of her drink. "Buying is a big decision, but it's also a much better investment. I'm working toward finishing my doctorate, so I don't know where I'll end up yet, which means I might end up buying in one place and needing to live in another. On the other hand, this is a good area with lots of possibilities for me once I graduate, so putting down roots here seems like a good idea."

I didn't know what I'd been expecting her answer to be, but it wasn't that. "I'm impressed. You've given this a lot more thought than many of the young clients I've had before. Those who can afford to buy generally just want the biggest place they can get for their money. It's a status thing to most."

"I don't care much about status." She offered me a small smile before draining the last couple of sips left in her glass. "Thank you for the card. I'll be in touch."

Stepping forward to set the glass down on the counter, she wiggled her fingers in a wave and took off without waiting for a reply. I watched her thread her way through the people and finally disappear through the door.

A part of me wondered if she would come back inside, and for the next few minutes, I kept a close watch on the door. I hadn't really been ready for that conversation to end yet. I hadn't even found out what she was doing her doctorate in, and talking to her had been the most fun I'd had in a while. *Should've gotten her number.*

I could kick myself for not getting it, but it was too late now.

A middle-aged couple who I'd pegged as serious potential buyers approached me and distracted me from my thoughts.

After them, a few more people came to me with questions about the property, the previous owners, and why they were selling. The open house only got busier as the afternoon progressed and I got busy doing what I did best, ending the day with no fewer than four offers to take to my clients.

When they returned home, we discussed the turn out and the offers, and by the time I left, I was fairly confident the place was as good as sold. I climbed into my car. The sun was starting to set, painting the sky in vivid oranges and pinks as I drove the few miles to my house.

It was only once I was settled on my balcony with a celebratory scotch in hand that I extracted my phone from my pocket to see if Elsie had reached out to me yet. It wasn't often that I gave a woman my number and she didn't use it almost immediately, but it seemed she was different.

There were a ton of messages, emails, and missed calls waiting to be returned, but not one of them was from her. I'd gotten a feeling she might be different after our brief conversation, but it seemed like she really wasn't like most of the women I'd met recently.

It was refreshing to know there were women out there who didn't fit into the mold I'd come to find annoying. *I really should have gotten her number.*

I'd thought I could kick myself earlier, but I was seriously tempted to do it now. She still had my number, though.

At least there was that. It put the ball squarely in her court, which wasn't something I was used to, but I was curious to see what she'd do with it.

CHAPTER 7

ELSIE

"How did it go?" Beth asked as I climbed into my car. "Did you find your dream house?"

I snorted. "I found someone's dream house, but it isn't mine."

After turning the engine over, it took a beat for her voice to flow through my speakers. "How so? Did the agent do that thing where the pictures they put up on the internet aren't at all what the place really looks like? I hate it when they do that."

"No, it wasn't that." I sat back in my seat and pulled Taydom's card out of my pocket. Holding it between both my thumbs and index fingers, I rested it on top of the steering wheel. "I don't think the agent on this house is like that. Honestly, it was my own fault. I misunderstood the advertisement he put up."

"Damn. What about the others? Didn't you say there were a few you wanted to have a look at?"

I sighed. "Yeah, I popped into a few of the open houses, but none of them are for me. I think I may need lessons in looking for property because there's so much I don't know."

Or you could just call the hot guy for help like he offered. I shook my head at myself.

If there was anyone who would be able to help me make sense of it

39

all, it probably was Mr. "legitimately the best agent in the city," but I just didn't know. He'd seemed nice enough, and I was pretty sure he would divulge all the hidden costs and things, but he was still an agent.

I thought about calling the number anyway, but then Beth's excited voice was back. "Oh, I can help. I've never bought a place myself, but like I said, I love looking at property and going to open houses. I've managed to teach myself a little bit about how it works. Wanna come over?"

"Right now?" I frowned as I looked down at the clock on my dashboard, but then I remembered it was a Friday afternoon and there was nothing and no one waiting for me at home anyway. "Never mind. Scratch that. I'll be right there."

"I'll pour the wine," Beth promised before hanging up.

Traffic had picked up since earlier and it took me much longer to get back than it had to get out to Bishop's Hollow in the first place, but I was surprised that even at peak time, the drive to the city was more than manageable.

Beth was waiting when I got to her small house and must have seen me pulling up because she opened the front door as soon as I parked. Grabbing my purse, I climbed out of the car and took the glass of wine she held out to me.

With her own in hand, she led me to the swing on her front porch and gestured for me to take a seat. It was one of those oval, hanging, reading chairs and I absolutely adored it. Beth always let me have it when I came over, and she settled on the plastic lawn chair she'd put in front of it.

"So tell me more. You said the place wasn't for you but why not? What do you feel like you need to learn?"

I tucked my legs in underneath me and cradled the white wine in my lap. "A few things. How to interpret the listings online, for one. It looks like there are a lot of costs involved that don't show up, and that can make a place that appears to be within budget fall firmly outside of it."

"That's true, but I'm sure you'll get it in no time." She explained a few of the more basic concepts to me and then frowned. "The agents at the houses you went to should have been able to tell you all this, though. Did you speak to them?"

I felt my cheeks grow warm and it had nothing to do with the wine I was drinking. "I kind of only spoke to one of the agents."

"What? Why? I mean, I don't mind talking you through it, but everything I just told you covers the most basic things they should tell you about each individual property. The utilities, for instance, obviously depend greatly on the area and house itself."

"Yeah, I know. It's not the utilities I'm worried about so much as some of the costs associated with transfer and that kind of thing, but anyway, Bishop's Hollow is a nice neighborhood, but I'm not sure it's my scene."

"Why not?"

"I felt out of place and ended up being super awkward in front of the agent I spoke to." I told Beth what had happened and chewed on my lips when she laughed. "It's not funny."

"It's a little bit funny. I wouldn't worry about it too much, though. Real-estate agents are a lot like lawyers. I think they're used to being made fun of."

"He did say not to worry about it, but I still felt really bad. I basically called him a thief to his face and I don't even know him."

She waved a hand, leaning forward as her gaze caught on mine. "If he said not to worry, don't worry. Besides, like you just said, you don't even know him. He wouldn't be in that industry if he hadn't developed a thicker skin than us mere mortals have. What's more interesting to me is why you're blushing like that. All this happened hours ago, and this is me you're talking to. You never blush when you talk to me."

I took a large gulp of wine and swallowed slowly, licking my lips when I was done. "It's just that I found him attractive, is all. I haven't felt that way since… for a long time."

She reached out to give my knee an affectionate squeeze, understanding warming her eyes. "I get it, honey, but it's not a crime to notice a good-looking man."

Sitting back again, she picked up her phone off the round metal table beside her. "What's his name, though? I need to see the man who's captured your interest."

"Taydom," I said, narrowing my eyes as I tried to remember his last name from the card.

As it turned out, Beth didn't need me to tell her. Her eyes went wide and she stilled. "Taydom Gaines? I mean, it's gotta be him. It's not a common name."

I snapped my fingers and nodded. "Gaines. Yeah, that was it. Do you know him?"

"Do I know him?" she muttered and gave me a look of exasperation and amusement. "I don't know him personally, but I do know *of* him. Every female in the city who has a pulse knows of him."

"Why?" I pointed at my chest with my glass. "Also, not true. I didn't know of him."

"Yeah, but you've been a bit out of it. For obvious and totally understandable reasons, but even so. He's one of the richest guys in the city, El. He's also one of the hottest, so I really wouldn't worry about having been awkward in front of him. I'm sure he's plenty used to it by now."

"Wait. Back up. Has he become one of the richest and hottest guys in the city in the last month? Why haven't I heard about him?"

She shrugged. "It's not like you've ever really kept up with the who's who of the city. Neither have I, to be honest. There was an article published last month in the Dallas Times that's shone the spotlight on him again, though, and it's lingering. I've known about him for a long time, but that's only because he does what he does. You can't be interested in real estate and not know who he is."

"God, I can't believe he's some kind of real-estate superhero and I came out and basically called him a thief." I groaned. "It's a freaking wonder he gave me his card at all. He must have been so offended."

"Wait." She held up a finger and tucked her chin in. "He gave you his card?"

I nodded. "He said he'd love to help me find my first house."

"I hope you took him up on his offer. He pretty much only deals in commercial property nowadays. If he was willing to help you find a place, he couldn't have been too offended. Plus, you couldn't have a better person helping you find a place."

"I'm not even sure if I want to buy yet, though. I didn't take him up on it right away because I didn't want to waste his time, but now it feels like asking for his help would be an even bigger waste of his time. If he's such a big deal, I shouldn't bother him with this."

She rolled her eyes at me. "He wouldn't have offered if he thought it would be a waste of his time."

"He's a real-estate agent. It's literally his job to help people find houses to buy. I'm sure he was just being nice."

"He's not exactly known for being nice." She laughed, eyes crinkling in the corners. "And weren't you listening? It's not really his job to help people find houses anymore."

As her laughter died down, she brought her fingers to her lips and drummed them as she wagged her brows at me. "You know, his card might be a good one to have, even if you don't end up buying a house."

"Very funny." I pursed my lips and leaned back into the soft cushions in the oval seat before releasing a heavy sigh. "I'm not saying I'd be opposed to the idea, but I doubt he gave me his card so I could use it to make a booty call."

She winked. "You won't know if you never try, but I hear you. Hang onto his card, though. Like I said, there's no one better to help you find a place to stay, and you never know when his number might come in useful."

"Yeah, I'll hang onto it." If I was going to spend my inheritance on property, I really did need good help.

If this Taydom guy was the best there was, I had to consider asking him for help if it came down to it. No matter how hot he was, I'd have to suck it up, give him a call, and do my best not to insult him again.

Just not a booty call because that really wasn't me.

Much later that night, after more teasing and tips from Beth and two movies during which I only drank coffee and water, I was ready to go home. It had occurred to me when we'd talked earlier about

Taydom's card that I didn't know what I'd done with it, but I figured it had to be in my car somewhere.

When I climbed in, I searched for it everywhere but didn't see it.

Great. Not only had I made a total dweeb of myself, but I'd also gone and misplaced perhaps the most important phone number I'd gotten in a long time.

Fuck.

CHAPTER 8

TAYDOM

"Are you fucking kidding me?" I muttered when Andrew opened his door shirtless and with his whole torso and face painted in the proud navy-and-gold colors of his favorite basketball team. "You look ridiculous."

"Thank you." He smirked at me and stepped aside to let me in. "I saved you some paint. You're welcome."

"Uh. No." I walked into the renovated warehouse he called home and bypassed the art supplies in his living room without a second thought, opting for heading to the kitchen to grab a beer instead. "For the record, I'm not going out with you decked out like that."

"We're going to the game, bro. Fans are expected to be decked out like this, so I'll repeat myself. I saved some paint for you. Get to it."

"There's no fucking way I'm going out with my face painted like a five-year-old." I twisted the cap off the beer and tossed it in the trash, then leaned with my hip against the countertop and pointed the bottle at him. "I'm not going out with you looking like one either."

Andrew's blue eyes lit up with humor as he folded his arms defiantly. "Well then, we're at an impasse, my friend. I'm not washing this off. It took me an hour to do."

"An hour that would've been better spent doing literally anything else." I shook my head as I took a long sip of my beer. I pushed off the counter and made my way to the couch. "Didn't you want to hit up some club after the game?"

"Yeah, so?" He ran his hands along the length of his abdomen and rolled and thrust his hips. "This just showcases the goods so much better. Don't you think?"

My hand flew up to cover my eyes, and I barked out a laugh. "I really didn't want to see that. Ever. And no, I don't think. I think it makes you look like one of those sports nutcases."

"Sports nutcases?" He lifted both his brows before he burst out laughing and picked his beer up off the coffee table. "I *am* a sports nutcase, in case you haven't noticed. It's part of being a man, bro."

"No, it's really not." Growing up, I'd played a lot of sports but never really had too much time to watch them.

Our old man lived and breathed for baseball, like so many others in my home state, but his love for it kind of put me off. Well, that, and the fact whenever Riley or I tried to join him to watch a game, he'd growl at us that if we didn't have enough work to do, he'd happily give us more.

The television was mostly used by my mother for soap operas and my father for his beloved baseball, while my brother and I only managed to sneak in a few shows here and there. It wasn't as bad as it sounded.

We were boys growing up on a farm. Dad was right. There was always a lot of work to be done, and whenever we had free time, I'd preferred to be either outside or busying myself with schoolwork anyway.

It had always been a priority of mine to get out of Woodstock, and I knew lying on the couch in front of a screen wasn't going to get me there. Since moving to the city, I'd gotten slightly more into sports, but I guessed it just wasn't part of my very DNA like it seemed to be a part of Andrew's.

He snorted at me now, rolling his eyes as he threw himself down on the couch across from mine. "One day, bro, I'm going to get you dressed up for a game. Just you wait."

"Wouldn't hold my breath if I was you." I laid my head back and sucked down more of my beer, my gaze on the exposed beams criss-crossing Andrew's ceiling. From the way they looked now, I never would have guessed how much work it had taken to get them restored. Just like the rest of the warehouse, the beams had been pretty rotten when Andrew had bought the place.

I'd thought he was crazy, but he insisted the neighborhood was being rejuvenated and that this place was capable of being turned into the most perfect man cave. Loathe as I was to admit it out loud, he'd been right.

The area had turned into a trendy spot for young professionals to live over the last few years. It was covered in bars, clubs, bistros, and coffee shops. It boasted quirky art galleries, bike paths, and organic grocers. They even had street murals.

All in all, I thought it was bullshit.

Andrew loved it, though, and I couldn't fault him on that. It was everything he'd ever wanted in a neighborhood, and the exposed brick walls and open-plan layout of his warehouse suited him to a tee, too.

It was a far cry from my estate out in the suburbs, not actually all that far from Bishop's Hollow, but I was starting to see the appeal. My house had been bought because it was a solid investment. It was a good place to live and had plenty of space for whatever I might need.

Andrew's had been bought as a den of iniquity or, as I liked to think of it, an over-sized play pen. But I had to admit that living here, cutting free, and simply being didn't seem all that bad anymore.

"Stop ogling my house," he joked. "It's not for sale. Not to you or anyone else."

"Dude, everything is for sale. The only question is the price."

He rolled his eyes at me and chugged his beer, pounding his fist into his chest when he was done. "Not this house. I wouldn't let it go if you offered me millions of bucks for it."

"Yeah? So you're still going to be living here when you're old and gray and married?"

He winced. "Don't say the M-word in here. You'll scare the place."

"If it's that easily scared, I don't want it anyway." I laughed and drained the rest of my beer. "We should get going."

"Yeah, soon. Let's have one more drink. We haven't pre-gamed nearly hard enough. I'm pretty sure I have a bottle of tequila around here somewhere. Give me a minute."

Sure enough, he was back less than a minute later with two more beers, a frosted glass bottle under one arm, and shot glasses in his free hand. He grinned broadly at me. "Let's celebrate."

"What are we celebrating?" I asked, accepting the beer he handed over to me.

He shrugged as he set down the small glasses and filled them, pushing one across the coffee table toward me. "It's game day, so we can celebrate that. How did your open house go yesterday? If you sold it, we could celebrate that as well."

"I got a few offers. One of them should get accepted, but I don't know for sure yet, and we shouldn't celebrate prematurely."

Andrew chuckled. "I bet you know all about premature *celebration*." The way he lowered his voice and emphasized the word after a brief pause made it clear that it hadn't been the word he really wanted to use.

"Fuck off. You have no idea what you're talking about."

"Hey, you can't blame me for thinking that. If I'd been dry for as long as you have, I'd have been premature too."

"Shut up." I groaned. "I've just been busy, and I'm bored as fuck with the usual. Get off my ass about it. Are we going to drink these before they get warm?"

"Yeah." He threw his shot back without toasting to anything and grabbed a fistful of his blond hair, eyes stretched wide open. "You're bored of one-night stands with hot-as-fuck women? What is wrong with you?"

"You and I have two very different definitions of *hot as fuck*." Without really meaning to, I found my mind drifting back to Elsie as I tossed my own drink down the hatch. "Speaking of which, there was a woman at the open house yesterday who was pretty hot."

"Yeah?" He spread his legs wide and popped his elbows on them, drink dangling between his fingers. "Was she waiting on her husband? The hot ones at those things always seem to be waiting on the wallet to arrive."

I snorted, but I couldn't argue. "Nah, she wasn't like that. From the sound of it, she's pretty independent. Smart too."

"If she's the whole package, why don't you call her? We can meet up with her somewhere after the game."

I sighed before taking another long sip of my beer. "I can't call her because I didn't get her number."

"Dude." He shook his head. "That's a rookie mistake."

"Yeah, well, there's nothing I can do about it now. I checked the guest book from the open house, and she didn't leave her details."

Andrew let out a disappointed sound, then lifted his arms in the air. "Hey, I'm sorry, but it sounds like it's just not your fate to sleep with her. Don't despair. We'll find you someone else to fuck later. I've got you."

"No thanks." I laughed. "I mean, thanks for the offer, but firstly, you know I don't need any help in that department, and second, I don't give a fuck about fate."

"Think of it this way. The bro-gods must be looking out for you. It has to be in your best interest that you have no way of getting a hold of her. She might have ended up pregnant and ruining your life or something. It might not be fate, but you should be thanking the gods anyway."

"Stop being so dramatic." I polished off the last of my beer and got to my feet. "Let's just get to the game, shall we? The alcohol is making you believe in those imaginary bro-gods again."

"Don't say that," he said in a stage whisper, glancing up and clutching both hands to his chest with the corners of his mouth inching up. "I'm sorry, you guys. Please don't punish him tonight. If he knocks this woman up, do you have any idea how much harder I'm going to have to work in the future?"

"I'm not knocking anyone up, Drew. Let's just go." I rolled my eyes at him again.

He just flashed me a smirk. "Fine, but when you do, don't expect me to fill in for you when you have to attend doctor's appointments and kindergarten plays, okay?"

"Deal." As if I'd ever be that goddamn stupid. I laughed it off, though, because it wasn't happening.

The day I either knocked someone up or asked Andrew to fill in for me was the day I'd start drinking heavily in the morning and calling my father every hour on the hour because even listening to him berating me for half of every day would be better than having to deal with the consequences of either one of those two things.

CHAPTER 9

ELSIE

"What are your plans for tonight?" Beth asked, lazily turning her head to face me as we lay on the lounge chairs in her backyard. She lifted a hand to shield her eyes from the bright rays of the sun behind me. "I hope you've got something more exciting planned than me."

"Unless working on ideas for my thesis qualifies as exciting, count me out." I adjusted the top of my bikini, which was barely containing the girls, even though I was lying still. "This is the most fun I'm planning on having today. You?"

"I'm taking the food truck out tonight. There's a basketball game and I'm going to park outside it. People don't want to spend that money at the arena on a hotdog, but I'm cornering the market."

"Good thinking. They've got to eat, right?" I smiled at my friend. "I'm sure you're going to do great. Your hot dogs are the best, and the truck is starting to make a name for itself."

"Thanks." She sighed when she caught sight of the time. "Shit. I've got to get going soon and I need to shower off all the sunscreen before I do."

"That's my cue then." I turned my face up toward the sun for one last minute, then swung my legs to the side and sat up. "Good luck tonight."

We collected the towels we'd laid out on the lounge chairs and walked toward the door leading into her kitchen. As I deposited my empty water glass in her sink, she turned from the door to face me with a slight frown marring her forehead. "I thought you had your thesis topic locked in."

"So did I." I lifted one shoulder in a shrug and pushed my sunglasses into my hair. "But my adviser wants me to revise a few things before classes start back up. It's a constant process until it gets approved by the committee."

She scrunched up her nose. "I still don't get why you wanted to keep studying."

"Yeah, I'm not sure I get it anymore either." I laughed. "But I started the program. Might as well finish it."

"Good point, but is the work you have to do tonight essential?"

I shook my head. "Honestly? No. Chances are, I'm just going to end up sitting in front of my computer, staring at the screen and not actually getting anything done. Or you know, I'll do research into something totally random instead. Last time, I spent two hours reading up on the different arguments surrounding whether unicorn horns have glitter in them or not."

"The internet sure is a rabbit hole."

"Absolutely," I agreed as I reached up and redid my ponytail. "Why'd you ask?"

"Do you want to come ride along with me instead? I know it's not nearly as interesting as unicorn horns, but at least we'll get to spend our Saturday night together."

"Yeah, that could be fun. I'm just going to have to go home to grab some clean clothes first."

She waved a hand at me. "We're the same size, and I have a spare shirt with the truck's logo on it for you. You came here in jeans before we changed, right?"

"Right."

"Then that's perfect." She smiled and jerked her head to indicate her hallway. "There's shampoo and stuff in the guest bathroom and towels under the sink if you want to get cleaned up."

"I know. Thanks." I followed her out of the kitchen and walked straight to her bathroom. She always left toiletries in there for me in case I ended up staying over, but she never mentioned it. I'd even found a brand-new toothbrush in the cabinet last time.

I used to carry a small bag of toiletries in my car, but they had run out after a few nights spent at Beth's shortly after… Well, they'd run out, and replenishing my supplies just hadn't seemed important. It did now, though.

As my brain had slowly started processing the absolutely terrible shock it had gotten and working through the grief, I noticed a lot of things I'd slacked on over the last month or so. But as I came back to myself, I was noticing silly things like toiletries and feeling proud of myself for the progress that meant I was making.

After my shower, Beth and I met in the living room and took off. The truck was a surprisingly smooth ride, and thanks to Beth's obsessive cleaning, it smelled like the pleasant Ocean Fresh freshener she used in the cab rather than a food truck.

"You going to look at more houses this weekend?" She glanced at me when we stopped at a traffic light.

"I don't know."

Red light spilled into the cab, causing shadows to fall over her face as she frowned. "Why not? You're not backing out of the decision you made, are you?"

"No, I just…" I scrubbed my hands over my face. "Yesterday was just a little overwhelming, you know? The reality hit me kind of hard when I was on my way home last night. I only have the money to move because of Mom, and I'd much rather have her. But I don't and I'm never going to again, and now, even my own body seems to be ready to move on, and I'm just… not."

"Finding a guy attractive isn't moving on," she said. "It's called living and being alive. You *are* allowed to keep doing both those things, even while you miss your mother. As for the money, you know she would have been thrilled with what you're planning on doing with it."

"I know. It all just got a bit much last night, but I'll be fine. I might take the rest of this weekend off and search again next week."

Her lips moved to the side and the dent in her cheek told me she was biting the inside of it. When the light finally changed, she shot me another look. "Okay, but just don't wait too long. You've only got a few weeks to find a place before the semester starts up for you. Again, if you need help, I'm here for you. Otherwise, just call Taydom."

"About that." I sucked in a breath and blurted the rest of my sentence out without taking another one. "I lost his card. I've tried looking his number up, but there's no mobile listed, and I don't really want to call his office. I'm pretty sure he wouldn't know who I was to return my call anyway."

"You lost his card?" She released a low, injured-sounding moan. "How?"

"I don't know. It was in my car. I was looking at it when I was speaking to you on the phone after I left the open house, but then I put it somewhere and I can't find it."

"You're hopeless." Another moan, then she smacked a hand against the steering wheel. "But the show must go on and a house must be found. I'll come with you tomorrow. We'll find another one of his open houses and just talk to him there."

"I already checked the website and there are no more open houses listed under his name for the rest of the month."

"Damn it." She bit her upper lip. "Okay, then you're just going to have to call his office. It's not such a big difference, right? He's a professional. He probably returns all calls to his cell and his office."

"I don't know. It feels like there is a difference. Let me think about it. Like I said, I think I'll take the rest of this weekend off anyway. Give myself a little time to adjust again before I continue the search."

"I love how kind you are to yourself," she said as she parked outside the massive basketball arena. "But I don't know where you find the patience to give yourself time when you know you need it. I'm not even the one moving and I can't wait until it's time."

I rested my head against the seat and laughed. "It can be frustrating, but it's worth it. Anyway, what do you need me to do to help tonight?"

"I'm going to get set up, but there's a lot more people here than I expected." Her eyes tracked from one side of the huge field that offered additional parking to the other. "Do you know the arena itself has parking, too? This is just the overflow, which means it's packed in there."

I whistled under my breath. The field extended far beyond the well-lit edge of it near where we were parked, and there wasn't a free space in sight. "It's going to be busy when the game lets out. That's for sure."

"Yeah." She rolled her lips into her mouth and narrowed her eyes as she thought. "Okay, this is what we're going to do. There are a couple of items on my regular menu we won't be able to offer. I just don't have the inventory to do it and it's better not to offer it from the get-go than having to explain to customers who have been waiting in line that we don't have it."

"What if we just sold out regularly?"

She shrugged. "That's different, but it's still a pain. We know tonight that we won't be able to offer a few things, so better to get rid of them altogether than to spend so much more time explaining that we don't have them."

"You're the expert here. I'll get the board out. You just tell me what needs to come off."

"Thank you. You're saving my life here."

"It's nothing you wouldn't do and haven't done for me." I smiled and hopped out the door before either of us got emotional.

Beth and I extended the awning of her truck and opened up the window. Then we wiped down all the surfaces and prepped the ingredients we could. Once that was done, I set out a variety of sauces on a plastic table outside while Beth did a few last-minute checks.

The game had already let out by the time we were done, and people were starting to leave the arena. They looked like ants pouring out of a nest, crawling everywhere and covering every surface I could see.

"Hey, let me know which items to take off the board," I said as I hoisted the second of two black boards that went outside the truck. There was another board on the inside, but Beth had already handled that one.

Loud music coming from the arena and starting up in many of the cars around us drowned out her answer. After making sure both boards were standing up around where I knew she'd want them, I headed back to the truck.

"Sorry." She smiled. "I tried yelling, but I guess my voice just didn't make it all the way to you."

Plucking one of the paper menus from the stack on the counter, she crossed off several items with a pen she had tucked behind her ear. "There you go. If you could take those off, that would be great."

"You got it." I took the menu and headed back to the boards.

Her regular menu was written on them in her loopy, neat handwriting. I held up the paper she'd given me and erased the chalk lines containing the items we wouldn't be selling.

"Elsie, is that you?" a smooth baritone voice that couldn't be mistaken for anyone else said from behind me.

I spun around to see that I had been right. Taydom was standing there with a foam finger in one hand and a heavily painted fan at his side.

Oh shit. Oh shit, oh shit, oh shit.

His eyes crinkled with amusement as he took a few steps closer to me. "Fancy meeting you here."

God, please don't let me make a complete fool of myself again. I didn't know if my prayer was going to work, but it was damn sure worth a try. I really, really didn't want to look like a complete idiot in front of this guy again.

I did have some self-respect and I desperately wanted to cling to it.

CHAPTER 10

TAYDOM

Elsie looked surprised when she turned around, and not pleasantly so. I couldn't remember the last time a woman had looked at me quite like she did at that moment, with a mixture of shock, alarm and, worst of all, distress.

I, on the other hand, felt pretty damn lucky right then. "What are you doing here?"

"Helping out with the food truck," she said, her voice wobbly. "You?"

"I came to catch the game." I stuck my thumb out and jerked it over my shoulder. "You know, just like all those other thousands of people over there."

She frowned, then rolled her eyes. I thought I caught the beginnings of a smile, but she wiped her face smooth too fast to be sure. "Oh, right. That's what all these people are doing here. I was wondering what was going on."

My brows rose. *Smart, cute,* and *funny.* "What can I say? We have these gatherings sometimes where we all come out to watch some grown men chase after a ball. It's considered to be fun by some people."

"Quite a lot of people, I'd say." She didn't try to hide her smile this time, and her entire face lit up with it. "You want a hot dog? I can help you skip the line."

"Only if you have it with me." I felt Andrew's disbelief at my side but I didn't look at him. This was a chance to fix my rookie mistake, and I wasn't passing it up.

Elsie hesitated for a beat, then shrugged. "Sure, why not? Let me just check in with Beth. I'll be back."

Andrew waited until she had at least turned around to step in front of me. "What the fuck, dude? Why are you trying to pick up girls at the food truck? I thought we were going out for that."

"She's the girl from the open house yesterday. The one I was telling you about earlier."

His eyes widened, the blue looking almost transparent in the bright light underneath the awning. "You'd better run then, bro. The universe has already tried to keep you away from her once. It won't interfere again, so run. Now. I'll distract her."

I lifted my gaze away from his to find her stepping into the food truck through a small door at the back. "I'd say she's pretty distracted, but I'm not running. The universe can do whatever the fuck it wants. I'm having a hot dog with that girl."

He threw his arms out to his sides, a knowing smirk pulling one corner of his lips up. "Fine. It's your future baby, dude. Not mine."

"Fuck off with that." I was about to tell him exactly where he could shove his bullshit when I realized I'd lost his attention.

His gaze drifted to the line forming in front of the counter, and he perked up. "Picking up girls at the food truck might not be such a bad idea after all. I think I see a tasty little morsel I'd like to try. See you later."

Without a backward glance, he strode up to a tall brunette who was as skinny as a rail. I rolled my eyes at him. *Hypocrite.*

Elsie moved through the crowd toward me carrying cardboard plates laden with hot dogs, grabbing my focus away from the friend who'd be getting an earful later. She smiled and gently lifted the plates when she reached me.

"Dinner is served." She smiled. "Just don't get used to it."

"I won't," I assured her. "That looks good. Thanks."

"No problem." She passed one of the plates over to me and nodded at the curb. "Want to have a seat in our super luxurious dining area?"

"Lead the way." A grin curled my lips as I followed her and sat down at her side. Tiny pebbles stuck into my ass and I was pretty sure there was patch of dry grass beneath me. The Ritz, this was not.

Thankfully, pebbles and grass had never scared me. Sitting like this even reminded me of home a little bit, which wasn't necessarily a good thing, but it wasn't all bad either.

"What are you really doing here?" I asked as I picked up a bun and held the open end closed. Then I bit into the relish and chili loaded dog.

She tilted her head, the lights all around us making her hair look like the black was streaked with gold. "I told you I'm helping out with the food truck."

"It makes perfect sense then that you weren't able to afford that house," I joked once I'd swallowed, glancing at her so she'd be able to see the humor in my eyes. "Might have been difficult getting a mort-gage that size on whatever one makes as a food truck helper."

"Beth does really well for herself," she informed me, but the corners of her lips twitched. "Not ten million dollars for a mansion well, but well enough."

"Who's Beth?" I glanced up at the brunette behind the counter, hands moving so fast I could barely see them. "I'm assuming that's her, but who is she?"

"My best friend." Elsie's smile when she said Beth's name spoke volumes. "She's been a real lifesaver recently, so I jumped at the chance of helping her out tonight."

A frown tugged at my brows. "Only to have me steal you away. I'm sorry. I didn't realize."

"No, it's okay." She turned that same smile on me. "It's more the setting up and taking down that I came to help with. It's small back there for two people and Beth's the whiz at actually getting food out. I wasn't planning on being back there with her anyway. I only get in the way."

"Ah, I get that." I took another bite, chewing as I watched Beth work. "It sure looks like she's in her element there. Personally, I hate having people in my office when I'm trying to get shit done."

"Same here." She let out a wistful sigh. "Well, back when I had an office and work to do. I'm taking a break to finish school, but I'm going to miss the kids."

"The kids?" I snapped my fingers. "Right, so you're doing your doctorate in education?"

Chuckling as she shook her head, she looked right into my eyes for the first time since we'd sat down. "No, it's not a bad guess, though. I'm studying psychology. I used to be a guidance counselor at a local grade school."

With her gaze still set on mine, it was easy to see her passion for what she did. Light came into her eyes and her expression softened. "Psychology, huh? That's admirable. I don't know if I could sit around listening to other people's problems all day. I mean, I know it's much more than that, but that's the general idea, right?"

"It's about helping people, and that's something I love to do. Everyone needs a little help sometimes. There's no shame in it, but a lot of people seem to believe there is. I think it makes people stronger when they can admit to needing help."

"I wholeheartedly agree." My fingers itched to touch the soft-looking skin on her face, to cradle her cheek, and kiss her to show her just how completely I agreed with her. "Yours is a profession I have a lot of respect for. I sure as hell wouldn't be able to do it."

"You help people, too," she said. "In your own way. Finding some-place for people to live and raise their families must feel pretty incredible."

"It does." I felt that same light I'd seen entering her eyes minutes before coming into my own. "I think I got addicted to it the first time I showed a house and it sold. These days, I don't get to help people find homes nearly as often, but finding space for them to grow or expand their businesses is pretty fucking exhilarating too."

"I can just imagine," she said, and I really believed that she could.

"Speaking of which, did you find another realtor to help you out? I was expecting to have heard from you by now."

Her cheeks grew pink and she suddenly seemed to find her untouched food extremely interesting.

Internally sighing, I shoved the rest of my hot dog into my mouth and chewed through the irrational stab of disappointment in my gut. When I'd finally swallowed, she still hadn't said anything.

"It's okay if you have," I said. "I just hope you've found someone who has your best interests at heart."

"I haven't found anyone else," she said, the words tumbling out of her mouth so fast, they almost became one. "I lost your card."

Hearing that pleased me more than it should have. "Well then, since you can't be trusted with numbers, give me yours and I'll give you a call."

"Really?" She arched a manicured brow. "You'd still be willing to help me? Aren't you, like, super busy or something?"

I nearly choked on a laugh. "Yeah, I am busy, but I'm also willing to help you. It is my job, after all."

"True." She pulled her bottom lip between her teeth, shifting to face me. "Thank you, I'd really appreciate your help. I'm sorry for losing your card."

"That's okay. There's a reason those things are outdated." I straightened my leg and dug into the pocket of my jeans to pull out my phone. After tapping in my passcode, I handed it over. "Here. Give me your number."

"If they're so outdated, why do you still use them?" She took the phone and typed in her number before handing it back, a grin on her full lips. "Wouldn't it have been easier to just program your number into my phone to begin with?"

"With your track record, you'd have just lost the phone. Consider it a public service. Replacing your phone would have been much harder."

I saw the tip of her tongue peeking out, but she seemed to think the better of sticking it out at me. It was too late, though.

I'd seen her tongue and it had sent my mind racing to the nearest gutter. My dick reacted to the images waiting for it in said gutter, of what that tongue might feel like on it, but I breathed through the impending erection and reminded myself that she was nothing but a potential client.

A playful swat to my bicep brought me back to reality. "I've never lost a phone, I'll have you know. The only thing I've lost this year is your card."

"Joke's on me then." I smirked, but for some reason, Andrew's warning played through my mind. She hadn't lost *anything* this year except for my card. Surely, that had to mean something, but so did running into her again.

Instead of heeding his ridiculous warning, I finished the other hot dog she had generously gotten me and turned back to her. "Tell me more about being a guidance counselor. I'm not afraid to admit that I got sent to mine back at school more than once. I had a knack for getting in trouble and they thought the poor woman would help me. I've never thought about things from her perspective before."

Elsie laughed but nodded. "It's an interesting job for sure. I've been doing it for a few years and most of that time was spent at one school, but more recently, I was helping out for a colleague on maternity leave."

She regaled me with stories of the kids she'd seen, not making fun of them but just telling me about them and the challenges they'd faced. At some point, I saw Andrew speaking to a different woman than the one he'd left me for, but he seemed fine, so I didn't bother motioning him over.

In between telling me stories, she asked about my job but, refreshingly, not about my family or upbringing. I noticed she didn't mention hers either, but since this was only our second conversation, I didn't bring it up.

I sure as hell wasn't ready to tell her anything about that, and I figured she felt the same way. When the brunette from the food truck stepped outside, I noticed the line was all but gone.

"That was fast," I commented before realizing that obviously, more time had passed than I'd noticed since sitting down.

Elsie looked up, blinked a few times, then shrugged. "Beth mentioned that sports arenas clear out fast after a game. Most people have plans after or whatever, but she thought it was worth it to come for those few who might want to grab an immediate bite to eat."

"Makes sense," I said, crumpling up my plate and holding my hand out for hers. She'd finally gotten around to eating while telling me about her job.

With both plates in hand, I got up and offered my free hand to her. She took it, climbing lightly to her feet and releasing my fingers immediately before dusting off her ass.

"I'd better get back to helping Beth, but I'll speak to you soon?"

"Sure, I'll be in touch about a house," I said.

"As long as you don't lose my number, you mean." She smiled. "Have a good night, Taydom. Thanks again for being so willing to help me."

A giggle rang out behind her when she took off toward her friend. I watched her go. Andrew walked up to me and raised a brow, his gaze flicking between mine and Elsie's retreating back.

He didn't say a word, but he didn't have to.

"Shut up," I growled and fished my keys out of my pocket. "Let's get out of here."

CHAPTER 11

ELSIE

"Why do you need another pack of highlighters?" Beth groaned as we stood in front of the stationery aisle. "You already have two."

"When you see the size of my textbooks, you'll understand." I opted for more of the bright colors over the pastels and added them to my cart. "Besides, whose school supplies are we shopping for?"

"Yours, thank God. I had more than enough of school in the twelve mandatory years to last me a lifetime." She flicked her curls over her shoulder. "You're a better person than me for volunteering for more of that torture."

"I like studying," I protested. "I'm going to miss it once I eventually graduate."

"I think you need your own help," she joked. "But here, have some more pens."

I laughed, but in all honesty, I'd just been about to add another box anyway. "Thanks. Now we can move on to files and sticky notes. If I can't organize properly, I'll never get around to graduation."

"Oh joy." Beth clapped her hands together with fake enthusiasm. "More school supplies. Just like I always wanted."

"Hey, you said you wanted to come." I shot her a smile. "I appreciate you being here, but you really didn't have to. As you can see, I'm more than capable of stationery shopping by myself."

"Yeah, but then I wouldn't get the scoop on you and Taydom from last night." She took over control of the cart and propped her elbows on the handle, her eyes never leaving mine. "I might have been too wiped out to talk much last night after the rush, but I'm all ears now."

"There's not much to tell." *Unfortunately.* "We talked, we ate, he took my number, and he's going to give me a call about a house sometime."

"What did you talk about?" she asked. "It had to have been an interesting conversation. You two were at it the whole time I was serving."

"It wasn't that long." I ran my finger along the binders of some notebooks and decided to add some of those to my loot. "It was, what, like twenty minutes?"

"It was more than an hour," she said dryly. "So spill, girlfriend. What did you talk about with one of the richest men in Dallas that kept him glued to your side for that long?"

"More than an hour, really?" I frowned. "It didn't feel like it was that long."

"Trust me. It was. An hour that felt like two lifetimes from the inside of my truck, but never mind that. I want details."

"We really didn't talk about much. We joked around a little. I told him about being a guidance counselor and he answered some of my questions about his job."

"It looked a lot more intimate than that from where I was standing. He couldn't stop looking at you."

"Bullshit," I said. "I looked around all the time, and even if he had been looking at me, it was only because we were having a conversation."

Beth sniffed. "No, I don't think so. It definitely looked like it was about more than that."

"It wasn't. He's going to help me find a house. That's it." Surprisingly, he also seemed to be a nice guy. It was contrary to what Beth had told me she'd read about him, but I'd always been one to form my own opinions about things and people. "He was really cool about it, too. Considering who he is, I thought he would be pissed about me losing his number or not calling him immediately, but he laughed the whole thing off."

"So you gave him your number?" she asked. "Why would you do that? Why not take his again?"

"Why would I take his again?" I countered as I loaded some lever-arch files in with the rest of my stuff. "He took mine. Problem solved. You said he would be the best person to help and he's going to help."

"Yeah, but now you've given up all the power already. You could have made him work for your number at the very least."

With a shake of my head, I laughed until a woman farther down the aisle shot me an annoyed look. "It's nothing more than him looking for a house for me, Beth. I don't need any power in that relationship. All I need is the money to either buy or rent whatever place he comes up with. If I even like it, that is."

Her face fell. "But you said you liked him."

"I said I found him attractive. That doesn't mean anything." More than attractive actually. Having spent some more time with him, I'd also learned that he was attentive, kind, charming, and witty. All of which were qualities that I liked in a man. "Trust me. There's nothing going on between us."

"Could there be?" she asked, hope sparking behind her eyes. "He wasn't the only one who couldn't stop staring. I really thought I saw some chemistry between you two."

"I'd be lying if I said I didn't feel anything with him." I'd felt a lot, but I was pretty sure he didn't feel the same way. He'd been polite, friendly, and pleasant enough, but he hadn't said or done a single thing that was flirtatious or otherwise indicated any kind of mutual attraction.

For a guy like him, I wasn't surprised. Despite my more *voluptuous* shape, I didn't have any body issues. I was really pretty confident for a bigger girl.

Did it mean that I pranced around in barely there skirts or in bikinis on beaches full of people? No, but I couldn't imagine I'd do that even if I lost the weight.

I loved my fuller hips and breasts, and though I didn't necessarily love the jiggling of my stomach or thighs, I didn't really look at them often enough to hate them either. The point was, though, that despite how I felt about myself, men like Taydom didn't look at me.

I was girl-next-door pretty. The bright emerald of my eyes and sleek black hair I'd inherited from my mother, along with the heart shape of her face and full lips, guaranteed that I got some attention, but I wasn't a stunner, and I was perfectly happy with that.

There was no changing it anyway. My body type was what it was, and no amount of dieting or exercise when I'd been younger had changed it, so I lived healthily but had stopped obsessing about the extra weight.

"What's the problem then?" Beth interrupted my thoughts. "You felt something with him and I'm convinced he felt it too. I was an outsider to your conversation, and as an outsider, I feel like I'm in a better position to judge body language."

"You were a biased outsider who knew that I thought he was attractive. I love you for it, Beth, but you're not completely objective."

She huffed out a breath as we moved slowly down the aisle. "I might not be objective, but I'm not blind, either. There was something there. I'm telling you now. Mark my words."

"Fine, consider them marked. It's nothing, though. I promise. He's just a nice guy and he's really good at his job."

"Sure, I can agree with you on the last part, but nothing I've read suggests he's a nice guy. If anything, he's known to be an aloof, evasive dick who gets things done. No matter what the cost."

I rolled my eyes at her. "Are you listening to yourself? That's what you've read. Isn't the press known for embellishing and creating mystery in order to sell their stories?"

"Maybe." She sighed and placed her hands on the handle of the cart, no longer nudging it along with her elbows. "But I don't think that's it. I've read a ton about this guy, and they've all reported the same things."

"He probably just knows what to say and how to act to sell news." Taking a bulk pack of sticky notes off the shelf, I turned to survey what we had so far. "I think we're almost done. You want to add some ice cream before we take off?"

She gave me a bright smile. "Of course I do. Who wouldn't want ice cream? It's hot as hell outside."

I laughed. "You make a good point. We'd better get some extra for our freezers too."

Saying those words made me think of something else I'd been considering but hadn't mentioned to her. Beth and I spent most nights these days staying over at each other's houses, and the more I thought about it, the more I realized she'd be the perfect roommate.

"When I find a house," I started, not really knowing how to broach the subject, "would you like to move in with me? You could save on rent and it'd be fun living together."

"It would be fun," she said, but her tone made her answer pretty clear. "But I'm fine in my little two-bedroom house. It's more than enough for me, and better yet, I don't have any responsibilities. My tiny lawn could go for a month without being mowed, and I never have to worry if I have nothing but wine in my fridge."

I couldn't help but feel a frisson of relief running through me. I'd been living on my own for a while now and I hadn't really wanted to give that up. "That's fine. I just thought I'd offer. You've done so much for me and—"

Her hand flew up to clamp over my mouth. "Stop it with all that already. You do just as much for me, and everything I've done, I've done because I wanted to. You don't owe me anything, least of all a place to stay."

"You would save on rent," I offered.

She rolled her eyes at me. "The truck's doing well enough that I can afford it. I appreciate the offer, babe, really. You're welcome to stay with me whenever you like, and I expect the same privileges at your place, but you don't have to worry about me."

My phone chiming distracted both of us.

Beth's eyes lit up. "Is that him?"

"I don't know yet." I laughed. "Give me a second to get it out of my purse."

Practically bouncing beside me, she waited impatiently to read the message, which was from the *him* in question. "It's Taydom."

"I knew it." She gave her butt a wiggle. "I knew he liked you."

I turned my screen toward her so she could see for herself that there was nothing going on between us.

Unknown: See? This is what you do when people give you their number. You reach out. Are you free tomorrow sometime so I can get an idea of what you're looking for?

"Girl, how is that not flirting?" She stared at my phone and jabbed a finger at it. "That's totally flirting. Don't message him back away. Wait a day or two. Take back the power."

"I told you I don't care about the power." I turned the screen back and typed a fast reply, sending it off before she could make me doubt myself.

Me: Sure. Tomorrow would be great. Since my time is flexible right now, what time works for you?

CHAPTER 12

TAYDOM

Elsie walked into my office looking like a wet dream come to life. A fitted navy top with white polka dots and a row of small buttons down the front showed more skin than I'd seen from her, and I liked what I saw.

A wide red belt was cinched around her waist, and a denim pencil skirt with low red heels completed the ensemble. Her hair was pulled back again, too. A high ponytail that left her face clear seemed to be her default style, and it suited her.

Her skin was smooth as porcelain, her cheeks were flushed, and her green eyes were bright as she closed the door behind her. There was a fifties, pin-up kind of thing going on with her today that was hotter than hell.

"I'm sorry I'm late, but you could have prepared me for the size of your building. I got lost trying to find your office. It's huge."

I pushed away from my desk where I'd been leaning with my arms folded while waiting for her. A smirk formed on my lips. "That's what I like to hear."

The flush on her cheeks deepened, but she didn't back down. "Oh, so that's what this is about. You got the big offices to compensate for something else. I get it. Don't worry."

I laughed, appreciating that she didn't back away from banter. "I'm not worried. I have nothing to compensate for. I assure you. I'd offer to show you, but you can at least buy me dinner first."

She lifted one of her hands and moved it around in a circular motion. "You have all this, and you want *me* to buy *you* dinner? I don't think so, buddy."

"Fine." I let out an exaggerated huff. "If you insist, I'll buy you lunch this afternoon. Let's go."

Leaving my jacket where it was hanging on a wooden stand in the corner, I moved toward the door. Elsie looked taken aback, a frown pulling her brows together. "Uh, where are you going? I thought you were just joking. We have a meeting here, right?"

"Yeah, but I thought we could talk outside of a business setting if that's all right with you." Uncertainty clouded her eyes and the corner of her mouth dipped in. "It's not a big deal. I wanted to get something to eat anyway because I haven't had lunch yet."

Her chest rose and fell on a deep breath, but then she nodded. "Okay. Yes. Sure. Let's go get something to eat."

I wondered what the hesitation was about, but I didn't ask. Instead, I waited for her to move toward the door. Then I opened it and followed her out.

Acting on instinct, my hand fell to her lower back and it was only when she stiffened that I realized what I was doing. *Fuck.*

What the hell was wrong with me? Whenever I was around this woman, I had these insane urges to touch her, and I really wasn't a touchy-feely sort of person.

Before I took my hand away, I felt Elsie relax into my touch and even slow down a little like she didn't want to lose it.

Now that's more like it. "How do you feel about Mexican?" I asked when we had pushed our way through the revolving doors in my lobby and walked outside. "There's a place near here that's pretty good, but their food is on the spicier side."

"I can do spicy," she said confidently, flashing me a smile. "In fact, spicy is my favorite."

Why does it sound like she's talking about something else? I nearly groaned out loud but caught myself before it came out.

I shoved my hands in my pockets then, needing to stop touching her even in that small way and realizing that Andrew was right. I needed to get laid. *Stat.*

Too bad the only woman who had captured my interest in a while was this one, and she hadn't even really wanted to have lunch with me. I doubted sleeping with me was on her agenda.

Why do I always have to want what I can't have? I'd have to figure it out later because Elsie was looking at me with a questioning tilt to her head now, her eyes narrowed. "Are you okay?"

"Yeah. Just zoned out for a second. Sorry."

"Already bored of me?" she asked, her tone teasing but a hint of something else in her eyes.

"No." *The complete opposite actually.* "I'm just hungry, and hearing you say spicy is your favorite made me lose concentration for a minute. Spicy is my favorite, too, and it was like I could already taste the flavors on my tongue."

Not necessarily the flavors of food and not necessarily only hungry for just that either, but that didn't make it any less true. Elsie chuckled and bumped her hip playfully against mine as we walked. "I totally understand. I take my food seriously as well."

A flush appeared on her cheeks again, and I wondered what it was about. Once again, though, I didn't ask. I definitely didn't feel the same way about my other clients as I did about her, but it wasn't like we were friends.

There were so many things I was curious about with her, but I didn't want to pry. Prying meant she might return the favor, and I certainly still didn't want that.

The smell of onion and cilantro met my nostrils when we walked into the small restaurant down the street from my office. Blue and orange walls and low lights hanging over the bar gave the place a Tex-Mex feel, and the vibe inside was almost homey.

Elsie released a contented sound beside me as we were ushered to a small table in the corner. She glanced at me. "It smells delicious in here. I'm suddenly glad that you were so hungry you decided not to do business in a business setting."

"I figured you might be." I took my seat after pulling out her chair for her, which earned me a surprised look. I shrugged. "What? I *was* taught manners once upon a time."

The corners of her lips quirked. "You're an enigma. Has anyone ever told you that?"

"All the time." I flashed her a devilish smirk and sat back in my chair. "Okay, so tell me, what is it you're looking for in a house?"

"Wow, straight to business, huh? Okay. Well, uh, I don't need anything too big." The emerald green of her eyes became a touch darker. "I'd like to have a guest bedroom, but it's not a deal breaker if a place only has one bedroom."

"Okay." I drummed my fingers against my leg. "What else?"

"The most important thing is that it's safe. I don't want to have to feel like I'm risking my neck every time I stick my head out the door."

"That makes sense." A crazy idea started taking root in my head. I had no idea where it had come from, but now that it was there, I couldn't shake it. "When we spoke the other day, you said you were taking a break from work while you finish school and that you weren't sure where you were going to end up. Where are your classes?"

"Central U," she said. "Why?"

"Fancy." I whistled when she mentioned the name of the university she attended. She had to be really smart to have gotten in there. "I always wanted to go to college, but I got caught up in building the company. Central U was my dream once upon a time, though."

"You seem to have done just fine without the education." She smiled and lifted her brows. "I mean, it's a great university but I don't know how you could possibly have been more successful than you already are."

"Yeah, I know, but acquiring more knowledge is never a bad thing."

"True." Elsie absently twisted the ring on her index finger. I'd noticed it was something she did when she was nervous or in thought.

Considering the offer I was about to make her, it was nice to know that I'd learned at least a few real things about her.

"So, you think you can help me find a place?" she asked. "I know safety comes at a premium, and I'm willing to pay it."

"You might not have to." *What the fuck are you doing?* "I think I know of the perfect place for you. There isn't a safer neighborhood in the city, and you're in luck because it's empty at the moment, so you could move in whenever you wanted to. It's got two bedrooms, a full bathroom, and the property it's on has a ton of amenities. There's a pool, a hot tub, a wet bar, a gym, and even a wine cellar, though you'd have to make nice with the owner to get access to that."

She sat up straighter, eyes widening. "It sounds like it would cost a fortune, but I'm definitely interested. When can we go have a look at it?"

"Right now if you want to. It also doesn't cost nearly as much as you're probably imagining it would."

"We could really go today?" Skepticism crept into her voice. "What's the catch?"

"There is no catch. Let's get some food. Then I'll take you." I grinned at her, but my mind was exploding with questions I couldn't answer.

What I had just done was completely and utterly insane, and I had no idea why I'd done it. There was just something about this girl that fucking got to me.

The way she'd said the most important thing was for her to be safe, combined with her speech last night about just wanting to help people, had flipped some kind of primitive switch deep inside me. It brought out a part of me that wanted to keep her safe, to help the person who was dedicating her life to helping others. I'd also remembered what she'd said about that cottage the other day at the open house, and it just so happened that I knew of an even better cottage that was available.

It was crazy and completely unlike me, but what was done was done.

"You'll take me?" she asked. "Like, you want me to go there with you in your car?"

"Sure. Why not? It would be stupid to take two cars when we could both fit into one. If we're supposed to consider the environment before printing an email, I'm pretty sure we have to do the same thing before driving."

"I don't really know you." Another ring twist as her teeth sank into her lips. "But you want me to drive with you and to go to a house with you alone? One that I don't know the address of?"

It took me a second to realize what she was saying, and my jaw practically hit the table when I did. "Trust me. I have way more to lose than you think I do if I tried anything with you." *Like my mom cutting off my balls with a blunt butter knife, for one.* "But if it makes you feel better, I'll give you the address and you can text it to whoever you want."

Her eyes darted between mine, but then she sighed. "Yeah, okay. I'll go."

Elsie didn't look entirely convinced that it was a good idea, but at least she'd agreed. God, what was she going to do when she figured out that there was a catch to this place, and more specifically, was she going to run for the hills when she realized what it was?

CHAPTER 13

ELSIE

The community Taydom drove me to after lunch was like something out of a novel. There was a heavy iron gate that guarded the entrance with some kind of intricate-looking crest on it. A security hut sat next to the gate in front of the thirty-foot-high walls that seemed to go on for miles on both sides of it.

Walls covered in ivy made the neighborhood look like some kind of country estate, and that alone immediately made me fall a little bit in love with it. I tried to imagine pulling up to this gate every day, knowing it was welcoming me home, and almost moaned out loud.

Taydom glanced at me as he pulled to a stop in front of it, a smug smile spreading on his lips. "Like what you see so far?"

"I love it."

I didn't see him press a button, nor did I see a guard, but the gate started sliding open without anyone questioning us. I arched an eyebrow at him, suddenly not so impressed by the amazing security.

"Does it open for anyone who parks here?"

"No." He scoffed. "Getting access to this community requires just about everything short of a blood sample."

"Then why did it open for you?"

"Magic." He smirked and wiggled his fingers for effect before wrapping them around his steering wheel again and gunning it through the gate.

Behind the walls, the neighborhood was just as beautiful as it had appeared to me from the outside. The street we drove down was lined with trees that provided a dense canopy overhead. Kids cycled without a care in the world and waved at Taydom as we passed.

"Do you know them?"

"Nah." He flicked his indicator on. "But people are friendly here."

Houses started appearing once we were farther into the community, and they were exactly what I would have imagined manor houses to look like. There were no walls or fences, only impressive buildings with perfectly manicured lawns and hedges separating one property from the next.

"Is this an older community?"

He nodded. "It was one of the first upmarket neighborhoods that was developed as a gated community from the get-go. Most people who buy here stay in here until they're carried out feet first."

"And you said it wasn't expensive." I rolled my eyes and shook my head at him. "This is beautiful, and it's everything anyone could want safety-wise, but there's no way I can afford it."

"Trust me. You can." He kept talking up the neighborhood as we passed through it. "As I'm not sure you noticed, we're almost adjacent to Bishop's Hollow. You mentioned the career opportunities there were good, so I figured you'd want to stay close by, even if the Hollow itself wasn't for you."

"Yeah, I'd love to." I liked hearing him talk like this.

At first, I'd been a little freaked out about the prospect of driving with him alone and going to a house where no one knew I would be going, but the truth was that I felt safe with him.

My concern hadn't really had anything to do with Taydom as an individual anyway. I'd never gotten a threatening or creepy vibe from him, but in general, I was wary of strangers. It might've sounded like more of a kid problem, but Mom had drilled it so deep into me how to take care of myself that I remained on high alert.

Now that she was no longer around and I was alone in the world, except for Beth, it seemed even more important that I didn't make any decisions that could put me in danger. Mom would never forgive me if I did.

Maybe I was a bit of a scaredy cat, but I had no one else to look out for me. I had to look out for myself, and even though Taydom was apparently rich and famous in these parts, I didn't know him.

Listening to him speak now, I realized it was silly of me to have been worried at all. It had been a knee-jerk reaction and not one he'd deserved. He was super professional and pointed out key points of the area to me until we reached what appeared to be the back of the community.

"You're really good at what you do," I said as he drove up a cobbled path leading up around the side of a mansion.

"It comes with the territory, but thanks." He gave me a smile, then turned his eyes back to the road. Dense trees rose up on either side of us and a bright green lawn surrounded the massive house beside us.

"Why would there be a little two-bedroom place next to a house like this?" I asked when it became clear that the house he was taking me to had to be on the same property.

"It's a guest house, but it's not used very often, so the owner recently decided to rent it out." He pulled to a stop in front of a single garage at the back of the property, next to what looked like a cottage. "Let's take a look, shall we?"

The little house was far enough away from the main house for both parties to have privacy, but not so far away that it felt isolated or lonely here. A sparkling pool sat between the two structures, a massive, separate entertainment area beside it.

"I have to tell you, I think I'm falling in love here. Please tell me you weren't kidding about it being affordable."

"I wasn't," he assured me. "The owner isn't renting it out for the money. More because it's a gorgeous place and it doesn't deserve to stand empty when there's someone out there who might appreciate it."

"I'm definitely appreciating it." I followed him from the car along a path made of flagstones that led to the front door. Rose bushes grew beside the path and it even had a little fountain in the middle. "This is like something out of a fairy tale."

"That was the idea when it was built," he said with an edge to his voice that I didn't understand. "Anyway, have a look. I know it's not big, but you said you didn't need big. There's a kitchen, dining and living room, the two bedrooms and a bathroom between them, but that's about it."

"It's perfect," I breathed as he gave me the tour. It didn't take more than a few minutes for him to show me the place, but I loved every inch of it. "I guess the only question left to ask is who owns the main house? What are they like?"

Taydom stopped walking when I asked the question, turning to face me with a sheepish grin spreading on his lips. The amber of his eyes practically glowed in the dappled afternoon sunlight shining in through the trees outside, and there was something bashful in them.

"Okay, so that might just be the catch."

"Why?" I frowned. "Is it some old man who likes to sunbathe naked or a crazy cat lady who talks to her dead husband's ghost?"

He laughed and dragged a hand through the dark brown strands of his hair. "No, thankfully not. To tell you the truth, it's me. It's my house."

My breath caught and my eyeballs nearly popped clean out of my head. "Are you serious?"

"Yeah." His eyes stayed on mine as he lifted his shoulders. "It's everything you were looking for, isn't it?"

"It's the most perfect place I've ever seen, and I would love nothing more than to live in it, but why would you do this for me?"

"Like I said, it's been standing empty and it deserves someone who loves it. As for why I'm offering it to you, it seemed like a good fit. I wouldn't want to put you into a mortgage while you're finishing your schooling, and finding a different place for you to rent when I've got this one just seemed redundant."

My arms folded across my chest as I looked up at him, his broad shoulders squared and the tanned skin of his forearms rippling as he looped his fingers into his belt. "There's something else to this. What is it?"

His chin came up as he stared at me down his straight nose, and a soft sigh finally parted his lips. "I remember what it was like to look for things with no help. You're willing to dedicate your life to helping others, which isn't something a lot of people would do. I'd simply like to offer you some."

Neither of us said another word for a long minute, our gazes locked together in the middle of the cool living room as the very air between us crackled. In that moment, I wanted nothing more than to wrap my arms around him, to hold this beautiful, confident man who apparently had a lot more to him than I would've given him credit for.

I wanted to press my lips to his and feel if they were as soft as they looked, but also to find out if he kissed with the same tenderness he'd just displayed or with the passion he had when he spoke about his job.

Taydom Gaines was known to be a dick, I'd learned, but the man standing in front of me now couldn't have been further away from that. It felt like the mottled sunlight had peeled away several of his layers and was giving me a glimpse of what lay underneath, and I really liked what I saw.

Nothing would happen between us romantically, I was sure, despite how the air seemed to zap and crack between us. But maybe he would become a friend.

The gesture he'd just made certainly made me want him in my life in some capacity, and honestly, the house he'd offered me really was like a dream come true. I might have to get over this attraction I felt toward him. With the pool between our houses, getting over it might also require batteries and some me time if I ever saw him in swimming trunks, but I was confident I could manage it.

There was no way I was allowing something as silly as attraction to put me off this house. It would be like living in a fairy tale without the prince, but I'd always believed those girls hadn't needed the princes anyway.

"Okay," I said finally, my voice barely above a whisper. "I'll take it."

CHAPTER 14

TAYDOM

The men sitting around my conference table had steely gazes and tight jaws. Each and every one of them was used to getting what he wanted, and right now, none of them felt like they were getting it.

I raked my hands through my hair and shook my head. "The capitalization rate on this property is excellent. The net operating income could be better, but it's high, and the area is becoming more popular by the day."

"Sure, Gaines." Cold, calculating blue eyes met mine from the left-hand side of the table, the potential-tenant side. "But not all commercial properties were created equal, as you know. The operational management expenses alone justify—"

A balled-up fist hit the table as the representative for the owners pushed back his chair and jumped to his feet. "That's bullshit and you know it."

"Gentlemen," I warned and pushed my fingers together on the table. "This is a negotiation, not fight night. Sit down, Ben."

He cut me a look, but he was in no position to argue. As it was, he should have been thanking me instead of making this more difficult.

Without me, the deal we were in the process of negotiating wouldn't have been on the table at all, and he couldn't afford for it not to be.

The last time we'd met with these people, Ben had come close to blowing the entire deal. Then he'd had the balls to come crying to me about his problems after. I'd promised him one more bite at the cherry and this was it.

If he fucked it up, I couldn't help him. He glowered at me but did as I asked.

"Right. Let's look at what it's going to take to get a yes from both sides of the table." I unbuttoned my jacket, took it off, and rolled up my sleeves. *Time to earn my money.*

Two and a half hours later, I had a signed contract in my hand. Mr. Sandler, the one with the cold blue eyes and the sharp tongue, was the last to leave the conference room.

"Thank you for your help, Gaines. We're happy to have worked with you. I've heard the rumors about why you're the best, and I have to say, I agree. You'll definitely be hearing from us again in the future."

"That's excellent news," I said. This deal had been hard as fuck to get down on paper, and three of my agents had failed before I'd stepped in, but it had been worth the time and effort.

The firm was getting a decent chunk of change and, more importantly, had gained another big corporate client. "I'd be happy to help you anytime. Just let me know what you need."

"We're looking into a Southern expansion within the next month or two. I'll give you a call with the details sometime."

"Sure thing." I grinned as he said his goodbyes. Then I collapsed into my chair and fist-pumped the air as I leaned my head back. *What a fucking day.*

Andrew sauntered into my office a minute later and released a low whistle between his teeth. "I just saw Sandler and his crew leaving. How'd that go for you?"

"We closed the motherfucking deal, baby." I lifted my hand for a high-five.

His brows rose, but he indulged my unspoken request and slapped his palm against mine. "Congratulations. I didn't think that was going to happen, if I'm being honest. Even with you at the helm, it was a long shot." He shrugged before his lips formed a smirk. "But you know, I could have done it, too."

I shot him a look and he laughed, holding both his hands up. "Yeah, yeah. Okay. Maybe you were the better guy for the job."

"Don't you know it?" I rubbed my palms over the stubble on my jaw and sat up straight again. "What's up? Did you need something?"

He shook his head. "Not really. I was curious when I saw those guys come in earlier, so I thought I'd check in with you this afternoon. Since you had a big win today, how about we go celebrate tomorrow afternoon? We can hang out at my place or we can go somewhere? It'll be Friday, so there should be a lot happening we can join in on."

"It might have been fun, but I can't. I already have plans."

"So cancel them," he said with his brows pulling together in a confused frown. "Just reschedule your meeting and we'll be good to go. Come on, man. Just this once, don't give me any shit about coming out. The Sandler deal is huge. It deserves to be toasted."

"I agree, it does deserve to be toasted, but it can't be tomorrow." I set my elbows down on the armrests of the chair and linked my fingers in front of my stomach, bracing myself for telling him the truth. "Unfortunately, these plans can't be rescheduled. I'm helping Elsie move."

He stilled, then shoved his hands in his pockets and arched a blond eyebrow at me. "Good on you for finding a client a place so fast, but since when do we help them move?"

"I'm making an exception for her."

"Why?" His head dropped to the side, his eyes curious on mine. "How did you find her a place so fast? Last I checked, we didn't exactly have many smaller places on our books."

Right, I'd told him after we'd run into her at the food truck that she'd said the place from the open house had been way too much. It was a conversation I was regretting now, but it was too late to take it back.

In any event, there was no reason not to be honest with him. I just wasn't particularly in the mood to take the shit I was going to get about it.

I lifted my chin. "She's moving into my guest house."

Andrew's jaw slackened as he absorbed my words. "Your guest house? As in the place you renovated and got ready for your mother when she visited?"

"That's the one." I sighed. "Obviously, she hasn't been using it much. It's just been standing empty, and now there's someone who can occupy it."

"I remember giving you shit about being a Momma's boy when you were doing it, but this is so much worse."

I laughed as I remembered just how much shit he'd given me for painstakingly fixing up the place. "It can't possibly be worse. You were all but convinced I was going to move her in with me permanently."

"Dude, you're the only grown-ass man I know who went through so much effort to make sure your mom would have somewhere comfortable to stay."

"True, but it's not like she can come through to Dallas for the day. If she ever left the farm, she'd have to come for at least a few days to make it worth her while. You don't know my mom, but she'd never come stay with me for days if she had to stay in the house. She'd think it's too inconvenient for me."

He nodded sagely. "Yeah, that's because it would be inconvenient. For all concerned. Could you imagine your mother running into the girl you were with the night before when she's doing the walk of shame?"

"No." I scrunched my face up in disgust. "If my mother ever was to come out here, I wouldn't be bringing any women home with me. Even if she stayed in the cottage."

Andrew's head tipped back as he laughed. "Yep. Absolutely still a Momma's boy."

"Nope. Again, you don't know my mother. If she ran into a woman on her way out of my house in the morning, she'd flag her down, make her some coffee, and start planning the wedding."

His eyes widened. "No shit? Then what are you doing moving a woman in with you?"

"It's not like my family has made the trip very often, obviously," I said drily. "Even Riley's only been out here once or twice, and it's been years since the last time. If any of them do come to visit by some miracle, I'll just tell them I'm renting the place out. It's not like she's moving in with me."

He tapped the corner of his mouth. "I didn't realize it had been that long since your brother came to town. Man, we had a fucking blast when he was here. You should invite him out again."

"He has a standing invitation and he knows it." My whole family did, but they hardly ever took me up on it.

My father hadn't been to visit me at all. My mother and brother came out the first few times I sent them tickets but had started refusing that I send them tickets at all these last few years. No doubt dear ol' Dad had instructed them to turn me down.

I could practically hear his voice in my head. *No Gaines needs charity, not even from another Gaines.*

Andrew tossed his hands out to his sides. "Maybe Riley will come if I tell him I need his help. We do need to get your head on straight, after all. You've invited a random stranger to live with you. That's serious."

"I didn't invite her to live with me," I growled, my mood darkening from all the talk about my family. "She's renting a place that happens to be on my property. My head has never been straighter."

The corners of his lips tilted down, but there was a spark of humor in his eyes. "Keep telling yourself that. I, for one, guess this is the beginning of the end of our friendship."

"Don't be dramatic. We've rented out places to thousands of people. This isn't any different."

His brows lifted to his hairline. "How is it not any different? It's fucking different, dude. Very fucking different."

"We'll have to agree to disagree then." I stood up and walked to the wall of windows behind my desk, turning my back on my friend.

Undeterred, he came to stand next to me. "We can do that, but I feel like I should still tell you that if she takes over your house and you need a place to stay, my door is always open."

"Thanks, but that won't be necessary." Hands sliding into my pockets, I surveyed the cloudless blue sky outside. It was the same sky that my parents were under, but I felt planets removed from them as I stood there on the top story of my high rise in downtown Dallas.

There were more people in the buildings all around me than in the entire town I'd come from. Pedestrians were making the best of the warm summer day on the sidewalks below, but none were just strolling. Everyone had someplace to be and people to see. It was another reminder that I wasn't in small-town Illinois anymore.

The pace of life in Dallas might not be as rushed as it was in some other cities, but it sure was a lot faster than back in Woodstock. I enjoyed it, but I knew my mother got overwhelmed, and my brother? Well, he could never wait to leave the city lights behind.

Andrew noticed that my mood had turned melancholic and clapped me on the shoulder. "Whether or not you think it's necessary, my offer stands. I'll let you get back to it."

He disappeared from my side and I heard the light slap of his shoes against the floor. Then the door closed behind him with a soft click. Finally turning away from the window about a minute or so later, I succumbed to checking in on my family without their knowledge.

I hadn't done anything creepy, like install cameras on the farm without them knowing—though I had been tempted once or twice. All I did was sign up for a few alerts on farming in Illinois and, more specifically, soybean farms.

My stomach dropped to my shoes at the first headline that came up after bringing up the alerts on my laptop. It was *not* good news.

Soybean farms in Illinois will not prosper this year. Definite profit losses ahead.

Well, fuck me. Looks like I might have to stop making up excuses about going home after all.

CHAPTER 15

ELSIE

"Are you really sure about this?" Beth asked as she taped up another box.

It was moving day tomorrow, and like the angel she was, my best friend was at my side helping me get packed.

I wrestled with the flap of a box containing nothing but scarves. "I'm sure. I needed a move. This will be good for me."

She let out a soft sigh and sat down on the box she'd just packed. Her gaze swept across my living room. "You're sure this is really what you want? It's not too soon, is it?"

"You encouraged this move," I pointed out as I looked up at her. "In fact, you were more excited about it than I was."

"Yeah, but now that it's actually happening, I just wanted to check in with you. You've lived here for a long time and your—"

"My mom helped me pick it out. I know." I brought my ponytail forward over my shoulder and absently braided the lower half of it. "That's one of the reasons why I need to move. There are too many memories of her here. Hanging onto those is making it harder not to imagine that she's going to be the next person knocking on my door."

Beth's eyes moved to the hooks behind said door. "I can see how that could make things harder. Remember the day she put those up?"

"Yeah." A fond smile spread across my lips. "She said we couldn't just be throwing our coats down on the couches when we came in."

"To be fair, we didn't just throw them down." Her smile matched mine. "We gently hung them over the back of the couch."

My eyebrows rose. "The way I remember it, we came in one night after one too many cocktails to celebrate the loan you got to start the truck, and we ended up shedding our winter garments as soon as we came in the door."

"Yeah." She chuckled. "But we didn't know she was going to come by to make a celebratory breakfast the next morning."

"I told her you were staying over." I shrugged but felt that familiar ache of missing her expanding in my chest. "We should have known she was going to come to make us blueberry and choc-chip pancakes. It was just her way."

"It was," Beth agreed.

Silence fell between us for several minutes after that. Both of us resumed with the packing, but while I didn't know what Beth was thinking about for sure, my mind stayed on my mother. I suspected hers did, too.

My suspicion was confirmed when she suddenly burst out in a fit of giggles. "Oh my God. Do you remember that time she sat us down and gave us that lecture about dust bunnies? She said bunnies are cute in petting zoos but gross in the home."

"You only got that lecture once," I said, grinning. "I got it all the time. That one and the one about making your bed even though you're just going to be getting back into it later."

"Giving credit where credit is due, all those little pearls of wisdom still play in my mind when I'm too lazy to clean the truck right away. I keep imagining her walking in and getting that indulgent smile on her face before she would gently start reminding me why it's so important to keep your space clean."

"Yeah, at least she was good about not making someone feel berated after one of her lectures." Tears stung the backs of my eyes and I dragged in a deep breath to keep them at bay. "I guess that's why her students loved her so much as well."

Beth must have noticed the crack in my voice. Suddenly, she looked at me over her shoulder from where she'd been folding clothes coming off hangers in my closet. "Are you still getting messages from them?"

I nodded. "Occasionally. They're slowing down, though."

Mom's employer had contacted me not long after her death to ask if it was okay for them to give out my email to some of her students. She had been loved among them and they'd asked if they could reach out to me to commiserate.

I'd appreciated it, and I loved hearing some of their memories of her and knowing what an impact she'd made on so many lives. Just like me, they'd be carrying what she'd taught them in their hearts and minds forever.

It was a way for her to live on, I supposed. It had also been comforting to know I wouldn't be the only one who would miss her.

Unfortunately, just like with everything else in this lonely journey, the messages of support had become less frequent and it felt like everyone else was moving on. I was too, in a way, but it didn't make me feel any less guilty about it.

Beth turned away from the closet and walked over to me, pulling me in for a big hug. "Just because they're not emailing you so often anymore doesn't mean they've forgotten her. Just like you and I haven't."

"I know." I returned her hug and held her tight before letting her go. "It's just hard sometimes, you know?" After wiping moisture from underneath my eyes, I took a deep breath. "But this isn't a pity party. Moving is a good thing. Let's not get wrapped up in memories right now."

"You got it." She moved back to my closet and carried on taking clothes off the hangers to fold, placing each item gently in the box behind her once she was satisfied. "So, since we're back on the topic of the move, what do you think Taydom is going to be like as a landlord?"

I shrugged but my teeth sank into my lower lip for a second. "I haven't really given it much thought. The cottage is at the back of his property and the main house is more to the front. Unless he's swimming or entertaining, I don't know if I'll be seeing much of him at all."

"You think?" She frowned. "If I was letting someone stay on my property, you can bet your ass I'd be checking in on them more regularly than normal for a landlord."

"I don't know. I mean, he's got to work a lot. To get to where he has, a person can't just twiddle their thumbs at home."

"Sure, but he's in the property game. His company offers management services as well, so he should be well versed in being a landlord. Plus, this isn't any old property you're renting out. It's his property."

"I didn't think about any of that," I admitted. "I probably should have, but if you see the place, you'll understand why I didn't. It's just so charming and perfect. The community is gorgeous, safe, and so well located. I'm willing to put up with a lot from a landlord if it means getting all those perks."

"Yeah, but," she gestured toward my closet floor, "what if he gets mad at you for not keeping the place clean? Which, if we're being honest here, seems to be the case more often than not."

"Whatever do you mean?" I asked, blinking innocently. "The floor of my closet is where the shoes go. Don't even try to tell me yours looks any better."

"It doesn't, but my landlord hasn't come by to do an inspection once since I moved in. He gets paid on time and I get someplace to stay. It seems to be working well for us."

"What makes you think it won't be the same with Taydom?"

She shook her head. "It's not that I don't think it won't be the same. We just don't know if it will be, and I wanted to make sure you'd thought about all these things."

"I get it. I would have wanted to make sure you'd thought it through as well. As much as I haven't really thought about the finer details of having him as a landlord, I'm not too worried."

A loud ripping sound tore through the air between us as she taped up another box. Between that and grabbing a new one to start on, she glanced at me.

"That's good to know. You know him better than I do, after all. If you're not worried, I'm sure I'm overthinking it."

"I don't think that you are. I really should have thought about it, but the truth is that I still would have taken him up on his offer. He'd have to end up being a really shitty landlord before I'd throw in the towel. Besides, thanks to him, I'm not locked into a contract. I'll be able to leave if he gets terrible."

Her spine straightened suddenly, eyes lighting up as she chuckled. "Yeah, I guess I'd put up with a lot to be able to live with a guy who looks like him too."

"I'm not going to be living with him," I grumbled. It wasn't the first time this was coming up. "Just like you don't live with your landlord."

"Mine is a seventy-year-old man with a beer belly who definitely won't look as good in his underwear as Taydom probably does."

I rolled my eyes at her and tried to ignore the picture of Taydom that my mind helpfully conjured up. "I wouldn't know what he looks like in any state of undress and I'm not going to find out."

"If you do, please take pictures," she joked. "Like, seriously, even if you see him in his swimming trunks. Record that shit and share it with your eye-candy deprived soul sister."

I snorted. "How are you deprived of eye candy? Just last week, you told me that there are at least three guys who frequent the truck that are, and I quote, to die for."

She sniffed and shot me a look with her brow furrowed. "None of them come to grab their lunches in their swimming attire, you know? All I get are nice smiles, pretty faces, and a glance at their hands when they reach out to take their hot dogs. It's not exactly great inspiration."

"Hey, hands can be sexy." Taydom's, in particular, definitely were. They were big, with long slender fingers that still managed to look strong—like they'd be able to crush anything that needed to be.

Even his fingernails, short, round, and clean, added to the appeal of those hands. They didn't look manicured necessarily, but he definitely took care of himself. Yet, despite how graceful and refined they seemed, I still got the feeling he wasn't all polished.

At lunch the other day, I'd noticed an assortment of small scars on his hands. Nothing so bad to indicate that he'd been cut up or something, but his hands definitely had stories to tell.

I liked that, and Beth seemed to notice.

"Let me guess," she said, her eyes alight with amusement. "You were thinking about a certain landlord to be when you made that comment?"

Blood rushed to my cheeks, but I lifted my shoulder in a small, nonchalant shrug. "Maybe, but he does have nice hands."

"I hadn't noticed." She laughed, but her face grew serious again soon after. "Which brings me to another point I was wondering if you'd considered. How are you going to feel if he brings girls home?"

"Fine." My stomach churned on the blatant lie, but I was determined to get over this ridiculous little crush I had. "We don't have that kind of relationship, so it wouldn't be a problem."

"What if he gets freaky with someone in the pool and you see them?" She wagged her eyebrows at me. "Other than remembering to snap a pic of his firm butt for your bestie if you can tear your eyes off it for a second, what will you do?"

"Not take a picture of it for you," I said, my tone snippy. "Or ogle him myself for that matter. The man deserves his privacy in his own pool and I won't invade it that way."

"I guess I'll just have to come to visit you often while it's still summer," she joked. "But okay. Again, I just wanted to be sure you'd thought about it."

"I'm not concerned about that kind of thing. Like I said, we don't have that kind of relationship. I don't think he's interested in me that way and I won't interfere in his private life if there's someone he does feel that way about."

Beth made a sound that made it clear she didn't agree with me, but I ignored it and went back to my packing. It would suck to have him parade an endless amount of women around the pool my new living room looked out on, but if that happened, I could simply keep the curtains drawn.

Nothing, not even petty jealousy I didn't have any real reason to feel, was going to deter me from the decision I'd made. I was moving into Taydom's guest house tomorrow and I was damn well going to enjoy living in the little slice of paradise he'd offered me.

No naked butts or midnight frolicking in the pool were going to stop me.

CHAPTER 16

TAYDOM

"Is that it?" I asked as I loaded the last of Elsie's boxes into the back of the truck I'd borrowed from a friend for the day.

She nodded and wiped her forehead with the back of her hand. Her face was red, but I was sure mine wasn't any better. It felt like it was eleven-million degrees out and we'd just spent the better part of the morning loading up her belongings.

Her black hair was piled on top of her head, and she wore a simple pair of black shorts and a black tank top. She looked good, even with the red face.

I was starting to think this girl would look good in anything, but much better in nothing. While her outfit wasn't revealing, it accentuated her curves and made my fingers itch to run along them.

"Thank God I don't have a shopping problem," she said, drawing my attention away from the small bead of sweat running down the side of her neck. "I can't imagine how awful it must be to move if you're one of those people who buys everything they see."

"I think they just get moving companies to do it for them." I closed the bed of the truck with a smirk aimed in her direction. "You know, just like I offered to get for you?"

"It really wouldn't have been worth paying someone for this." She motioned at the tied-down boxes. "I even told you that Beth and I could do it by ourselves. Unless you've conveniently forgotten that little detail."

I tapped one of my temples. "I never forget the little details. It's one of the things that makes me so good at what I do. As I told you before, it's no trouble to help you. I was simply reminding you that you had another option available to you."

"None that was viable." She flicked her gaze up to her apartment building and I could have sworn I saw her eyes water up, but then she blinked and offered me a smile. "Should we get going? I'm sure you're looking forward to getting this over with."

"No way. Helping friends move is what I live for on Saturdays." I walked around to open the door for her, smiled wide when she shot me a questioning look, and motioned for her to get in. "What's that for?"

"Two things," she replied once I was settled behind the wheel. "Firstly, you referred to us as friends, and secondly, you got the door for me."

Her eyes were focused intently on me as I twisted the key to start the old clunker. For some reason, she seemed to stare at my hand as I flexed my fingers over the stick when I shifted it into gear. Interesting.

Now wasn't the time to wonder about it, though. "We are friends, aren't we?"

She shrugged and finally lifted her gaze away from my arm to focus on the side of my face as I eased into the traffic. "Sure. I guess. Does that mean I can borrow a cup of sugar when I need it?"

"That's a neighborly thing, so you're welcome to borrow sugar. Considering that your neighbor is also your friend, you also get wine-borrowing privileges."

She chuckled. "While that's definitely a perk I'm going to end up taking advantage of, never let Beth hear that you made that offer. Your cellar would be drained within a month."

"You haven't seen the size of my cellar." I winked, then groaned when I realized how my playful, though completely accurate, comment must have sounded. "Sorry, that came out sounding like I meant it as a reference to something else."

Elsie laughed. "It really did, but you're forgiven. I know you didn't mean it that way."

The certainty in her voice made me glance at her. There hadn't been much flirtation between the two of us, but something about her tone bothered me.

It was almost like she didn't believe I'd want to engage in flirting or innuendo-laden conversation with her. Crazy, considering that my dick had started pressing up against my zipper when I'd noticed the way she was looking at my hand. I couldn't help but wonder if she was thinking about what it might feel like on her.

It wasn't like I could tell her that, though. I wasn't about to make her rethink moving by suddenly starting to hit on her. So I settled for getting to know her better. Maybe eventually, she'd start feeling the same chemistry between us that I did, and once that happened, maybe we could do something about making it go away.

Besides, helping her move had been good for distracting me from what I'd learned yesterday, and I wanted to stay that way. "So, should I be expecting many parties over at the cottage from now on?"

A soft, cute little snort came from her side of the cab. "The college I go to isn't exactly known for its active social calendar, so no. Why? Would it have been a problem if I said yes?"

"No. I really wouldn't have minded. I was just curious about whether I should study up on how to talk to frat guys or expect my grass to get spun out in the midst of a showdown."

"I think you watch too many movies." She laughed, and I caught the end of a headshake in my periphery. "Also, if they were my parties these frat guys would have been attending, what makes you think you would have been invited?"

"Ouch." I lifted a hand to my chest and rubbed the spot over my heart. "That hurts. I thought we'd established that we were friends?"

She dipped her head in agreement. "True. I'm sorry. If I undergo a change in personality and also change schools, you will be the first person invited to my party."

"Thank you." I grinned. "When do your classes start up again?"

"Monday." She turned to face the window when we started getting closer to her new neighborhood. "Thank you for helping me get my car out here earlier and for all your help with the move."

"No problem." The city started growing smaller behind us and the buildings beside the freeway were less densely spaced. Green treetops and wide-open spaces loomed up ahead, bringing a smile to my face. "I'm glad you decided to take me up on my offer. We're going to have fun living together."

"We're not going to be living together," she protested automatically, almost as if she was as tired of hearing that phrase as I was.

My laughter bounced off the windows of the otherwise silent cab. "I was kidding, but I'm assuming I'm not the only one who got the talk?"

"Definitely not." She relaxed back in her seat, her features softening with every mile that went by. "What about you? Am I going to be hearing any raging parties happening at your house?"

"The most raging it gets at my house is when Drew comes by to watch a game." Sadly, it was true.

Elsie opened her mouth, presumably to ask something else, but then decided against it. She released a contented sigh instead when I turned off at our exit, then shifted to face me again. "What made you decide to buy a place out here anyway? There are much hipper, livelier neighborhoods around for a guy like you to live in."

"A guy like me?" I knew these roads like the back of my hand, and since there wasn't any traffic, I figured it was safe to look at her for a moment.

She chewed the inside of her cheek before giving me an apologetic smile. "I didn't mean it as an insult. It's just that you're young and successful, not bad looking and—"

"Not bad looking, huh?" When I saw the apples of her cheeks color, it dawned on me what she might have wanted to ask before deciding otherwise. "Thank you. You're not bad looking either."

It was the understatement to end all understatements, but it was better than freaking her out by telling her what I really thought.

"I lived in one of those hipper neighborhoods before this place came on the market. I bought it pretty much the same day I found out it was for sale. I liked the space and vegetation, trees all around, and not feeling like I was sleeping a foot away from the person next door. Don't get me wrong. I still like going out to grab a drink and all that, but it's not really my scene for everyday living." Wanting to answer her unspoken question as well, I added, "There was a time that I lived up to the playboy reputation I used to have but not anymore."

"That's a surprisingly non-explicit way of saying it," she remarked, but I didn't miss how tension eased out of her jaw. "You didn't have to tell me that, by the way. It's none of my business."

"No, but we're friends and we're about to be neighbors. You have a right to know what you're in for. There are a couple of teenagers that live in the houses on either side of us. Whenever their parents go away, they throw the expected house parties. Other than that, you're in for peace and quiet."

"What about the house itself? Is there anything you expect of me there?"

I frowned as I shook my head from side to side, gently stepping on the brakes as we rolled up to the gate. "Nothing. It's your house, Elsie. I'm happy to help you fix whatever needs fixing, but I'm not going to tell you what to do or when to do it."

"Good to know." She grinned as the gate started sliding open. "I can't believe I get to call this home from now on."

Her hand shot to squeeze my thigh as she bounced in her seat. It didn't look like she even realized she was touching me, but I sure as hell realized.

The shorts I wore were made of a thin fabric, and I could feel the warmth of her palm on my skin. Her pinky finger was also only inches away from my junk, which didn't help matters much.

My muscles stiffened as I tried to fight the effect of her innocent touch. It was only then that she seemed to notice that she was, in fact, touching me.

With her cheeks reddening to the same hue they'd had just after we'd spent the morning hauling her boxes downstairs, her eyes widened and she yanked her hand back. "Jeez. I promise I'm not usually so touchy-feely. I just got excited."

"Feel free to get as touchy-feely as you want." *Wait. Fuck, Taydom. You could have waited until the gate was fully closed behind you.*

Elsie laughed my comment off. "It's good to know that success hasn't made you lose your sense of humor. Although I guess you'd remember what you felt like the first time you drove through these gates and knew you were home."

"Yeah, sure. That's what it was about." I almost rolled my eyes at myself, but I busied my mind with planning the impending offloading instead. "When we get there, I'll grab the boxes if you can just tell me where they need to go."

"Nonsense. I'll help get everything inside. Then you can go do whatever it is you do on Saturday afternoons and I'll get busy unpacking."

"We'll see."

Elsie ended up ignoring me and carrying the boxes she could while I heaved the heavier ones inside. This morning, Beth had brought over the few pieces of furniture that had belonged to Elsie that she'd had in her former apartment in the food truck, so at least all that was already done.

As I hoisted up a black garbage bag filled with something that sounded like it was filled with bells, something sharp sliced through my finger. "Fuck."

"What?" she called from inside the cottage. The garbage bag was one of the last things we'd needed to carry inside, but now I was bleeding all over the path leading to her new front door.

"I think I cut myself." Gently setting the bag down on the floor—to the side so it wouldn't get blood on it—I lifted my hand. "Yep. Definitely cut myself."

A jagged-looking cut sat on the side of my middle finger. It wasn't deep enough to require stitches but it was definitely deep enough that I was going to have a new scar to add to my ever-growing collection.

I sighed, more annoyed than anything else. Elsie ran up to me, face pale as she watched blood trickling down my palm and over my wrist. "Oh no. Oh God. I'm so sorry. What—"

She cut herself off when her gaze dropped to the bag. "Shit. I should have warned you. My Christmas decorations wouldn't fit in any of the boxes I had leftover."

I winced but not from the pain. "When we tell other people about this, can we please not tell them that I sliced myself open on a fucking Christmas decoration?"

It didn't appear that she'd heard me. She touched her fingers to my uninjured hand instead and gripped it tightly. Panic seeped into her voice and her eyes were wild. "I know where my first-aid kit is. Come with me. I'll fix you right up. I can't put in stitches, obviously, but I can—"

"Relax," I said once she'd sat me down on the couch and went in search of her kit. "I'm fine. I just need to run it under some water until the bleeding stops. Trust me. This isn't my first cut and it won't be the last."

Thankfully, she didn't stop to question me. She kept chattering nervously as she ripped open a box in her kitchen and came back to me. In addition to her kit, she also carried a bowl of water and some paper towels.

"How'd you find all of that so fast?"

She shrugged. "Adrenaline. Now open your hand and let me get to work."

She sat down so close to my side that she was practically in my lap, but I didn't mind. Her touch was so gentle that I almost didn't notice she was fixing me up until she was all done.

Instead of watching what she was doing, I watched her. The way her eyelashes fanned across her cheeks as she kept her gaze on my hand. The way her chest was heaving as if she was running a marathon.

And okay, I also had a pretty decent fucking view of her cleavage from here. A fact that I couldn't ignore and not something I could stop looking at. Thinking I was safe to stare, considering how attentive she was being to my wound, turned out to be wrong.

Her throat cleared, and when I lifted my eyes, it was to find hers on mine and an arched dark eyebrow. "Enjoying the view?"

"I was actually." I smirked, but then I noticed that her eyes had dropped again. Only this time, it wasn't to my hand.

She was looking at my mouth, her chest still rising and falling faster than normal. When her tongue dashed across the fullness of her lower lip, my resolve crumbled.

I'd wanted this woman since the first time I'd laid eyes on her. While I wasn't the prolific ladies' man Andrew was, I knew what she wanted at that moment. A kiss.

It was the first definite sign that she wanted me too, and I wasn't going to let the opportunity to taste her pass me by.

Bringing my hand to her face, I cupped her chin and lifted it until her eyes were back on mine. Electricity passed between us and the air itself thickened with tension. "I'm going to kiss you now. If you don't want me to, this is your chance to say it."

When the only response I got was a soft moan and another swipe of her tongue across her lip, I lowered my head and brought her mouth to mine.

Sweet baby Jesus. Finally, fucking finally, but holy shit has this kiss been worth the wait.

CHAPTER 17

ELSIE

*H*oly hotcakes in heaven.

If there was one thing every girl knew, it was that kisses could either be the mother of all disappointments or the very best feeling in the world.

Unfortunately, despite what romance novels and movies wanted us to believe, it was very often the handsome cocky guys who disappointed. Beth and I had discussed the conundrum numerous times and believed it was because they thought their looks, money, or whatever else made up for the fact that they'd never bothered to ask what they were doing wrong. It was almost like they thought possessing one or more of those attributes would make up for any shortcomings they had in the kissing department.

Newsflash, boys! They don't.

Taydom, on the other hand, kissed like he had a doctorate degree in the art. And with him, it definitely was an art form.

Sparks exploded behind my eyelids when they lowered of their own accord, and an angelic choir started singing in my ears. *Hold the presses, people. The hottest guy in Dallas, who's also one of the ones with the most money, actually bothered to slow down to learn how to kiss at some point.*

It was a revelation, but it was also dangerous. My nipples peaked against the lace of my bra, and my panties grew damp, but he wasn't even really touching me. Not like I wanted him to anyway.

Both of his hands were way above the waistline. One large palm was fitted to the back of my neck while the other was on my back.

As enveloped by him as I was, it was impossible to miss the expensive, woodsy yet spicy scent of him. It shouldn't have been possible for him to smell good after he'd spent all morning lugging my stuff around, but there was only the faintest hint of fresh sweat.

Somehow, that only added to the intoxicating cocktail of his aroma. *Note to self: find out what deodorant rich people use.*

I wasn't sure I smelled anywhere near as good as he did, but I couldn't bring myself to care. With his strong arms encircling me and his magic mouth on mine, I would vow never to wear deodorant again if that was what it took.

Eww. Take that back.

I did, but at the same time, I also yanked myself all the way out of my head and focused on the man who was kissing me. His hand had dropped from my back to caress my sides and he now had one thumb brushing the underside of my boob. *Ooh, he's good, this one.*

A moan fell from my lips between kisses, only to be echoed by one of his own. The next moment, a large hand found my thigh and expertly hooked around it to spin me so I could be laid back on the couch.

I obliged the request without him needing to put it into words, wrapping my hands around his neck and bringing him with me. His upper body pressed against mine, but his lower half remained in the same position he'd been in before.

"No." My voice was breathy but insistent.

Taydom broke the kiss immediately, his hair messy from having my fingers in it and pools of regret in his eyes. "No?"

Oh, God. No. "No, not that *no.*"

"I'm sorry." He frowned. "I was taught that no meant no. I told you to say no if you didn't want me to kiss you. You said no."

"I didn't say no to you kissing me," I whispered. "I said no because you…"

"I what?" he asked, the muscles against me flexing as if he was about to pull away.

I locked him into place with my body and lifted my head to kiss him again, but he only lifted his farther. A hint of laughter was entering those gorgeous brown eyes now, though, making the golden flecks seem bright again. "I'm not putting my lips back on you until you tell me what you were saying no to."

Heat crept to my cheeks. "I, uh, I was saying no because your legs were still—you know—*there*."

"Well, yeah, they're attached, you see?" he teased, lowering his head so that his lips brushed against my neck with every word he spoke. "If you want something from me, just say it."

Tingles ran down my arms and goosebumps appeared on my flesh from the soft caress of his mouth. My thoughts scattered, but the ache below my belly reminded me of what it was I wanted. "You weren't getting on top of me."

I felt his head tilt and his body froze above my own, not even his chest moving to breathe. "Do you want me to? I'm fine with just kissing you, Elsie. Really. I'm not some boy who can't control himself."

"Maybe I don't want you to control yourself," I breathed. "In fact, I very much want you to lose control."

"Be very careful about what you say next because it sounds like you want me to fuck you." His voice was low and raspy, slathered in want and coated in need.

I pulled my head back against the pillow and slid a hand between our chests to push him away slightly. My body protested the loss of the weight of his, but I was hoping it would be back there soon.

When his half-lidded eyes rose to meet mine, I pressed a kiss to his lips and spoke against them. "That's because it's exactly what I want."

I felt the rumble of his answering groan in my hand still on his chest. It traveled from there, up my arms, and into my chest before making its way lower and settling at the apex of my thighs.

"What are you waiting for?" I asked. A tiny pang of worry hit my gut when I realized he hadn't exactly told me what he wanted. The mere fact that he'd kissed me first didn't mean—

"Stop overthinking it, baby," he rasped out as he moved back and held his hand out to me. "Trust me. I want you. I was taking a minute to make sure this wasn't a dream and to decide if I wanted you on the couch or the bed."

"The bed's not made yet," I said before the former part of his sentence sank in. "Wait. Why would it be a dream?"

He tugged me to my feet with his lips curving into a smirk. As soon as I was standing, he pulled me into his arms, flush against his hard body. I realized then that every inch of him was hard. Painfully so.

One of his hands traveled up my back to grab the ends of my ponytail, giving it a light pull to indicate he wanted me to look up at him. He waited until I did before leveling me with his gaze. "Because I've dreamt about fucking you pretty much every night since we met."

"You have not." I gasped, and I wasn't even a gasper. He looked like he was serious, though, which I figured was pretty fucking gasp-worthy.

He grinned and shook his head, then smacked my behind before letting me go. "I never joke about dirty dreams, babe. Now come on before I change my mind and fuck you right here."

"What's wrong with right here?" I asked but took the hand he held out for me again and followed him to the bedroom. "Wait. The bed's not made up, remember?"

"It is. I got you new bedding yesterday. They've been washed, too."

"You got me new bedding?" I frowned when we walked into the bedroom and I noticed that he was right. The bed was made up with bedding that definitely wasn't mine.

It was beautiful, though. A deep purple with turquoise paisley patterns edged in black. Pillows matching the colors of the comforter stretched almost halfway down the mattress, and when I ran my fingers along the linen, it was softer than anything I'd ever slept on before.

Taydom watched me patiently but with lust and hunger darkening his gaze. "Yes, I did. I didn't dream I'd get to see you on them, but I couldn't resist."

"What did you dream then?" I asked as I turned to face him.

"It'll be way more fun to show you." His slightly swollen lips curved into a devilish smile. Closing the distance between us in two long strides, he brought his hands to my face. "May I?"

"Yes," I said with absolutely no room for doubt in my tone. "Please show me."

His grin widened as he moved around me, stopping once he was behind me and standing so close to my back that I could feel his heat. I didn't quite understand what he was doing behind me at first, but then his lips came to the column of my throat and it was too difficult to even wonder.

Big hands closed over my hips. His fingers splayed as they flexed and his mouth lavishly nipped and licked and kissed all the skin he could reach. My head rolled back and landed against his broad chest.

Taydom's arm slid around my waist and he pulled me closer, his lips leaving my skin to come back to mine. While he kissed me senseless, I felt his featherlight touch on the hem of my tank top. He rolled the fabric up slowly, exposing my flesh inch by inch.

The cool air in the bedroom met my heated skin, and more goosebumps rose as if he had managed to use the very air itself as part of his seduction technique. I wasn't complaining, though.

When he finally reached my breasts, he stopped the slow ascent of my shirt and took one in each hand. His thumbs flicked my hardened peaks, and as I moaned, so did he.

Patience apparently wearing thin, he yanked my shirt off the rest of the way before peeling my shorts off next. Standing in front of him in just my underwear wasn't nearly as intimidating as I thought it would be.

He broke off the kiss to walk around me, his pupils dilated. Thankfully, I wasn't the only one breathing heavily as he took me in.

"Even better than my dreams," he said, placing one hand on the center of my chest and using it to push me back against the bed.

I went willingly but wound my arms around his neck so he would lie down with me. He spread out over my body, his weight making me sink deeper into the mattress.

Feeling him like that made my own patience decide to up and go, leaving me a clawing, writhing mess who couldn't wait any longer. "Taydom."

"Yeah, I know. Going slow isn't fun anymore." He pulled back to look into my eyes, dropped a kiss on my nose, and then, thank all the gods, got busy.

My bra and panties were just about ripped clean off my body, and his clothes followed. My mouth dried up when I caught sight of the body he had been hiding beneath all those pesky layers. Holy shit, he was perfect. As I'd suspected, his muscles weren't bulky or bulging, but they were certainly there.

His broad shoulders and chest tapered down to a narrower waist while his arms were toned and lean. His abdomen was ripped, and every line that made every girl salivate was there, right down to those cut hipbones.

"Damn," I breathed. My gaze dropped to the smattering of hair below his belly button, the happy trail that was partially obscured by a very large, very enticing erection. "I thought going slow wasn't fun anymore."

"It's not." He groaned as his eyes raked over every inch of me, the same as I'd just done to him. "Jesus Christ, woman. You're gorgeous."

I wanted to argue. In comparison to him and the standards he had to be used to, I couldn't be anything special. The way he was looking at me stopped me from saying anything, though, because it was like he'd never seen anyone or anything more beautiful than me.

"So are you," I said and reached up to pull him back to me. "Are we doing this or what?"

"Oh, we're doing this," he replied before sealing his mouth over mine. Our bodies came together like two pieces of a puzzle, like they had been made for each other.

As good as Taydom was at kissing, he was even better at sex. From the minute he buried himself inside me, I was climbing toward the stars.

He never stopped kissing me, not until those very same stars exploded behind my eyes and the angelic choir reached their crescendo. Taydom tensed above me, his moans mingling with my own as he speared me with the sexiest look I'd ever seen and followed me over the edge.

Even so, I soon learned that he wasn't done. Using his mouth, his hands, and eventually his cock again, he gave me more pleasure than I'd previously thought I was capable of.

When he was finished rocking my world, he collapsed on the bed beside me.

The sun was starting to set outside as I rolled to my side to face him. "Wow. We were at that for a while."

He smirked and hooked his arms behind his head, his hair mussed and his lips now well and truly swollen. "Yeah, but we waited long enough for it."

"True." I smiled as we lay there in the darkening room catching our breath.

Taydom rolled over and pressed kisses to my forehead, my eyes, and finally my mouth. His eyes blazed into mine when he pulled back. "I'll let you get settled in. Otherwise, I'm going to keep you busy all night, and you're not going to get the chance to unpack. I'll be right next door if you need anything, okay?"

"Okay." I lifted my head to give him one last kiss, then watched as he covered his fine ass in clothes again before giving me a wave and walking out.

Nothing between us had felt awkward after at all, but now that I was alone, it dawned on me what I had done. I had sex with my landlord on my first night here.

That can't have been a good idea.

CHAPTER 18

TAYDOM

Maybe Andrew had been right all along. I'd been a miserable bastard to be around this last couple of months, but I was on top of the world this morning. It turned out I really had just needed to get laid. Or rather, to get laid by Elsie.

No other woman would have done the trick. Hell, now that I'd had her, I wasn't sure another woman would ever do the trick again.

Not that I wanted a relationship, with Elsie or anyone else, but there could be some definite benefits to being friends and neighbors with her. It was something I would keep in mind. All I knew was, despite what I'd hoped for, one time with her was not going to be enough.

Just the thought of her was making me hard, and I was at the goddamn breakfast table. Grown-ass men who possessed even a sliver of self-control did not get hard at the breakfast table, but it seemed Elsie had broken something in me.

I blamed her dusky pink nipples and smooth, soft skin against mine. She kissed like an angel and fucked like a devil, and I'd be damned if I didn't admit that I fucking loved it.

Since jerking off at the breakfast table wasn't an option, not even in my current state, I shoved all thoughts about Elsie forcefully out of my mind. As much as I would have loved to go over there and give her a proper Welcome to the Neighborhood wake up call, I didn't think we were anywhere near the point where she'd want to wake up with my dick inside her.

There was more to it than that, though.

After what I'd read about Illinois last week, I needed to check in with my parents. I swallowed the bite of cereal I'd just taken and picked up my phone.

My mother answered on the fourth ring. "Well, would you look at that? He does know that a phone works both ways. How are you doing, sweetheart?"

"I'm good, Mom. Really good." This time, I wasn't even lying. "How are you?"

"Oh, we're fine." I had a feeling that my mother, on the other hand, was lying. "Do you know this is the first time you've called me without me calling you first?"

"Really?" I frowned. "That can't be right."

"It is." A soft sigh came through the line. "I miss you, Tay. Thank you for giving me a call, but what is this really about? I doubt you called me out of the blue just because you miss me, too."

"I do miss you, Mom." Hitting the button to put her on speakerphone, I set the device down and rubbed my temples. "I just, uh, I read something on the news and I was worried about you."

"Worried about us?" She chuckled, but the sound was nervous. I could see her perfectly in my mind's eye, leaning against the wall beside the phone, head bowed and hand clutching the top button of her shirt. "Why would you be worried about us? It's our job to worry about you, sweetheart. Not the other way around."

I bowed my own head and ran my hands through my hair. "That's the thing, Mom. I am worried about you and I think I have damn good reason to be. I saw the predictions for soybean farms in your area this year. It's serious."

I heard a sharp intake of breath, but she didn't deny it. She paused for a long minute instead. "It's been a difficult year, and we've been through some hard times, but we're a strong family, honey. We'll make it through."

Frustration made me grip my hair tighter. "You don't have to worry about it, though, Mom. I can send you some money. Enough money to ease your minds and get you through the rest of the year without having to worry."

My mother didn't answer me immediately. In the silence that followed, I heard my father's voice in the background. This wasn't the first time I had offered to help them. In fact, it was such a regular occurrence that it seemed my father didn't even need to be on the call to know what I was saying.

"Do not let that boy send us any money. If he wants to help, he should be on this farm with us. Since he isn't, we don't need his help." He spat the words like they tasted bitter on his tongue.

I sighed. This was what it always came down to, the fact that I wasn't there.

Growing up, my father had always told my brother and me that one day, the farm would be ours. The thing was that I never wanted it. I'd told him so more times than I could count.

While I'd still been living there, I'd done my part. I worked day in, day out, and I never complained. Whenever I went home, I still did what I could.

After I'd left home and came to Dallas, I sent them money every month. My paychecks weren't great at the beginning, but I sent them more than I could really afford to.

I felt like shit for leaving Dad and Riley with all that work and I figured they could hire someone with the money. It didn't take me long to realize they weren't cashing the checks.

I called them about it. We argued, and Dad told me if I really cared at all, I'd come home. I'd help by sharing the workload, just like I always used to do.

That was the first time we'd had the argument, but it sure as hell wasn't the last. To this day, Dad hadn't accepted a cent of my money. I hired a team for them once, but Dad chased them off his property.

Machinery I purchased got returned. Nothing I tried had worked, but I couldn't give up.

My mother's sweet voice cut into my thoughts before I could come up with yet another different angle. "Don't send us money, sweetheart. Your money is yours. We couldn't take it."

I clenched my jaw and ground my teeth together. As usual, she didn't blame her refusal on my father. She always protected him. Hell, she always protected us all.

What I needed to do was to get up there to have it out with my father face to face. After I'd read that first article in the news about the state of the soybean industry, I'd kept reading. Dozens of articles said the same thing. This could be the year that we saw farms that had been in families and part of communities for generations fold.

While nobody in my family had been honest with me about the true state of their financial affairs in a long time, I knew they were more indebted than they liked to think about. I couldn't sit back and watch them lose the farm because my Dad was too proud to accept my help.

Unfortunately, I needed a reason to go visit them now. If I couldn't come up with something legit, Dad would probably shoot me on sight. He'd know what I'd gone there for and he wouldn't let me within five hundred feet of the farm without me staring down the barrel of a gun.

"Okay, Mom. Whatever you say." I screwed my eyes shut and searched my head for an excuse that wouldn't immediately make them suspicious. "I wanted to talk to you about that, but there was actually another reason I called."

"Oh?" She sounded surprised. "Glad to hear it, sweetheart. What's up?"

"I, uh—" I grasped at the first thing that popped into my head and said it without thinking it through. "I want to bring my girlfriend up there to see you."

"Your what?" There was a banging noise, which I suspected came from her dropping the phone. Some muffled sounds came next, and she was back. "Oh, darling. You haven't told me you have a girlfriend.

Who is she? What's she like? Do you have a picture you can send me?"

I chuckled, feeling like I was only going halfway to hell because of this. Mom sounded so happy and excited that it had to make up for the fact that I was lying to my mother, right?

"She's great," I said. "You're going to love her."

"That's it? You're not going to give me anything other than 'she's great'?" She sighed. "Well, I guess that's fine for now. It's more than we've ever gotten from you before. You've never brought a woman home before, so even vagueness is better than nothing."

"I'm not being vague. I just don't want to ruin the surprise." Since it was going to be a surprise to me too, I couldn't ruin it anyway.

"When will you be coming?" she asked.

Mentally running through my calendar, I shut my eyes. "We should be able to take some time to come up there within the next month or two."

"So soon? That's wonderful, honey. We can't wait."

"Neither can we." After I'd hung up the phone, it occurred to me that I might have just bitten off more than I could chew.

It was all very well and fine to promise my mother a visit from myself and my girlfriend, but finding a girl to play along with the idea might prove to be a touch more difficult. I massaged my temples as I wondered how the fuck I was going to get out of this.

Perhaps I could tell them the week before I left that she had broken up with me. That seemed to be the most viable idea.

I would still go because I would have already bought my ticket and arranged for the time away, but no girl would join me. Although my mother would still pepper me with questions, I just wouldn't have the answers to them.

I was still pondering my conundrum when a light knock sounded on my kitchen door. Looking up, I called out, "Come on in."

Logically speaking, there was really only one person it could be. It might have been one of my other neighbors, but they hadn't popped in since I'd moved here years ago. It was, therefore, more likely to be Elsie, and it turned out I was right.

Her dark hair was pulled up into its usual ponytail, and her face was devoid of makeup. She wore a loose-fitting, billowy pair of shorts and a white shirt. A slight flush tinged her cheeks as she met my eyes.

"Hey. I, uh, I was wondering if I could take you up on that offer to help if anything needed fixing."

"Sure." I pushed the empty cereal bowl away. "What do you need?"

"Some of the cabinets don't close properly. I thought it was better to find out if you had time to help me fix them now than to leave it. Once my classes start up again, I won't have too much time."

"Yeah, of course." I stood up and motioned for her to precede me out of the kitchen. As we walked out, I wondered if I might just have found the answer to my problem.

CHAPTER 19

ELSIE

"I think the problem is that they're not level," Taydom said as he opened and closed the bathroom cabinet a few times. He was on his haunches, his head tilted as he narrowed his eyes. "Yeah, that's definitely the problem."

"Can you fix it?" I asked, not sure how much a real-estate agent knew about being handy.

He chuckled and turned his head to look at me over his shoulder. "Yes, I can."

"You sound like Bob the Builder," I joked.

"Doesn't mean it's not true." He pushed to his feet. "Let me go grab a few things and I'll be right back."

I watched as he disappeared into the bright morning and turned right toward a shed at the edge of his property. Sunlight glinted off his pool and prisms reflected on his tanned skin.

He was shirtless, which didn't do much to help with my resolution to not jump his bones again. Light blue drawstring pants hung low on his hips, accentuating not only his golden skin but also that behind I'd come to appreciate so much.

I still wasn't sure if sleeping with him had been a good idea, though. It wasn't something we needed a repeat performance of until we knew where we stood. I planned on talking to him about it at some point during the morning. I just wasn't quite sure how to broach the topic.

A few minutes later, he came toward me again. *Carrying a freaking toolbox.*

With the morning light behind him, the caramel undertones of his hair became more obvious and his muscles bunched as he carried his tools to my house. Even more impressive, the toolbox actually looked used.

It certainly didn't seem like he'd bought it just to have it but had never opened it before. The plastic was faded and scuffed, and once he opened it, it was obvious that the tools inside weren't brand new either.

"So," he said as he crouched down on the bathroom floor again and began rummaging around for something. "How was your first night? Sleep well?"

"Yes." My mouth went dry as I watched him work. It was incredibly sexy to me that he wasn't just a businessman. He was actually handy as well. "You?"

"Like a baby." He grinned as he plucked a screwdriver out of the box and started fiddling with the door. "Although from what I've heard, apparently it's more accurate to say that I slept like a baby's father."

I laughed, surprised again by his casual sense of humor. "I've heard that, too. Just so I know, you don't have any firsthand experience in that, right?"

"Definitely not." He grinned. "Not that I'm aware of anyway. You?"

"No." I'd always wanted children, but that had been when my mother had still been around. I wasn't so sure anymore. Raising kids without her around to advise me or guide me was just too overwhelming for me to even think about right now.

Taydom let out a relieved laugh. "Good to know."

"Just for interest's sake, do you want to have any children one day?"

"I think one person only has so much luck in one lifetime. I seem to have used up my quota in business. Somehow, I don't think children are in my future."

"That's an interesting way of looking at it." That had to have been the most neutral answer to the question I'd ever heard, but it was a good one. "What if you got to have a say? Would you say yes?"

He deflected the question by tinkering some more, then scooted back and tested the cabinet a few times. "There. That should do it."

"Wow. That was fast."

He moved the door back and forth and it was definitely working better now. Curious about his deflection but fully understanding that we weren't really at that point in our relationship yet, I let it go.

"Where did you learn to do that?" I asked.

"Let's just say I didn't grow up rich or in the city. At my house, if you wanted something done or fixed, you did it yourself. Was it just this cabinet, or were there more?"

"A few more in the kitchen."

He nodded and placed his tools back in the box before walking out.

I trailed along after him, wishing I knew what to do to help.

"Can you show me?" I asked. "You know, just so I don't have to bother you with something like this next time."

"It's no bother." He gave me a smile and dragged his free hand over his hair before setting the toolbox down again. "To be honest, I like doing stuff like this. It takes me back to a much simpler time in my life."

"How so?" I didn't want to pry, but I figured he could always just give me another non-answer if he didn't want to talk about it.

Taydom hesitated for a minute, then shrugged his broad shoulders as he worked on the cabinet above the sink. "I grew up on a farm in Illinois. My family has been on that farm for generations. It's hard work, but it's a good life, you know?"

My teeth sank into my lower lip before I shook my head. "Not really, no. I've never even been on a farm."

"You haven't?" His eyes widened. "I can't even imagine that.

Farming is such a big part of who I am that I'm pretty sure a decent percentage of my bloodstream is made up of dirt and soybeans."

I flipped the switch on my kettle and propped a hip against the counter as I waited for it to boil. "Why are you here then? In Dallas, I mean. Not in my kitchen. Your life here seems lightyears removed from that of a farmer."

"It is," he agreed quietly, working in silence for a minute after. "As much as it's a part of me, it's not what I wanted for my life. I was always the cliched one in my family when it came to that."

"The small-town boy who couldn't wait to escape the small town?" I asked.

He nodded. "Everything I did, I did to give myself the best chance at getting out of there. I kept my grades up and applied for a few business courses all over the country. I've always had an interest in property, but I wasn't going to be picky. Eventually, I got accepted into one of the courses here in the city, got financial aid to be able to do it, and the rest, as they say, is history."

"Wow." My eyebrows rose. "I'd read that you were self-made, but I don't think I fully grasped what that meant until right now."

"You've read up on me, huh?" Luckily, he didn't sound angry or put out by it. If anything, there was a definite hint of amusement in his tone. "I should have read up on you, too."

I let out a decidedly unladylike snort as the kettle came to a boil. "You wouldn't have found much about me to be honest. I don't even really have social media. I'll tell you whatever you want to know, though. In the meantime, would you like some coffee?"

"Yes, please." He replied without hesitation. "Okay, so first question for you. Why did you look me up?"

I frowned as I grabbed two clean mugs from the drying rack. I'd washed all my cutlery and crockery early this morning, even though they'd been packed away clean. I just didn't like the idea of eating off something that had been boxed up without cleaning it again.

"I don't think you would have found the answer to that on the Internet," I said as I located my instant coffee in a different cabinet than the one I'd thought I'd packed it in. "How do you take it?"

"Black, no sugar." He swapped the tool he'd been using out for another, swinging the door in front of him to check it. "It's a good thing I can just ask you whatever I want to know, then."

I rolled my eyes, but it didn't make him any less right. "I didn't look you up at first. Beth considers herself a bit of an armchair expert in the real-estate market, and as soon as I told her I'd met someone called Taydom at an open house, she told me a little bit about who you were. I only really looked you up when you asked me to move in here. Just to make sure there were no news articles about animals or children disappearing in your immediate vicinity."

"Well, thank God you didn't search for plants. Those tend to shrivel up around me."

"You're a farmer who can't keep plants alive?" My tone was incredulous as I finished fixing his coffee and put it on the counter beside him. "How does that work?"

"I can't keep potted plants alive," he corrected, nodding his head in a thank you as he picked up the mug. "Which is why I've never tried an animal or a child."

"I guess that's a good point." I laughed as I stirred my own coffee. "I had a dog when I was growing up and I adopted a cat when I first moved out of the house. I did okay with those, but I've never tried a child."

"We had animals on the farm when I grew up, but they weren't solely my responsibility. That's why I didn't count them. I did do okay with them, but I can't really claim that as my win."

"Scratch the dog off my list, too, then. He was my Mom's. I only helped out."

"You still get the cat, though. Where's it now? Living with your mother?"

The crack in my heart ached with emptiness. "No, she was old when I adopted her. The vet had to put her down about two years later. Cancer."

"I'm sorry," he said and turned around, genuine concern in those gorgeous golden-brown irises. He frowned when he realized my eyes were wet. "Whoa. Fuck, Elsie. Why didn't you tell me this was such a sensitive topic for you? We could have left it."

"It's not about the cat," I said miserably. "It's my mom. She passed away just about two months ago now. It was sudden. A heart attack. It just sneaks up on me sometimes."

Taydom blinked a few times in surprise, then set his coffee down and strode over to me. He opened his arms and folded them around me as he pulled me to his chest, holding me tight. "I'm so sorry. I didn't know. We didn't have to talk about any of this."

"It's okay," I mumbled against his warm skin, smelling that same divinely masculine scent as yesterday. "Thanks for the hug. I think I needed it."

"Anytime." He held on to me for another couple of minutes before letting me go. When he did, he put his big hands on my shoulders and dipped down to look into my eyes. "You good?"

"Yeah, I'm fine." I managed to offer him a small smile, at which point he must have decided that I wasn't going to try to slit my wrists with the spoon in my mug and let me go.

When he went back to the cabinet he'd been busy with, I lifted my mug and watched steam rising from the surface. "Tell me about your family. What was it like growing up on a farm?"

"It was heaven and hell, all wrapped up in one sweaty package." He grinned. "Being a kid on a farm is the absolute best. You get to be outside all day, it's expected that you're going to get dirty, and you even get praised for it. We had a lot of chores from a young age, but that taught us about working hard and responsibility."

"That does actually sound pretty cool." I took a sip of my coffee once it seemed like it wasn't going to burn my mouth off anymore. "You said we?"

"My brother, Riley, and I. He's two years older, which was both a good thing and a bad thing."

"Where's he now?"

"Still on the farm," Taydom grunted, and though I didn't know him very well, I could tell we were nearing territory he didn't want to venture into. "What about you? You're an only child, right? What was that like?"

"Well, I'm not as maladjusted as people claim only children will be, so I guess that's a good thing," I joked to lighten the mood. I told him all sorts of stories about growing up and my mother.

After he finished fixing up the cabinets, we had another cup of coffee or four together. We just talked and got to know each other better.

When he eventually stood up and told me he needed to get to work, we were both jittery but smiling. As we said our goodbyes at my front door, Taydom took me into his arms again.

I remembered thinking on the day that he showed me this place that I wanted him as a friend, and it felt like we were getting there. The only problem was that we'd already done so much more together than friends should.

"I'm sorry if I ruined anything by what happened between us yesterday."

His chest vibrated as he laughed and I felt his head shaking above my own. "You didn't ruin anything. Get out of your own head. You just have too big of a brain."

I couldn't help but smile at that. "Message received. I need to stop overthinking it."

"Exactly." He released me but dropped a kiss on my forehead before stepping away. "Good luck at school tomorrow."

"Thanks. Have a good week."

He smirked. "I always do. I'll see you around, Elsie. Let me know if there's anything else you need."

CHAPTER 20

TAYDOM

The week was in full swing and it wasn't even nine on Monday morning. Clutching my phone to my ear as I tried to hear over the cacophony of horns, people, and life in general downtown, I pushed open the door to my favorite diner.

"Yeah, I'll be there at four on Wednesday and I remember about dinner tomorrow night." Scott kept droning on about my engagements for this week while I pointed to the items on the menu I wanted for breakfast.

The waitress nodded and filled my waiting coffee cup, giving me a smile before she left to put in my order. Scott eventually told me that he'd enter all my new appointments in my calendar and double-checked a few details before hanging up.

My phone had barely hit the table when it rang again. This time, the name that came up on the screen surprised me.

"Riley?" I asked, not used to receiving calls from my brother. "Is everything okay there?"

His low, familiar laughter met my ears. "Everything's fine. Don't worry, little brother. I'm not calling because the apocalypse is happening."

"Good to know," I said, a smile tugging at the corners of my lips.

Riley was a mix between my mother and father. We used to be close, but we had grown apart over the years since I moved to Texas. "How are you?"

"Fine," he answered after a brief pause. "We're holding up."

My insides went cold. Riley and I might not be as close as we once had been but I still knew him well enough to know that he was blowing smoke up my ass. "How bad is it?"

"It's not your problem anymore, Tay," he said, and I swore he sounded exactly like my father at that moment. "I'm not calling about us or what's going on here anyway."

"Yeah?" I asked as I took a sip of the strong but lukewarm coffee the waitress had poured for me. "Why are you calling then?"

"Mom told me you called. She said you were bringing a woman home."

"What about it?" *Damn it.*

I hadn't brought up the subject about helping me out with that to Elsie yet. Listening to my brother now, though, I knew I should have. Riley had a sixth sense for when I was lying, and at least if I'd spoken to her about it, it might not have been a flat-out lie any longer.

"What about it?" He snorted. "Be serious, Taydom. You've never brought a woman home before. It seems suspicious that you'd suddenly want to bring someone now with everything that's going on."

"What can I say? It's not my fault I found someone I'm serious about now." *Fuck.* I was suddenly lying left, right, and fucking center. It wasn't how I was raised and I sure as fuck never imagined it would come this easily.

Guilt settled like a giant monkey on my back, but I shook it off. If lying got me a chance at saving the farm, then so be it. *Greater good and all.*

"You're serious about this woman?" Suspicion practically dripped from my brother's tone. "Mom's really excited about this, so it better be true."

"What else would it be?" There was something wrong with me. Every word I said was a shovel, digging myself in deeper and deeper.

"A ploy to come home so you can give Mom and Dad money," Riley said, cutting through all my bullshit as usual. "If that's what it is, I'm going to be fucking upset. Just so you know. Mom hasn't been this happy for months, so if you—"

"It's not a ploy," I insisted. At this point, sticking to my guns was the only choice I had. "It's real, Riley. I've met someone that makes me happy, and I want her to meet you all."

Okay, so finally there was some truth in what I was saying. Elsie *did* make me happy. Spending time with her was fun, and considering she was the only person, except for Andrew, who knew anything real about my past or my family, I didn't mind introducing her to them.

Maybe it was a gross exaggeration that she was my girlfriend, but she was a girl, and she was becoming my friend.

Riley didn't respond immediately. My brother could be as broody as my father, though. He didn't mince his words, and he didn't waste them.

"Well, okay then," he said finally, his relief clear as a bell. "I'm happy to hear that you've found someone. God knows it's taken you long enough."

"Says Woodstock's most dedicated bachelor." Riley was known around my hometown as being unobtainable. He'd always been that way.

I didn't know why or when he'd made the decision not to date and to give his life to the farm instead of a woman, but he'd never wavered from it. Last I had heard, he had "some acquaintances he blew off some steam with from time to time," in his words, but nothing more than that.

He laughed again. It was one way in which he took after my mother. Riley laughed loudly and often with those he trusted the most. To the rest of the world, he could come across as a closed-off bastard, but nothing could be further from the truth.

I supposed I was the same, not that I ever really thought too much about it. We simply were the way we were.

"The difference between us, little brother, is that Mom hasn't given up on you finding love. I played her game, went out on the dates she set me up on, and when nothing took, she yelled that I was impossible and hasn't bothered me about it since."

Damn. Once this little charade of mine was over, I'd have to see what I could do to follow his example and get her off my back once and for all.

"How's Dad?" I asked. Inevitably, talking about one of our parents led to talking about the other. I figured I might as well ask.

Chances of getting an honest answer from Riley when it was about our Dad were slim to none, but I had to give it a try. He surprised me today, though.

Letting out a heavy breath, he hesitated before giving me more than he had in years. "To be honest, that's why I thought you were working some angle with Mom. I thought she'd told you how upset he's been."

"She didn't," I confessed. "Wouldn't talk about him at all actually. Just said he was fine."

"Yeah, well, he's not." His voice suddenly sounded strained. Tired. "It's getting worse as the season goes on. He's getting more and more upset. Stress hangs over his head like a fucking thunder cloud, but he refuses to talk about it."

I whistled under my breath and shook my head. "That's nothing new. He's as stubborn as a mule, that man."

"Especially when it comes to you, Taydom. You left us, and I get why you did it, but don't expect him to be happy about it."

"I don't expect him to be happy. I don't even expect him to be proud of everything I've accomplished, but I do expect him to shove his pride someplace where the sun doesn't shine if it's about the survival of the farm."

"We're not quite there yet," Riley said, but it didn't sound like he even believed himself.

"Sure, bro. I'm sure you're not."

Silence fell between us. I let my head fall back against the cushioning of the booth and listened to the ever-present hum of the diner.

On his end of the line was nothing but absolute silence. It wasn't surprising, but it did make me wonder how he was really doing up there by himself, on the farm with only our parents and the occasional "friend" for company.

Before I could ask him about it, he told me he had to go and ended the call. A few seconds later, the waitress brought over my breakfast in a brown paper bag and smiled when I added a hefty tip to my check.

Once I was back at my office, I was still thinking about my family. I scrubbed my hands over my face and unwrapped my sticky buns, even though my appetite had vanished.

As I thought back over the conversation I'd had with my brother, my mind snagged on the part when we'd discussed Elsie. I hadn't known her for a very long time, but I'd developed something of a soft spot for her.

My tenant and neighbor had already become part of my life in such a way that it was difficult to remember what it had been like without her. Glancing down at my watch, I wondered if she'd be in class yet and decided to send her a quick text.

Me: Hope you have a great first day at school. Thinking about you.

I briefly debated adding kisses, realized it would be a terrible idea, and hit send before I could come up with any other stupid ideas.

Her reply came through a few minutes later and made me frown at my screen.

Elsie: Who is this???

Just a few seconds after that, I received another text from her and discovered that even over a few simple words on a text, she could make me laugh.

Elsie: Just kidding, Taydom. Thanks. Thinking about you, too.

Something jolted in my heart as I read her words, causing my laughter to stop abruptly as I rubbed the spot.

Jesus. Fuck. What the hell was that?

CHAPTER 21

ELSIE

Getting back into the routine of being a full-time student wasn't easy. Contrary to what most people believed about older students, we didn't imagine we were still kids and were acutely aware of the differences in age between others on campus and us.

Students who looked like children surged all around me, laughing and chatting in a carefree way. It made me simultaneously jealous of them and grateful that the worst possible thing that could happen to me had already happened.

The only thing I felt a sense of jealousy about was when I watched the couples walking past me. They strolled along hand in hand, looking at each other with these dopey looks on their faces that I envied.

I didn't know them, I didn't know how long they'd been together, or whether they would last, but seeing them reminded me that I'd never had that one true love. I didn't know if I ever would.

After the first few weeks, though, I barely noticed them anymore. I lost track of time during the day as I got absorbed with lectures and schoolwork and collapsed into my bed exhausted every night.

Taydom and I had coffee together many mornings, grabbed dinner together occasionally, and had spent one or two weekends working in the entertainment area of his backyard together. We texted back and forth, but while we had started touching casually more often, we hadn't hooked up again.

Our relationship had developed into an easy yet flirtatious friendship, and I'd have been lying if I said I hadn't wanted it to become something more. Friends with benefits sounded like a good label to me, but I hadn't brought it up with him yet.

I'd caught him looking at me with heat in his eyes on more than one occasion, but he hadn't made a move on me. I suspected that it was because I'd told him how much it meant to me to do well in my classes and that I felt like I had some catching up to do.

I was all caught up now, though. In the majority of my classes, I'd even gotten ahead, which was something I was immensely proud of.

As my last class of the day let out a little bit early, I decided to head over to the food truck. I hadn't spent much time with Beth since my classes had started back up and I missed my friend something terrible.

We'd seen each other so much in the couple of months after my mother's passing, not seeing her for weeks now made me feel like I was missing a limb. She had moved her truck again and was now trying out a location near my campus at lunchtime. Apparently, it was the best spot she'd found so far.

Since it was hours after the lunch rush, the truck was quiet when I arrived. A wide grin spread on Beth's face when she saw me and she waved like a crazy person.

"Oh my God, stranger! It's so good to see you." She hopped out of the back of the truck and came over to envelop me in a hug. "How have you been?"

"I'm good." I returned her hug, then waited while she grabbed us a drink each before sitting down at a small plastic table she had placed outside. "How's business?"

"Girl, I should have looked into the college crowd years ago. I have a steady stream of customers starting mid-morning that only runs dry by about three. It picks up again after five and keeps going until about six-thirty before all the students are gone. It's wonderful."

"I'm glad." I cracked the top off the bottle of soda she passed me and took a long drink. "At least you found out about it now and not never."

"That's what I've been telling myself." The smile finally started fading from her face as she took me in. "What about you? How's school going?"

"The workload was killing me, but now that I've gotten back into the swing of things, it's all good."

"How is it being back on a campus full time?" She winked. "There are a lot of potential boy toys around here that I've seen."

I laughed and shook my head at her. "It's been interesting to say the least. I mean, I'm glad I'm doing this thing for myself, but it's hard to see the social side of things. Everyone on campus is so much younger and so... free."

The corners of her mouth turned down and her brow furrowed in sympathy. "I can see how that could be depressing. Try to look on the bright side, though. You've got the benefit of having real-life experience. We were bright eyed and bushy tailed once, too. Now we know better."

"True," I said, flashing her a weak smile. "Anyway, let's change the topic. I don't feel like being depressed right now. We haven't seen each other in way too long to spend our time that way. What else is new with you?"

She pursed her lips and moved them from side to side before shrugging. "Not too much. I went on a couple of dates, but they were all duds. What about you? How's the new house?"

"It's great." I released a contented sigh as my smile grew stronger. "I can't think of a better or more perfect place for me. Honestly, it's like going home to a sanctuary every night."

"And Taydom?" she asked with a coy grin spreading on her lips. "How's he been since you moved in?"

I had known the conversation would eventually move on to him and I was ready for it. Having not wanted to tell Beth what had happened between us over the phone, I was bursting at the seams to fill my best friend in.

"We slept together," I blurted out without any tact whatsoever. "On my first night there, no less."

Her eyes widened. "Are you serious?"

"Yes." I knocked my shoulder into hers. "I was worried about it just after it happened, but things haven't been awkward between us, and oh my God, Beth, it was so great."

She still seemed to be processing what I had said. "You slept with Taydom Gaines?"

"Yes." I reached out to poke her in the ribs when her expression remained vacant. "Hello? Beth? Are you there?"

She swatted my hand away and laughed. "I'm here, I'm here. I'm just... shocked. I already knew you were attracted to him and that he was attracted to you. I just didn't think either of you was going to give in so fast."

"It was pretty damn fast, all right." I giggled as I covered my face with my hands and shook my head. "All my stuff wasn't even in the house yet."

"Elsie," she exclaimed and threw her arms around me in a side hug. "That's awesome. I'm so proud of you."

"You're proud of me for sleeping with someone?" I asked, my voice muffled by her arm.

"Yes." She nodded firmly before releasing me. "But not because you slept with him really. I'm proud of you for going after what you wanted and for not feeling guilty about it."

"It hadn't even occurred to me to feel guilty." How in the crinkling crabsticks had I forgotten to feel guilty?

Beth slapped my arm but not hard enough to hurt. "Don't even think about starting now."

"It's just, how could I not even have thought about it?"

"Because it was great and something else that you did for yourself. You don't need to feel guilty about living your life, El. We've been over that. Now instead of burrowing yourself into a hole, give me details. I want all the details."

I shot her a look. "I can't give you all the details."

"Okay, let's just start with the most important then." She held her hands up and spread them until they were about a foot apart. "Stop me when I get into the right ballpark."

Her hands started moving closer together.

"Beth!" I grabbed one of her hands and forced it back to her side as she dissolved in a fit of laughter. "I'm not telling you that."

"Why not?"

"It's private." My cheeks grew uncomfortably warm. "But you weren't far off to begin with."

Her laughter abruptly ended as she gaped at me. "No way. That was like, twelve inches. Is that even possible?"

I shrugged. "Obviously."

When she gaped at me once again, I couldn't hold it in anymore. "I'm kidding. Jeez. Relax."

"Oh, I'm betting you were super relaxed after, if it's anywhere even near that. Although I've got to tell you, I don't really believe you."

"Of course you don't. Twelve inches is ridiculous and would probably constitute some kind of rare medical condition."

She swatted my arm again. "I knew it. Enough messing around. Give me the real details."

"There's not much to tell you. It happened. It was incredibly satisfying. Then he left."

"Has it happened again?" She frowned. "You've been there over a month now."

"I know, but I've been busy, and he has too. We've spent a ton of time together, but things haven't progressed that far again."

"Do you want it to?" She cocked her head as she waited for my answer.

I didn't even have to think about it. "Yes."

"Does he know that?" Chewing on her lower lip, her eyes darkened with worry. "Please tell me you guys talked about it before it happened."

"Sort of. We checked in with each other to make sure we both wanted it and that kind of thing. But it's not like we sat each other down and had an intense conversation about the future of our relationship. Or lack thereof, in our case."

"So he doesn't know you want it to happen again?"

I shook my head. "No. It hasn't come up."

"Did you mean to make a punny?" She wiggled her nose and laughed. "But okay. I get it. It's not an easy conversation to have with someone."

"It's really not." Before one of my essays had been due, I'd seriously considered booty- texting him but I just couldn't bring myself to do it. "I mean, what words does one even use for something like that?"

"I can think of a few, but I don't think you're going to be able to work any of them into casual conversation."

"Yeah, I think I know which ones you mean." I laughed. "Maybe I should put it this way. I know the words. I just don't really know how to string them all together in a way that doesn't make me look like a hussy."

"You're not a hussy." She shook her head. "You're, like, whatever the complete opposite of a hussy is."

"Are you calling me a prude?" I lifted my eyebrows. "Because from where I'm sitting, I'm the one trying to get it on with someone while you're just laughing at me for it."

"Fine." She rolled her eyes. "You're not a prude. Maybe the next time you're spending some time with him, just tell him you've been really stressed, and you need his help to relieve it."

"Good idea. Should I also download a soundtrack from a porno, and do you think I should start playing the first song before or after I make that statement?"

"You're impossible." She took a sip of her drink before her expression turned serious again. "Hey, just, uh, you know, keep your eyes open. Don't do something silly like go falling for him. He's a rich playboy. He's not the man you spend the rest of your life with."

"I agree." I really did, but sometimes, I wondered if we were right. There was a lot more to Taydom than what met the eye, hidden depths I had only just started to explore.

When I got home later that afternoon, he had yet another surprise in store for me. On my kitchen counter was a gorgeous bouquet with a handwritten note in his own scrawling handwriting, saying that he hoped my day was awesome.

Somehow, that just didn't seem like a playboy thing to do. Unless I was misunderstanding the meaning of playboy, and if I was, were they really as bad as they were made out to be?

Because Taydom certainly wasn't. If anything, it was starting to feel like he was too good.

CHAPTER 22

TAYDOM

"One word for you, brother," Andrew said as he sauntered into my office. His grin was as wide as the Milky Way and his arms were spread out at his side. "Nightingale."

"As in the last name of the nurse or the bird? I'm going to need a little bit of context." I was distracted by the contract lying on my desk. I had been reading through it for an hour and I really wanted to finish it before I went home.

My best friend tutted at me with a shake of his blond head. A smirk curved his lips. "You're hopeless, man. I'm not talking about the nurse or the bird. I'm talking about the new karaoke bar opening tonight."

"No." I rubbed my tired eyes and waited for the sting to pass before looking at Andrew again. "If you were about to ask me to go, that's my answer."

Gracefully lowering himself into a chair, he straightened his tie and crossed an ankle over his knee. "Why not? I'm going and you haven't even heard the best part yet."

"Yeah?" I cocked my head. "What's that?"

"They have a crazy happy hour going on. I'm talking about the kind of specials that will have people lining up down the block. Yours truly is on the list and I can bring a friend. Be my friend please? Women love karaoke. I guarantee the pussy at this place—"

"No." I pointed at the hundred-plus-page contract I was reviewing. "I don't give a damn about that. It's been a long day and I've done nothing but work. I'm exhausted. As soon as I'm done here, I'm going home. I need to sleep, Drew. I'm sorry but not tonight."

Andrew pouted, but he must have seen the resolve in my eyes because he raised his hands and shrugged. "Okay. It's your loss, but I can see I'm not going to change your mind. Let me know when you get bored as fuck after getting home. I'll see if I can get you in."

"Sure, man. Thanks." My shoulders lowered as I sighed when he left my office a few minutes later. It really had been a long week and I was looking forward to getting home.

Elsie had been busy as fuck since classes started back up. We'd spent a lot of time together since she'd moved in, but it was sporadic. I never knew if or when I was going to see her.

Even so, I couldn't deny that I hoped I'd run into her tonight. Nothing sexual had happened between us since that first day but I sure as hell still wanted a repeat performance.

Knowing how much pressure she was under and how much she was struggling to adapt held me back, though. No matter how much chemistry simmered between us whenever we saw each other, I wouldn't push her.

With all that in mind, I was pleasantly surprised when she came out as I pulled up the drive. It was later than when I usually got home, but it seemed she had been waiting for me.

Twilight had fallen and the sky appeared pinkish. The treetops were shadowy guards keeping watch over the house and rustling in the warm breeze.

Warm orange light spilled out of Elsie's cottage as she stood in the open door.

"Hey," she called when I got out of my car. "Long day?"

I slammed the door shut behind me. "The fucking longest."

"Yeah, I can see that." A slow smile spread on her lips as her eyebrows rose. "You look like a zombie."

135

"Thanks, you look great too," I teased, but she really did.

Her hair was damp from a recent shower and was pulled up in a high knot behind her head. Soft sweatpants hung from her hips, and on top was the signature tank top I'd learned she loved putting on whenever she got home.

She'd claimed once that having to wear one was because of "big-boob problems." Apparently, other women could forgo a bra all together, while she still had to rely on something built in or wearing a bra.

A plethora of responses had been on my lips and my hands had twitched to show her just how much I loved what she had referred to as *problems*. I'd kept them by my sides, though.

"I know, right?" she joked back without skipping a beat. "The Zombie is a total trend around here these days."

I laughed as I lifted my laptop bag out of the trunk and slung it over my shoulder. I turned to face her. "Which begs the question, why are you out here? Shouldn't you be catching up on some sleep?"

"It's not that late." She rolled her eyes and grabbed the dishcloth I hadn't noticed hanging over her shoulder. Twisting it between her hands, she dropped her head back to indicate her house. "I made some dinner, but we can do it another night."

"No way." I patted my stomach as I secured the laptop with my free hand and walked toward her. "I'm starving. Whatever you made will beat the noodles I was about to throw in a pot."

"That's good because I don't actually think I could have refrozen the pot stickers and I'm pretty sure the salad I made wouldn't have lasted."

She turned and headed into her house, leaving the door open behind her. I shut it after walking in, slinging my bag off my shoulder and setting it down near her front door.

"Pot stickers and salad, huh?" I salivated as I followed her to the kitchen. "Any chance you've got some hot sauce with that?"

"Do I have hot sauce?" She scoffed and winked at me over her shoulder. "Is Taydom Gaines the king of real estate in this city? Is

Woodstock a farming town? Is your mother the best cook in four counties?"

"Okay, okay." I groaned and put my hands up in surrender. "The answer has to be yes."

"Of course it is." She walked over to her fridge and pulled out a fresh Asian salad, along with two clear little bowls filled with a bright red sauce. "Have a seat. This is my treat. The table's already been set."

The stool scraped as I pulled it out and sat down. Scents of coriander, pork, and chili hung in the air, and I had to bite back a moan. "If you're trying to seduce me, it's working."

Elsie's head tipped back as she laughed. "I've heard that the way to a man's heart was through his stomach."

"His heart?" I cocked an eyebrow as I loosened my tie. "I'm not so sure about that. His bed? Definitely."

She removed a pot from the oven. "Well, I think a lot of women confuse the way to a man's heart with the way to his bed." Amusement danced in her eyes as she put the pot down on the counter and opened the lid to release more of that delicious aroma. "Come and get it then. We'll see where it leads."

Slap me silly and call me Sonny. This was the first time she was openly flirting with me. I couldn't say I minded it at all. In fact, it was more like the complete opposite.

Elsie had dimmed the lights in the house so that the entire open area making up her living and dining room was lit with only that soft, warm lighting. Soft French music flowed from the radio in the kitchen and she looked happy, relaxed even, as she took two plates out of a cabinet.

Her body swayed gently to the music as she dished up for us, and I was fucking mesmerized by her. Every movement and every curve called to me like it was a siren's song and I was a poor sailor.

With her neck exposed from her hair being up, the shadows elongated her throat and dips appeared beneath her cheekbones. The sway and sashay of her body seemed to be completely unintended, like she just couldn't help but move to this music.

Her clothes might not have been sexy in the traditional sense of the word, but she didn't need skimpy or elaborate clothing to make me want her. Everything about her this evening was enchanting, tantalizing even.

"You know that I meant you should come and get your dinner and not me, right?" she joked, eyes twinkling in the dim light. "Stop looking at me like that and come get your food."

"It was the food I was looking at like that." The hell it was, but I wasn't going to pass up on the meal she'd prepared for us. Other people might have tried for sex first, but not me.

First off, I was perfectly happy to just have a meal with her. Secondly, growing up the way I had meant that I always appreciated having food on the table. Having it go to waste was bordering on a sin in my book.

Ironically, it was one of the few sins I had a real problem with. Obviously, premarital sex wasn't something I batted an eyebrow over, and after all I'd accomplished, greed probably wasn't either.

No matter how much I gave back, I still had more than I could ever need or use in seven lifetimes.

Food wasting when I knew how much had gone into growing it, when I knew what farmers went through to make a fraction of what shit cost in the stores, that was something I wasn't okay with.

"This is delicious," I said once Elsie and I were seated and I'd swallowed my first bite. "Absolutely perfect after a week like this. How did you know?"

"I figured that if your week had been anything like mine, you might need a good dinner. Besides, I missed you. We haven't seen each other much this week."

My heart gave another odd tug. *Fucked. That's what I am. Totally fucked.* "Yeah, I practically lived at the office this week. We have a big deal closing and the sellers have nominated an idiot for a lawyer. They insisted on using some friend of the family, despite my advice, and we're all paying the price for it."

"I'm sorry." She made a face, her adorable features all scrunched up. "Is there anything I can do?"

"Can I hire you as my company psychologist when you're done

with school? That way, I could legitimately have people's heads checked sometimes."

She laughed and shook her head. "I told you. I want to keep working with children."

"The people I work with *are* children," I said. "Seriously, most of my clients act like oversized spoiled brats."

She peered up at me from under her eyelashes as she chewed. Once she'd swallowed, she took a sip of water and shook her head again. "Oversized spoiled brats aren't my game. I like the undersized ones. It feels like I stand a chance at helping them."

"Some of my clients are skinny. That counts as undersized, right?" I pointed at her with a chopstick. "Before you say no, let me give you some examples from just this week."

Elsie and I laughed nonstop for the rest of our meal. It wasn't until our plates were cleared and in the sink that we stopped comparing notes and grew serious for once.

I swatted her on the ass with a dishtowel. "You cooked. I'm doing the dishes. It's not negotiable."

"Not negotiable, huh?" She planted her hands on her hips as she came to stand next to me, grabbing for the pot in my hand.

I held it way up high above my head and tried to look stern. "Not negotiable."

"But you're my guest," she protested as she stood up on her tiptoes and extended her fingers to reach. "That means we leave the dishes to soak while we have an after-dinner drink. Then you leave and I wash up."

"Nope. Technically, we both live here. Equal living for equal perks."

Her nose scrunched up. "How is doing the dishes a perk?"

"You only do dishes at home and where you're really comfortable, right?" I grinned when she dropped back to her feet. "With you, that counts as a perk in my book."

She was still standing really close to me, her chest almost all the way up against mine. "With me?" Her voice was small and just a little breathless as her eyes found mine. "You're too smooth. Do you know that? It's not fair to charm people out of doing their own dishes?"

"Everything's fair in dishes and war," I said as I lowered my hand to place the pot in the warm water.

"I don't think that's the saying," she murmured, her gaze still locked on mine.

"It is for us," I replied.

We surged forward at the same time, her arms coming around my neck as mine slid around her waist. Our lips met in a frenzy of pent-up need and long overdue desires.

She tasted heavenly, the zing of the chili still on her tongue. I moaned as I kissed her deeper and hauled her up against me.

However this night was about to play out, her lips weren't the only thing I was tasting. I'd been dying for her for over a month and I was planning to get my fill.

CHAPTER 23

ELSIE

Kissing Taydom felt like coming home. It made no sense. I hadn't known him for a very long time, didn't have much shared history with him, and admittedly, there was a lot I still had to learn about him.

But somehow, someway, being in his arms felt like home. After just that one night with him, I already felt like his embrace was familiar.

I melted into him, my hands messing up his soft hair as I tilted my head back to give him better access to my mouth. Neither of us seemed to be able to get enough of the other. We were pressed so close together, it was like we were trying to merge into one.

His hands were splayed across my back, fingers flexing as he held me to him. Need began building deep inside me, a slow burn that spread from my core to my extremities.

I tightened my grip on Taydom's hair, eliciting a low groan from the back of his throat. Running his hands up my back, one came to rest on the side of my throat while the other tugged at my hair.

A second later, I felt a slight pull at the elastic band in my hair and then it came tumbling down around my shoulders. He wasted no time burrowing his fingers into the clean strands, moaning into my mouth as he held my head in place.

The need building inside me skyrocketed when I felt him growing hard against my stomach. The kisses became heated. No longer just a kiss we'd both waited too long for, it became one that was leading somewhere.

Our hands started wandering and exploring. Taydom's muscles tensed under my roaming fingers. Then he let out a low sound and started moving. Without breaking the kiss, he walked us backward, and it took my lust-addled brain a minute to realize he was navigating us toward my bedroom.

Once inside it, he kicked the door shut behind us and spun me around until my back hit the hard wooden surface.

I would have crashed into it, but Taydom's arms around me took the brunt of the impact. He pinned me to the wall with his hips and reached for my shirt, fisting the material at the hem and rolling it up. When it reached my breasts, he lifted the fabric away and created enough space between us to lift it over my head.

Our lips parted only for the time it took for my shirt to come off. Then our mouths fused together again. Wanting his skin against mine, I returned the favor and got off his shirt as fast as I could.

Thankfully, he was still wearing the button-down he'd had on for work, and freeing him from it didn't involve breaking our kiss again. Once that was done, I started groping for his belt.

He moved his hips back a fraction of an inch to give me enough space to undo it. Then his hands joined mine between us and his pants soon hit the floor. Sliding my hands into the waistband of his underwear, I lifted the elastic away from his skin and pushed it down.

Taydom stepped out of both, completely naked now and fully erect. I couldn't see him, but I could feel him against the exposed skin of my belly, hot and impossibly hard. His lips crashed to mine over and over again before his mouth left mine.

"Taydom," I whispered on a soft moan, but when he sucked a hardened nipple into his mouth through the lace of my bra, I cut myself off. My teeth sank into my lip as I arched my back to press myself more firmly into his mouth.

His hips anchored me against the door. I was completely

surrounded by him, and I couldn't believe how good it felt. Better than good. It was amazing.

One hand pinched my other nipple and the other lowered to my butt. He gripped me hard before letting me go so he could push my shorts down. My panties followed soon after.

As soon as those barriers were removed, he ran his hand up the length of my thigh. It came within inches of my aching pussy. Then it disappeared again. He repeated the teasing touches a few times, effectively turning me into a writhing, moaning, desperate mess.

"Taydom, I can't. Please." My voice came out breathy and tight. I hardly recognized it, but the sound of it prompted him to grin against my skin before he removed his mouth from my breast.

His golden eyes met mine. They were pools of liquid heat that were as filled with want as I imagined mine were. He didn't say anything as he dropped down to his knees in front of me. Faced by the evidence of what he'd done to me, he groaned and licked his lips.

"Please, Taydom. Now. Please." I shoved my hands into his hair. Every nerve ending in my body was on fire and I felt slippery wetness between my legs.

Taydom dipped his head forward and placed soft kisses on my inner thighs, his lips firm as he closed his eyes and took a deep breath. Embarrassment warmed my skin until I saw the look of utter bliss on his face when he turned it up to face me.

As he did, he raised a hand and finally pressed his thumb to my throbbing clit. My knees nearly buckled as pleasure ricocheted through me.

"Yes," I gasped when he circled the aching bud once.

He pulled back to give me a wicked smile as he spread me apart with his fingers and licked through my core.

"Holy shit. Yes. Please don't stop." I moaned far too loudly for him not to have heard me. He didn't respond, though.

His tongue came up to swirl around my clit as he pushed one of his fingers into me. I was so wet that he was met with no resistance. A tempest of delicate pleasure swept through me. Sparks flew behind my eyes as he licked me again. The long strokes of his tongue had me

143

trembling. My chest heaved, tension winding so tightly in my belly that I could hardly breathe.

Taydom picked up his pace then, obviously realizing how close I was getting to the edge. His steady, sure lapping drove me wild. My hands tugged at the thick strands of his hair as a storm of pure, exquisite sensation overtook me.

His tongue thrust into me just before another finger joined the first. My hips bucked against him as I writhed under his mouth. The tension in me coiled so tight, I knew it was about to snap.

My thighs began to shake, and loud moans escaped from my lips one after another. Another stroke of his tongue, followed by rubbing his fingers against a sensitive spot inside, sent me hurtling over that euphoric edge.

"Taydom. Oh, fuck, Taydom." I screamed as he licked me through my orgasm.

When it started to subside, he didn't give me time to recover. He wound his arms around me once more and lifted me clear off my feet.

Carrying me over to the bed in only three long strides, he set me down on my knees. His hands came to my hips before he turned me over and bent me forward with a palm flat against my back.

"I need to fuck you now. That okay?" Every line of his hard body was tense, his muscles locked. He was breathing hard and his voice was harsh, sharp.

I needed him so badly that I felt achingly empty without him inside me, even though he'd just given me one of the most powerful orgasms of my life.

"Fuck me," I breathed, reaching around to unhook my bra before I braced myself on my elbows.

Taydom lined himself up behind me, his thick cock pushing against my entrance. He took a deep breath, gripped my hips, and slammed into me without any further teasing or warning. A deep growl rumbled in his chest as he buried himself fully inside me.

I wiggled my ass and arched my back to allow him to go as deep as I could take him. A loud, rough groan came from him and he began to move. Each stroke hit me exactly where I needed it. He stretched me out and filled me up in the most delicious way.

His hips moved like a piston, his rhythm never once breaking. He moaned and moved faster, rubbing every nerve, every highly sensitized inch of me. Heat spread through me as another climax built.

I was so close, but I needed more. "Taydom!"

"I'm right there with you," he rasped out. He fucked me harder, bringing his hand to my clit and pressing the rough pad of his thumb against it.

I cried out and dropped my head as he circled me and adjusted his pressure until my body started shaking. My muscles tightened, and with one last powerful thrust of his hips, I tumbled into oblivion again. Mind-blowing pleasure shattered my thoughts and overwhelmed my senses as I came on his cock.

Groans and moans were spilling out of his mouth as his face contorted with pleasure. I felt him tense. Then his fingers dug into my hips as he pulsed deep inside me. "Fuck. Elsie. Yes. Fuck."

An almost animalistic growl came out of him, and he filled me up with his release before his muscles went slack. "Holy fucking shit."

"You can say that again," I mumbled as I collapsed on my mattress.

Taydom followed me and drew me into his arms. "Holy fucking shit." He grinned and planted a kiss on my sweaty forehead. "That was incredible."

"It was," I agreed, but as I felt the combined result of our climaxes slick between my legs, something occurred to me. "We never talked about this, but we didn't use protection last time."

He stilled against me, the grin vanishing from his lips. "Fuck. I never... I never even thought about it."

"To be honest, I didn't either." Both of us had acted recklessly and irresponsibly without even noticing. I had never been so swept away by someone that protection never even crossed my mind. "I'm clean. I've never done anything like this before, but I get checked every few months anyway."

He relaxed some, but his jaw was still tight. "Yeah. Same. Are you on some form of birth control?"

"The pill," I said as I snuggled into his chest. "We were unbearably stupid, but if we're both clean and I'm protected, I think we're okay."

"I'm sorry." He sighed as he held me tighter. "I don't know what the fuck happened. I should have thought about it."

"This isn't just on you. We've both had a lot on our minds, I guess. We'll be more careful next time, but there's no point dwelling on it. We can get tested together sometime if you want?"

"That's probably a good idea." He kissed me gently and rested his forehead against mine. "I know it's not just on me, but I am sorry."

"So am I." I closed my eyes and put an arm around him. "But we're going to be fine."

I was surprisingly calm about this. In the back of my mind, I knew it was probably because I was in some form of shock, but I just couldn't process it right then. Not when he was holding me so tenderly and we fit so perfectly together.

When I opened my eyes again, Taydom's were closing. I planted a soft kiss on his lips before wiggling free. "I'm just going to go get cleaned up. I'll be right back."

"Wait. Let me go get a washcloth."

I saw he could barely keep his eyes open.

"No, it's okay. Rest. I'll be back in a minute."

He objected again, but I slipped out of his hold before he could stop me and made my way over to the bathroom.

Once I was done, I walked back into my bedroom to find him passed the fuck out. I poked him a few times, but he didn't move.

Smiling as I shook my head, I decided to let sleeping billionaires lie. I doubted either of us had planned on ending this night sleeping in the same bed, but I only had the one, and we were way past any possible morning-after awkwardness anyway.

Instead of overthinking it or worrying about what it meant for our relationship that we'd be sleeping beside one another, I crawled in next to him.

With Taydom's rhythmic breathing beside me, I drifted off to sleep within a few minutes.

CHAPTER 24

TAYDOM

When I woke up, I was feeling warmer than usual. Like I'd fallen asleep with a hot water bottle in my bed. Only the hot water bottle was the size of a person and it was pressed up right against my side.

As I opened my eyes, I realized that it was because it wasn't a hot water bottle. It was a person. Elsie, to be exact.

Blinking in the early morning sunlight streaming into her room, I couldn't quite believe that I'd fallen asleep in her bed. That had never happened to me before.

I didn't sleep with women. I didn't sleep with anyone actually. My mother had once told me that, even as a child, I'd rarely wanted to sleep with them or with my brother.

Yet I'd fallen asleep with Elsie.

What was more important was that I'd slept well. Really well.

I didn't even really remember falling asleep. Sure, I'd been exhausted, but somehow, I doubted that was the only reason for having gotten the best sleep I'd had in ages.

Having Elsie in my arms as I woke up, I suspected that she was the reason for my peaceful slumber. Her hair was loose and spread out behind her on the pillow. A soft, relaxed expression graced her beautiful face and made her look even more gentle and innocent than usual.

One strand of her hair was lying across her cheek and I lost the fight against the urge to brush it behind her ear. She stirred when I did, and a second later, those gorgeous green eyes slowly opened.

Unlike me, she didn't seem surprised or confused at all to wake up with me in her bed. Her lips curled into a sleepy smile. "Good morning."

"Morning."

She rolled over and out of my arms, then extended her hands high above her head and curled her body into a half-moon shape as she stretched lazily. The movement made her back arch and her chest press against the sheet covering her.

"Sleep well?" she asked, smirking when she saw my gaze was firmly rooted on her chest.

I couldn't help it. I could make out the outline of her nipples, and I was crossing my fingers that the sheet would slide off to reveal them.

"Taydom? My boobs don't have the answer to my question. How'd you sleep? You passed out before I even made it back from brushing my teeth."

"Yeah, sorry about that." I tore my eyes away and sat up, partially to hide the tent starting beneath her sheet but also because this wasn't my bed. Lazing around in it wasn't an option. "I didn't mean to invade your bed for the night. I just conked out."

"That's okay." She flashed me a smile as she sat up beside me. "I was going to throw you out, but I couldn't lift your big ass."

"Big ass, huh?" I ran my fingers through my hair and swung my legs to the side. "That's funny. I don't remember you having any complaints about my ass last night."

When I stood up, I could feel the weight of her gaze on me before I covered said ass with my boxer briefs. Turning my head to give her a smirk of my own over my shoulder, I saw her tongue swipe across her plump lower lip.

"Now who's having trouble keeping their eyes where they should be?" I gave my butt a little shake for effect.

Elsie burst out laughing as she covered her eyes with her fingers. "You can't blame me. I might not have been able to lift your ass, but that doesn't mean it's not a good one."

"Thanks." I picked my pants up off the floor, then took my turn to watch as she stood her naked body up out of the bed and made a swipe for her pajamas. "Yours isn't too bad either."

She covered herself much faster than I had, but her smile never left her lips. "Thanks. Do you want some breakfast?"

"Depends. Were you going to make something anyway? Otherwise, I can just grab something at my house."

"It's the most important meal of the day. I never skip it. Come on. I think I've got some bacon we can fry up, and if you ask nicely, I might even be able to whip up some pancakes."

"Are we talking about getting down on my hands and knees nicely? Because if I'm going to be getting on my knees, I have some ideas about what I could do while I'm down there." I grinned and rounded the bed, my hands closing around her hips to hold her still just as she yelped and tried to take off.

"No. You're not doing that." She laughed as she squirmed to get out of my grip. "If you do, we're never going to get around to breakfast and I'm starving."

"Suit yourself." I dropped a kiss on her forehead before letting her go and holding out a hand to her. "Let's get out of your bedroom then. Being in here is giving me ideas you apparently don't want to carry out right now."

She took my hand and gave it a squeeze. "Maybe later. Let's get some sustenance in us first."

I shouldn't have been surprised about how natural it felt to be with her first thing in the morning. Everything was different with this girl. Somehow, everything felt easy and natural with her. The craziest thing of all was that not even that thought scared me.

We settled into making breakfast together like we'd done it a thousand times before. I stuck to getting the condiments ready, the table set, and taking care of the dishes left over from last night.

Elsie opened a package of bacon and got that in a pan. Then she started mixing ingredients for her pancake batter. We talked while we got breakfast ready, which made it feel like this was how we started every day.

"What are your plans for the rest of the weekend?" she asked as she dipped a ladle into the batter and scooped some into the pan. "More sleep? You looked like you could use it yesterday."

"If I can get it, I'll take it. I have a lot of work I still need to get done, though. Monday will come with its own challenges, so I better get ahead of it or I'll never catch up."

Spatula in hand, she tilted her head and propped her hip against the counter as she waited for the first bunch of pancakes to start forming bubbles. "Is that normal for you? Always having to stay ahead?"

"Pretty much." I shrugged. "I don't mean to sound cocky, but when you're at the head of a company the size of mine, the work never ends. I can't afford to become complacent and there are a lot of people who depend on me to keep the wheels turning."

"I've never thought about it that way," she said as she flipped the first pancakes. "In my mind, the head honchos don't really do much."

I laughed. "It's not only you. Most people seem to believe that. Maybe later on, I'll become nothing more than a figurehead, but that's not true now. If I slow down, I'll have to employ a bunch more people to set things up so the cogs can keep turning."

"But you could do it." She checked a pancake with the spatula, deemed it ready, and slid them onto a plate before starting on a new batch. "Theoretically, I mean. You could employ those people so you could lessen your own load."

"I'd have to have a fucking good reason to do it. It would require an overhaul of the structures we currently have in place and some other things, but theoretically, yes, I could."

"You do have a fucking good reason to do it, though. I can't imagine you see your family often with the way things are at the moment."

The mention of them made my stomach churn, but it was also the opening I had been waiting for. "No, I don't. I haven't been back to Illinois in years."

Her eyes widened. "Have they come to visit you then?"

"Nope. Farmers don't get much time off either." I cleared my throat. "I'm actually planning a trip there in a couple of weeks. You should come. It could be fun."

As casual as my tone was, no one would have ever guessed how much I had riding on her reply.

Her eyebrows drew together as she gave me a strange look. "You want me to come home with you?"

"Yes. Why not? You deserve a break too."

Several emotions crossed her face, but they were mostly in the region of surprise.

Hope unfurled like a living thing in my chest, but then she shook her head and my heart sank.

"You're right," she said. "It could be fun. I'd love to see where you grew up and to learn about farming. Everything you've told me about it so far sounds fascinating, but I'd have to check with the school first."

"You're not saying no?" I asked.

She smiled. "I'm not saying yes, either."

It didn't matter because I had a feeling she would be saying yes very, very soon. Crossing the kitchen in two long strides, I lifted her into my arms and spun her around. "But you're not saying no."

She laughed as she pulled back, her hands on my shoulders and her hair forming a curtain around us as she looked down at me. "You're insane. Do you always invite women home with you after you've slept with them?"

"No, because I've never slept with anyone." The words came out before I could stop or rephrase them.

Elsie's lips parted in disbelief and she wiggled until I set her back down on her feet. "It's not possible that you never slept with anyone before me. I mean, I just can't believe that you were a virg—"

"Oh, God no. That wasn't what I meant. I've *fucked*. I just haven't slept with anyone after."

She frowned deeply. "Seriously?"

"Seriously."

Her frown dissolved into a smile. "Well, I'm not sure if that's a compliment or not that I was your first. Maybe I was just that boring that you couldn't keep your eyes open."

"It definitely wasn't that," I assured her as I watched her slide the second batch of pancakes out of the pan. The bacon was done as well, as was everything I had gotten ready.

Elsie and I ate at the dining-room table, talking and laughing until our plates were cleared and I caught a glimpse of the time. I rubbed my palms on my thighs and pushed to my feet.

"Thanks for breakfast and for letting me invade your bed, but I should get going." I helped her carry our plates back to the kitchen and to clean up before saying my goodbyes. "Remember to let me know about Illinois. Find out which dates will work best with your class schedule and we'll make the trip then."

"Thanks." She smiled and came over to me, rising up on her toes to wind her arms around my neck. "And thanks for inviting me to come."

"No problem." I returned her hug and brushed a featherlight kiss against her cheek. "I'll see you soon, okay? Go get back in bed. I wasn't the only one exhausted after last week."

"Maybe I will." She pulled back to look up at me. "You should get some more sleep too. Look after yourself, Taydom. You won't do me any good if you drop from exhaustion before I get to experience farming firsthand."

"You got it." I pressed another kiss to her forehead, then let her go. "Have a good weekend, Elsie."

I didn't remind her again to let me know about Illinois, but until she did, I would be checking my phone every minute to see if her answer had come through yet. If she ended up saying no, I was fucked. There were no two ways about it.

CHAPTER 25

ELSIE

"Are you sure you need so many onions?" I asked Beth as she loaded two more bags into her cart.

We were stocking up on supplies for the food truck. I couldn't quite wrap my head around just how much produce she needed.

She chuckled as she picked up four bunches of green onions as well. "I'll probably be back before the end of the week for more. Onions, gherkins, and tomato relish make my world go round."

"Yeah, but really?" I eyed the cart. "That's a lot of onions. We're going to use half the space in my trunk just for this."

"Hey, I didn't force you to come with me for my inventory restock." She arched an eyebrow at me. "I know you said you wanted to spend some time together, but we could have done that later. So spill, girlfriend. I know there's more to it than that."

"I did want to spend time with you," I said as I pushed the cart after her when she moved to the next shelf. "But you're right. I also need to talk to you about something."

"Yeah? What's that?" She glanced at me over her shoulder. "Does it have anything to do with your hot landlord?"

I groaned. "Am I that obvious?"

She shrugged, but the corners of her mouth lifted. "Yeah, you kinda are. It's either school or Taydom with you these days."

"Well, I mean, those are the only two things going on in my life. Besides, I listen when you talk about the truck and people you date."

"True." She winked. "But let's face it, you're a little more into him than I have been with any of my last few dates."

"Maybe," I admitted as chewed on the inside of my cheeks. "That's kind of what I wanted to talk to you about. I'm not sure what's happening between us, but he's invited me home with him."

"As in, he wants you to meet his family, home, or into his house, home?"

"Meeting his family," I said, watching her eyes grow bigger in surprise. "Yeah. Tell me about it."

She cocked her head, and her eyes remained round as she stared at me. "You know he's notoriously cagey about his family, right?"

"What?"

She nodded. "I'm being serious. All anyone knows about him is that he comes from Illinois. That's it. He refuses to answer any questions about his family or his past."

"Wow." I frowned. "That's weird. He's told me a bit about them. It actually seems like he's close to them. Well, to his mom and his brother at least. He hasn't mentioned his father much."

"Interesting." She plucked a bag of tomatoes up and added it to the cart. "It's not only interesting that he talks to you about things he's said time and again that he doesn't like getting into, but also that he's actually invited you home with him."

"Yeah, I don't know if it's interesting but it is weird." An entire bucket of crushed garlic followed the tomatoes while I spoke. "Isn't it a little soon to be meeting his family?"

She lifted one shoulder. "Depends. Is he taking you as a friend or a girlfriend?"

"A friend, I think. We haven't exactly discussed the status of our relationship, but it's hardly reached the stage where we're boyfriend and girlfriend."

"Then you have nothing to worry about," she said as she hooked her fingers around the front of the cart and pulled it after her. "Friends don't have to wait for any required amount of time before they can meet the parents. Friends who fuck? Well, I'm putting them in the same category."

"Are there actual rules about this stuff, or are you making it up as you go along?" I teased. "Because it sure sounds like you're making it up."

She rubbed the space between her eyebrows with her middle finger, a discreet way of flipping me off right in the middle of the fresh produce market. "Fine. Have it your way. I might be making it up, but consider this. If you introduce a significant other to your parents, they assume it's because you're serious about this person. A friend, on the other hand, is just a friend. It doesn't have them planning a wedding for you in the near future."

I snorted. "There's definitely no wedding in our near future."

"Exactly, which means meeting his parents is no big deal. When are you going?"

"He's going in a few weeks. I haven't decided yet if I'll be joining him, hence the need to have this conversation with you." I sighed as I reached up to twist my ponytail around my finger. "Would it be weird if I went? I've only known him for a few months. Meeting his parents feels like a big deal, even if it is just as his friend."

She shrugged. "I guess it could be weird if you make it weird. Don't make it weird and you'll be fine."

"You really think that?" I lifted my brows. "Because I don't think it's only up to me not to make it weird. He might make it weird or his family might not believe that we're just friends."

"To be fair, you aren't really just friends. You are also lovers, so they wouldn't be entirely wrong not to believe you."

"There's no love involved." I shook my head, but my heart did kick a bit at the denial. "Okay, there might be the tiniest amount of feelings involved, but it's definitely not love."

She shook her head at me. "I didn't say it was. I just said the two of you are lovers, which you are. If you don't like the term *lovers*, I guess we could just call a spade a spade and call you fuckers."

She cackled with laughter when a woman walking by gave her an admonishing look. I waited for the poor lady to pass before giving my friend's shoulder a light slap.

"Thanks a lot for that."

"What? She doesn't know who we're talking about." She nudged the cart a few steps forward with her hip. "Anyway, let's not get off topic. He wants you to go home with him. Otherwise, he wouldn't have asked. So what if you do engage in some extracurricular activities of a carnal nature? You like him. Go meet his family and assess whether there could be anything more between the two of you than there already is."

"I have to meet his family in order to do that?" I felt a deep frown settling between my brows. "Because it seems to me that one should first assess what, if anything, is between them, and only then should family be met."

"You're overthinking this," she said as she reached up and tapped a finger against her temple. "What's the worst that can happen? You go, meet some new people, get out of the city for a few days, and spend some extra time with a gorgeous billionaire who is your friend and also gives you orgasms from time to time. There's no downside."

I hesitated before replying. Beth wasn't wrong, but it wasn't as simple as all that either. "What if it changes something between us? I like us the way we are now. I don't want anything to change. Plus, what if his parents don't like me? There's a potential downside for you. Despite the distance between them, Taydom is close to his mother. If she doesn't like me, I could lose him."

"He's in his thirties. I doubt he lets his mother choose who he's allowed to play with, regardless of how close they are."

"You never know." I helped her hoist a massive bag of potatoes into the cart, then realized it was just about full. "Whenever my mom didn't like someone I was spending time with, I seriously reconsidered my opinion about them. I respected her and her instincts, and if I'm being honest, she wasn't wrong once. Also, do I need to grab another cart?"

She shook her head after glancing at the shopping list she had clutched in her hand. "No, we're good. Almost done. We just need to make a stop at the bakery on the way back to my place."

After stuffing the list into her purse, she lifted her gaze back to mine. "Your mom had killer instincts. I get that, but if she told you to stay away from Taydom after spending only a few days with him, would you have done it?"

"I don't know." I wanted to say yes and I wanted to say no, for differing reasons, but I just wasn't sure which one would have won out. "My point remains, though. There are definitely possible downsides to this."

"Look," she said as she placed her hand on her hip and gave me a stern look. "It's just a trip, my friend. You're not getting married to him. I doubt the trip will change much between you and it gives you the opportunity to travel a bit while you're still young. You've never been to Illinois, right? Go."

"You're right," I said finally as we walked to the checkout counter. "I've never been there, and I probably am overthinking it, but I can't help it. I just wish my mother was still around so I could ask her for her opinion as well."

Beth slung her arm across my shoulders and gave me a hug while we walked. "I understand, but I think she would have agreed with me. Don't be afraid to say yes because of things that haven't even happened yet. If you want to go, go. Don't let the fear of the unknown hold you back."

I dragged a deep breath in and then released it slowly. As I thought back to how I had felt in Taydom's arms, the sense of rightness I got whenever we were together, and how much I enjoyed just sitting and talking to him, the answer wasn't actually all that unclear.

While I wasn't in love with him or anything crazy like that, I did like him and I couldn't deny that my feelings ran deeper than what I was ready to admit. I wanted to spend more time with him. I wanted to see where he'd grown up and meet the people who had raised him.

He'd invited me to do just that, so on some level it had to be what he wanted too. Without any rational reason not to, why the hell couldn't I agree to what we both wanted?

"You know what? You're right. I'm going to say yes."

Beth let out a victorious squeal and threw her arms around me again. "You're going to Illinois, baby. Yeah!"

I giggled into her dark brown curls and returned her hug. "I guess I am. Ready or not, here I come."

CHAPTER 26

TAYDOM

Bright blue sky stretched as far as the eye could see. It was a cloudless day, perfect for taking a fishing trip with my best friend.

Andrew and I headed out to the marina early and rented a boat. Once our lines were in, we kicked back with a beer and waited for something to happen.

Neither of us were serious fishermen, but we still liked to do it. Sitting out on the water, getting some sun, and being outdoors was relaxing and not something we got to do every day.

A mud-colored ballcap covered Andrew's blond hair, and sunglasses covered his eyes. He lifted his hands to curl the end of the cap as he turned his head in my direction.

"What's eating at you?"

I frowned behind my own pair of sunglasses. "What do you mean?"

"Come on, man. I know you, and something's bothering you." He pointed at me with the neck of his beer. "You've barely said ten words to me since you picked me up."

"Sorry. I've just got a lot on my mind." Such as the fact that Elsie hadn't given me an answer yet. It had been a week since I asked her to come to Illinois with me, and the only time we'd discussed it again, she'd said she was still waiting on word from one of her classes.

Andrew crossed his arms over his faded T-shirt. "Am I going to have to drag it out of you?"

"No." I drained what was left of my beer and reached for a new one in the cooler between our seats. "Things aren't going well at home."

His cap moved as his brows lifted. When he pulled his sunglasses down to the tip of his nose, I saw concern darkening his blue eyes. "Why? What's going on?"

"The industry my parents are in has taken a hit and the farmers are feeling the pinch. I didn't even hear about it from them. I had to hear about it on the news."

He whistled under his breath. "That sucks. What are you going to do?"

"I have a plan, but it kind of hinges on Elsie."

"Elsie?" He frowned. "How does a plan to help your parents hinge on the girl you're renting the cottage to?"

"She's a little more than just a tenant, man." In fact, since that night that we'd slept together, I'd come to the conclusion that she was a lot more than that. "I told you we were friends."

He rolled his eyes before pushing his glasses back up. I saw my own reflection in the mirrored shades, but I could still feel his gaze on me as he waited for me to explain. "You know my parents wouldn't accept any help from me financially, so I might have lied to them a little to give myself an excuse to go up there."

"An excuse to…" He trailed off before he snapped his fingers and a wide grin spread on his lips. "Oh. That's why your plan hinges on Elsie. You're going to use her as the excuse."

No one ever said Andrew wasn't sharp, but the way he had phrased it irked me. "You've got the gist of it, but I'm not using her. I told my mother I had a girlfriend I wanted to introduce to them, so I asked Elsie to come home with me, but—"

"I'm sorry, but how is that not using her?" I saw a frown line forming above the top of his glasses. "Would you have invited her with you otherwise?"

I cleared my throat. "No, probably not. Fuck."

He chuckled as he leaned back in his chair. "Well, you're in too deep now to change anything. If you've already told your mom you're bringing someone home, you've got to bring the girl home. Plus, you've also already asked her to go with you."

"Yeah." I sighed and pinched the bridge of my nose. "I know. I just didn't think of it as using her. I don't want her to feel like that's what I'm doing."

Fuck.

I hadn't seen things from that perspective at all. While it was true that I wouldn't have invited Elsie with me otherwise, I also really did want her to come with me. I was looking forward to showing her around the farm and spending time with her without either of us being distracted by work or school.

I wasn't necessarily looking forward to going head to head with my father, and I still hadn't quite figured out how I was going to give them the money, but knowing Elsie might be going with me had put a silver lining around the entire visit. And not just because she would be an excuse to go or a distraction from them while we were there.

Elsie feeling I'd used her if and when she realized what was going on hadn't been my intention at all, but I could see why Andrew would think what he did. From the outside, that was exactly what it looked like I was trying to do.

"Your brain is going to explode if you keep thinking that hard," he joked. "Dude, it's no big deal. If you're going to get money to your mother, you're going to have to make the trip. It's that simple."

"I still don't know how I'm going to get her to accept the money, and frankly, it is a big deal to me. Elsie has become important to me. I really don't want her to think everything I've done since we met was because I was playing some long game to get her to help me con my family."

"What does it matter what she thinks?" He sat straighter and yanked his sunglasses off his face to glare at me. "Also, did you just say she's become important to you? What the fuck, man?"

"Calm down to a mild panic." I waved a hand at him. "I'm starting to care about her, is all. That's why it matters to me what she thinks. It's nothing to get worked up about, though."

"Nothing to get worked up about?" He shook his head, his mouth dropping open. "That's bullshit and you know it. You don't do relationships. That's why you're my favorite wingman. You can't go falling for some chick who's going to stop you from coming out with me."

"Dramatic much?" I rolled my eyes. "She's not going to stop me from doing anything and I'm not falling for her. I just care about her and I don't want to hurt her feelings."

"Caring about chicks leads to falling for them," he grumbled. "I can't believe I'm going to have to find a new wingman. You suck."

I laughed as I reached out and patted his shoulder. "Poor Drew. If it comes to that, I promise I'll help you vet the candidates. Better?"

"No." He shook my hand off before smirking at me. "On the plus side, if you and your billions are off the market, that might mean a lot more willing pussy for me. Too many women are obsessed with you, you know? As soon as they find out what I do or who I work for, it's all Taydom, Taydom, Taydom."

"You jealous, bro?" I quirked an eyebrow at him, trying my best to hold back a grin. "Because if so, you could work a little harder and make those billions for yourself."

"No thanks. We've talked about that, remember? I'm not jealous. I'm simply pointing out a fact. If there is no chance they can get you, all those pretty girls hanging around me hoping to get to you might just decide to fuck me. It's a win-win situation really."

"I only have one problem with all that. I'm not off the market and I'm not going to be. Jesus. All I said was that I was starting to care for the girl. I'm not about to go down on one knee for her. You know how I feel about all that."

He laughed and held out a fist for me to bump. "Hell yeah, I do. I just needed to be sure you haven't changed your mind."

"Definitely not." Although that wasn't completely true.

Over the last few days, I had often found myself wondering what it would be like to be with Elsie for real. When I walked into my empty house after a shitty day, I thought about what it might be like to find her waiting for me. When I woke up in the mornings, I played the memory of the one morning I had woken up to her beautiful face over and over again in my mind.

Somehow in almost all of the small, everyday moments, I found I had Elsie somewhere on the brain. Whether it made any logical sense for her to be there or not, I still found myself thinking about her.

The other morning, I'd walked into my office, and the first thing I did was imagine her sitting on my couch having a cup of coffee with me before going to class. Then I started imagining bending her over my desk and fucking her from behind, and well, then I'd had to forcibly shove her out of my head since I'd wanted to avoid walking into my morning meeting with a raging hard-on.

Elsie had only been in my office once, and yet it seemed like she haunted me there now, too. It was a fuckup of a situation and totally unlike me, but for some reason, I liked it. I liked thinking about her all the fucking time.

There was probably something very wrong with me but I didn't even care.

None of these thoughts made their way out of my mouth, though. I was still figuring it out for myself and Andrew would freak the fuck out if I told him what was really going on in my head. Also, there was this overly possessive part of me that didn't even want to share intimate thoughts about her.

Messed up? Absolutely.

We hadn't even talked about being exclusive or at all about what was going on between us, yet I went crazy at the mere thought of talking too much about her with another man. At this point, if I was to see her with another guy, I was pretty sure I'd lose it.

Andrew's voice drew me out of my thoughts. "Just don't tell the girl anything. She'll never know that you were using her to help your family. If you care about her, fine, but your family has to come first. I might not have all the details, but if they're not doing well, you have to take care of them."

"I know," I agreed. "Despite the fact that they make it insanely difficult to take care of them, I know I have to. I just have to figure out how to do it."

The other thing—which was something else Andrew didn't need to know—was that it wasn't only my family I wanted to take care of. I wanted to take care of Elsie as well, and I knew I could. I just had to make very sure that she didn't end up seeing things from Andrew's perspective instead of mine.

"You'll figure it out," Andrew said confidently. "You thrive on anything that's insanely difficult, so I know you'll come up with a plan. I just can't wait to hear what it is."

"Thanks, man. Neither can I." I just wished another layer hadn't been added to the plan I didn't have. If Elsie felt like I'd used her or had been using her all along, she'd be really hurt.

The very last thing I wanted to do was hurt her. The worst part of it was that this plan I had yet to formulate had the power to do a lot of damage to the hearts of the only two women I really cared about.

Lucky fucking me.

CHAPTER 27

ELSIE

A s I sat up in bed, it felt like there was a hook behind my navel and whoever held the other side of it tugged as soon as I was upright. Nausea rolled through me, making me break out in a cold sweat as my mouth watered.

I groaned and folded myself into a ball, dragging in breath after breath to quell the feeling. It took a few minutes before it started subsiding, and a few more after that before it felt safe to move.

The clock on my nightstand glared at me with angry red numbers on the display. They were red every morning, considering that it was the color of the backlight, but they'd never felt quite so angry and judgmental before.

God, I must be coming down with something.

I didn't have time to be sick. As those judging numbers just loved to remind me, I was already running late. I had to get to school or risk missing my first class.

After hauling myself out of bed and into the shower, I raced through my morning routine and made it out of the door just a few minutes later than usual. Thankfully, this seemed to be a sweet spot for traffic and I made it to campus just in time for my class.

Abnormal psychology was one of my favorite classes. It was one in which I seldom felt bored, but I just couldn't seem to focus on what Dr. Martin was teaching that day.

Despite the fact that I'd gone to bed early every night of the week, I felt exhausted. My eyelids felt like they'd been lined with lead and my brain just wouldn't hang onto thoughts.

"The first criterion of abnormality is the violation of social norms," the professor was saying as that hook yanked the back of my navel again.

My hand flew to my mouth as I tried to keep myself from getting sick all over my desk. It didn't feel like a false alarm, so I hastily grabbed my things and shot Dr. Martin an apologetic look before fleeing from the room.

Her brows furrowed on a frown, but she didn't try to stop me. I hadn't had much contact with her since classes started back up, but I'd had her for a couple of courses over the years and she knew I wasn't one to bail in the middle of a lecture for nothing.

I dashed down the hall with my sneakers squeaking as I took the one corner separating me from the bathroom. Shoving the door open with my shoulder, I crashed into the first available stall and sank to my knees.

My satchel went tumbling to the floor, but I couldn't bring myself to care. *Urg. I'm feeling so shitty.*

The latest bout of nausea passed eventually, but I didn't go back to class. I didn't want to take the chance of having to cause another scene if I had to leave abruptly, and if I was coming down with something, I didn't want to spread it to others.

Between the classes I'd already be missing when we went to Illinois and the trip itself, I really hoped whatever I had was some kind of twenty-four-hour thing. *Possibly even a twelve-hour thing, if I'm lucky.*

I made my way out of the building, surprisingly feeling perfectly fine again all of a sudden. I decided to go to the health center just in case. There was definitely something up with me, and if I was contagious, I needed to know.

Our campus wasn't a big one. The size of the health center reflected our relatively small student population. The quaint brick building was situated in the middle of a patch of trees that made it look a little like something out of a fairytale.

Weird, considering that it was a mini-hospital, but I'd asked the administrator about it once. He said it had been chosen partly because the environment it was in was already calm. Apparently, that helped patients with all kinds of ailments to remain calmer themselves.

I'd done a lot of sessions there as part of my program and I smiled as the small bell above the door tinkled when I walked inside. Jeanette, the same receptionist who had been there since I was an undergrad, widened her eyes in surprise when she looked up to see me.

"Hey, Elsie. I didn't know you were scheduled for more sessions this semester. I thought we'd only be seeing you again next semester." She smiled. "How are you?"

"I'm good. You?" I clutched the strap of my satchel as my palms grew sweaty. "I'm not here for a session actually. I'm feeling a little under the weather. Thought it was best to get checked out. I really can't afford to get sick right now."

Her hazel eyes softened in sympathy. "I hear you. There never does seem to be a good time for it, though. Have a seat. Someone should be with you soon."

I nodded and motioned toward the stack of clipboards lying on the counter in front of her. I knew the required forms to be filled would already be clipped to them. Jeanette always seemed to be prepared to handle a stampede of new patients, even if it was more of a trickle on most days.

"Should I fill that in?"

She grinned. "That would be great. Thanks, honey. Let me go check in the back how long it's going to take someone to get to you."

"Thanks." I grabbed a clipboard from the stack, took a seat facing the windows, and completed the form while I waited.

Jeanette was back a few minutes later. "April says she'll be with you just as soon as she's done."

"Okay, great." I watched people sauntering past the building and heard the bell jingle a few more times during the wait. The health center was constantly busy. The trickle of students never quite seemed to let up.

Thankfully, the staff was also efficient and the waiting times were never terrible. April called my name a little while later, flashing me a smile from where she stood in the doorway.

"Hey, Elsie. Come on through. I've set up exam room two for us. What's up?" The fiery-haired doctor had become something of a friend to me and it was a relief to know I'd be getting checked out by someone I knew.

Her kind brown eyes tracked my movement as I got up and made my way to her. As she looked me up and down, her brows pulled together. "Are you okay? You look a little pale."

"I feel pale," I said, offering her a weak smile. "I'm okay. I'm just not feeling my best."

"In that case, you've come to the right place." She lifted her hands and placed one on either side of the stethoscope hanging around her neck. Her head dipped to the side. "Come on. Let's get you checked out."

A nurse I didn't know waited in the exam room, smiling as we entered. "I heard we're looking after one of our own today."

"Not quite," I said. "Just a student who's spent some time here, is all."

April motioned toward a bed in the center of the room and patted the mattress. "Hop on up, girl. Why don't you tell me what's been going on with you?"

The nurse moved behind me as I climbed onto the bed and faced April. I gave her a quick rundown of my symptoms and told her they'd only started this morning.

"Well," she said, once I was done with my explanation. "It could be any number of things. There's a stomach bug traveling around campus at the moment and a pretty bad flu doing the rounds, but we need to account for another possibility."

"Like what?" I frowned. The expression on her face had gone from relaxed to concerned and I noticed her exchanging a glance with the nurse.

She rolled her lower lip into her mouth. "Have you been sexually active recently?"

My brows rose as my cheeks flushed. "Yeah, I, uh, I guess. Yes. Why?"

The corners of her mouth pressed in and she dragged in a deep breath. "We have to consider that you might be pregnant."

I felt the blood that had just rushed to my cheeks leave my face as fast as it had shot up there. My fingers and toes grew cold and my mouth was suddenly drier than the Sahara Desert.

"But, I, uh, I'm on the pill." My heartbeat sped up until it felt like the thing was trying to win a Nascar race. "I can't be… you know."

Sympathy softened her features as she lifted a shoulder. "Even if you take it exactly the way you should, it's not infallible."

Exactly the way you should. Her words echoed through my mind as I thought back over the last few months since my mother's death. I'd been fairly consistent with taking my pill at the right time of the day, but I *had* skipped some days.

"Fuck," I mumbled, a heavy sigh falling from my lips as I tried to wrap my head around the possibility. "What now?"

April's soft hand closed over my forearm and she squeezed as she offered me a comforting smile. "Now we draw some blood and run some tests."

I nodded, but it was like I was hearing her from underwater. I switched into autopilot mode after that, holding out my arm like a good little girl.

I barely felt the pinch when April inserted the needle, and a few seconds later, I couldn't believe she was already done. "Anything else?"

She shook her head. "Nope. We'll run this in the lab and let you know the results as soon as we do."

"How long is that going to take?" I asked, my voice strangely monotone.

"A few days." An apology flashed in her eyes. "With the stomach bug and the flu in the air, in addition to all the normal tests we run, the lab is slammed at the moment. There's also a health drive this weekend, so we'll be here, but we'll be busy."

"This weekend?" I blinked as I struggled to comprehend what she was telling me. "It's only Wednesday."

"I know, but there's no way I can speed the results up. I guess you could go get an over-the-counter test if you're worried, but we're already running the blood test. It's miles better than any test available at the drug store." She laid a hand on my shoulder. "I'll give you a call personally as soon as your results are in. You have my word. I wouldn't make you wait until Monday if I get them earlier."

"What do I do until then?" I asked, numbness spreading through me.

"Go home," she said softly. "Get some rest for today. If you're feeling up to going back to class tomorrow, do it. Don't say anything to anybody until we know for sure. It might very well be one of the bugs going around campus."

"Okay." I felt my head bouncing up and down, but I didn't remember wanting to nod. "Thanks, April. I'll be waiting to hear from you."

"I know. I promise I won't make you wait a minute longer than necessary." She gave my shoulder a squeeze, then waved and went off to do what it was she did after delivering potentially life-altering news.

As for me, it was all I could do to put one foot in front of the other. My mind was racing through a flurry of thoughts, but I couldn't grab onto any.

When I eventually made it back to my car, I took April's advice and headed straight home. Once I got there, I shed my clothes, drew my curtains, and got into bed wearing my most comfortable pajamas. Whether it was disbelief or shock that sent me into complete shut-down mode, I didn't know.

All I knew was when I woke up again, it was dark. I made my way to the kitchen, had some dry toast and a cup of tea, and went back to bed. I needed time to process, and just like I'd been after the last greatest shock of my life, I gave myself the time I needed.

CHAPTER 28

TAYDOM

The soft hum of the air conditioning was the only sound in my office as I tried to determine what else I needed to take with me. My desk was covered in stacks of paperwork, but a lot of what I'd had to get done from Illinois could be done on my laptop.

I'd already packed it up and had double-checked that I had soft copies of all the documents I needed. Andie, my assistant, had also assembled a few thin files I had to take and had placed them neatly into my laptop bag.

Dragging my hands through my hair as I narrowed my eyes at what remained on my desk, I released a slow breath and nodded. That was it.

The only thing I was still missing was a girl to take with me. Elsie hadn't given me an answer, but we'd been texting, and she'd alluded to having a good surprise for me. I was crossing my fingers that it meant she'd heard back from that last class she'd been waiting on and that we were all clear.

Doubt ate away at the back of my mind, though. There had been complete radio silence from her since yesterday morning. She hadn't returned my texts and hadn't taken my call when I tried that.

Last night when I'd gotten home, all her lights had been off and there had been no sign of movement. I wasn't sure what to make of it all, but I'd also decided not to jump to conclusions.

Her class schedule was pretty packed on Wednesdays and I refused to become one of those creepy clingers who needed to hear back from someone within a minute. My plan of action was pretty simple. If I hadn't heard from her by the time I got home this evening, I'd head on over there and find out firsthand whether she was coming.

She knew I was leaving tomorrow and that I hoped she'd be on the plane with me. We would be gone for a week, which I hoped would give me enough time to talk some sense into my family.

My door opening grabbed my attention away from my musing thoughts. Andie strode in, her blonde hair pulled back into a severe bun and her blue eyes wide as she gave me a tight smile. "All set?"

"Just about." I drummed my fingers on my lips and smirked at her. "The only thing I'm still short is a woman to take home with me. My mother is expecting a girlfriend, but I can't seem to get hold of the only girl I know who is also a friend."

Curiosity came as a sharp gleam into her eyes, but she knew better than to ask why. A slight line appeared between her eyebrows. "If you need a woman to go with you, I could accompany you."

"Thanks for the offer, but no thanks." I sat back in my chair and laced my fingers together. "I might be in a bit of a tight spot, but I'm not interested in you that way, and I know you feel the same."

"True, but an assistant is supposed to assist. Therefore, if you have a problem that I can help with, it's my job to do whatever is necessary." She dipped her head slightly. "If you need me to come with you, I will do so."

Andie ruled our offices with an iron fist. The only person she ever showed this kind of subservience to was me, but I'd seen that other side of her. I knew who she really was, and as loyal as she was being by offering, I could never take her up on it.

Being away from the office on a farm away from a lot of modern amenities and in a place where heels were a body part and not footwear, Andie would not be happy. Plus, I'd meant it when I said I wasn't interested in her. We had zero chemistry. There was no way my family would buy us as a couple.

"Again, Andie. Thanks, but no thanks. I really do appreciate your offer and I know that if I asked you to, you would help me with this in a heartbeat. This is a personal problem, though, not a professional one. It's not on you to assist me with it."

She gave me a firm nod and a grateful smile spread out across her face. "Thank you. Enjoy your trip, Taydom. I'll be in touch."

"Talk to you soon." I waited until the door closed again behind her before gathering my things and following her out. The coming week would officially be the longest I'd been away from the company since I'd started it, and leaving set me on edge.

Even though I would be reachable telephonically, I had given over the reins temporarily to Andrew. He would handle the meetings where personal representation from our upper management would be required. He'd only agreed to help because he knew how important this trip was to my family. Otherwise, I was sure he would have told me to go fuck myself.

Knowing that I needed to drop by to see him before heading home, I programmed in the address for the open house he was having when I climbed into my car. The engine purred to life and I followed the disembodied voice navigating me to a neighborhood I didn't know very well.

It was another of the trendier areas, which was much more Andrew's scene than mine. The condo he was trying to sell was in a newly renovated building and took up both of the uppermost floors.

Even knowing as little as I did about this neighborhood, I figured it would be an easy sell. In fact, I was kind of expecting to walk in and have him tell me he'd received offers on the place already.

What I didn't expect to walk in on was what appeared to be the remains of a house party instead of an open house. There were red solo cups everywhere and empty bowls containing oil stains. I could only assume they'd once held potato chips.

"What the fuck is going on in here?" I asked Andrew's back. The man himself was standing with his hands on his hips, facing the view outside through floor-length windows.

He turned to me with a self-satisfied smirk on his lips. "What do you mean? I just closed the deal."

"It looks terrible in here." I motioned in the direction of the dining-room table. "There's sushi rice all over that thing."

This was why Andrew wasn't doing as well as he could be. Sure, he'd sold the place, but with this kind of approach, there were only so many types of clients that would deal with you.

He waggled his brows at me. "That's because the sushi was a massive hit. I couldn't bring it out fast enough."

"Except for the fact that you're not in the catering business." I shook my head and squeezed my eyes shut, lowering my chin as I dragged in a calming breath. "You know what? Forget I said anything. Congratulations on the deal."

"Thank you." He grinned. "What are you doing here?"

"I came to make sure we were still good for the trip. You've got everything you need?"

He rolled his eyes at me. "You've triple-checked all that with me, bro. Trust me. We're good."

"You will let me know if there's anything you need or any questions you can't answer?" I hooked my thumbs into my pockets and arched an eyebrow. "Andie will be available to you as well. I went over all the most important details of the meetings with her this morning. Then she offered to come to Illinois with me anyway."

"You haven't heard back from Elsie yet?" He ran a palm along his cheek. "That sucks, man. Especially for someone who's not used to hearing the word no."

"Fuck off. I hear that word all the time, but I haven't heard it from Elsie. Unfortunately, I haven't heard the word *yes* either." I sighed as I lifted my shoulders. "I thought she was going to say yes, but now she's ghosting me."

He shook his head. "Just go alone, man. If she's playing games with something this serious, it's better that she doesn't go."

"She's not playing games. I still haven't told her anything, and besides, if I go alone, I'm going to piss my family off. Riley is likely to shoot me in the fucking kneecaps for getting our mother's hopes up. My father will chase me off the farm if I try to talk to him about money with no independent witnesses present."

"I could come," he offered with a sly smile. "We could pretend you misspoke and you meant to say you were bringing your boyfriend. I'm comfortable enough in my sexuality to do it."

I laughed. "Thanks for the offer, but I'll tell you the same thing I told Andie. I'm not interested in you that way. Mom would never buy it."

He shrugged and straightened his tie. "Your loss. I would have made an excellent boyfriend for the week. If you've turned both me and Andie down today, what are you planning on doing? You're leaving tomorrow. That doesn't leave much time for you to come up with someone new."

"No. It doesn't. The other problem is that even if she does come and she finds out why she's there, she's going to be pissed."

Andrew inclined his head. "That, she is, but you know my thoughts about that. Just don't tell her and you're golden."

"It feels like I'm making the wrong decision no matter what I do," I said. "I'm damned if I take her and damned if I don't."

"It's not ideal, but you'll get through it." He clapped his hands together. "Now, are we going to have a drink to celebrate the sale?"

"A quick one, then I've got to get home. Elsie and her decision await me."

If she said no, I had a long night ahead of me, figuring out what in the hell I was going to tell my mother. If she said yes, I had a long night ahead to figure out how to tell her my plan without her feeling used.

Taking a short break to have a drink with Andrew wasn't going to change any of that. It might grease the wheels in my brain a bit, though. At this point, I would take all the help I could get.

When I finally pulled up outside my house a couple of hours later,

Elsie came out to greet me. I couldn't deny that I was nervous about what she was going to say.

I was going to have to roll with the punches, though. I'd gotten myself into this and now the only way out was through.

I might just need a few more drinks before the night is out.

CHAPTER 29

ELSIE

Headlights hit the windows at the front of my cottage, which meant Taydom was finally back. I had been waiting for him in my living room, only one lamp providing soft light for the freak-out I was having.

I wiped my sweaty palms on my drawstring pants and drew in a shaky breath. This was the moment I had been waiting for all day.

I'd gone to class, but waves of nausea still rolled through me every so often. I was also still more tired than usual. Despite all of that, I had decided to stick to my plan of going to Illinois with Taydom.

If there really was a baby growing in my belly, I wanted to know the family it would be born into. Besides, the reasons I'd decided to go in the first place hadn't changed. At the same time, if I had the stomach flu, I didn't want to create unnecessary chaos in Taydom's life by leading him to believe I was pregnant.

I didn't know how he would take the news—if there was any news at all—but I had decided to wait for the results before I said anything, and that was exactly what I was going to do. In the meantime, I still had to tell him about Illinois.

Rising slowly, I took a few deep gulps of air. Just because I had decided to tell him didn't mean it would be easy. Frankly, I had been freaking out the whole day.

But my mother had taught me well. I refused to create a crisis where there wasn't one, and I refused to let what was out of my control take over my life. The reality of the situation was that Taydom and I had both been irresponsible. If our actions had consequences, we would have to deal with them together when the time came.

A baby wasn't something I had been planning for, nor was it something I wanted at this point in my life. It was possible that grief over Mom was making me more complacent about this than I should have been, but I had only just started processing the greatest shock of my life.

Her death had been so unexpected and so untimely that I was still reeling. I was trying to get back to my life, or some version of it anyway. I had moved, gone back to my studies full time, and started developing feelings for a guy, but none of that meant I had learned to live without my mother. None of it meant that I was back to the way I had been before, which was probably why I was wondering if I might be pregnant in the first place.

It didn't excuse my carelessness. Nothing would, but whatever happened, I could handle it. I had to. If Taydom and I had conceived a life, I would take care of it.

A baby might not have been in my immediate plans, but I'd always wanted a family. Taydom hadn't seemed entirely opposed either. He'd simply said he thought his luck had run out.

It was food for thought, but not the kind of thought I had time for right then. Every free minute of my day had been spent wondering about this, but now it was time to face him.

I'd prepared myself for this moment all day and I was determined to act naturally. Until I had something concrete to tell him, it would be Elsie-as-usual.

I opened my door as he was parking and saw the flare of surprise in his eyes to see me. Exterior lights lit up his garage and parking area, and he was facing me, so it wasn't difficult to see his expression.

He was definitely surprised, but he also seemed relieved to see me.

I had avoided speaking to him while getting myself together, but I hadn't expected a couple of days without contact to have had any impact on him at all.

Obviously, I had been wrong.

"Hey, you," he said as his lips spread into a soft smile. "I was starting to wonder if I was ever going to see you again."

"It's only been a few days." I left my doorway and walked over to him. "Sorry for not replying to your texts. I've been a little out of it."

He frowned. "Why? What's wrong?"

"I'm just getting over a cold. Nothing to worry about." Sharp needles of guilt stabbed at my gut for playing it off that way, but it was the best I could do.

Concern tightened his expression and darkened those golden-brown eyes. "You sure you're okay? You should have told me you were sick. I would have brought you soup or something."

A tiny piece of my heart melted. "Thanks, but I just kind of slept through it. I didn't mean to worry you."

"As long as you're feeling better." He motioned toward his house with a jerk of his thumb over his shoulder. "You want to come in?"

"Sure." My hands started trembling again, but I managed to muster a smile and hoped he wouldn't notice my anxiety. Just because I'd decided not to stress him out unnecessarily didn't mean it was going to be easy being around him when potentially, I was keeping a massive secret.

"I've still never been inside your house. You're going to have to give me a tour."

His eyes narrowed as he frowned. "What? Really? How is that possible?"

"I don't know." I shrugged. "I guess we've just never gotten that far. We always end up hanging out at my place or in the entertainment areas."

"You're right," he said slowly, then reached out to grab my hand. "We're rectifying that right now. Come on."

His strong, warm fingers closed around mine and I instantly felt comforted by that one small touch. It was incredible how alone I'd felt over the last two days.

I could have reached out to Beth or responded to Taydom, but I'd needed the time alone. Regardless, human touch was something I had craved. My mother always used to hug me when I was feeling down, and it was her arms I really missed during this time, but Taydom's hand in mine was something.

It was more than something. At this moment, it was everything.

Instead of heading toward the back door which faced the garage and my place, he led me around his huge house. "If I'm giving you a tour, we're doing it right and going in through the front."

"You never gave me a tour of the showhouse either. Am I about to get treated to the full Taydom Gaines experience?"

He grinned. "I think you are."

Without letting go of my hand, he rummaged around in his satchel and produced a set of keys. The front door was an intricately carved wooden monstrosity with strained glass panels throughout. I'd never noticed it before, but it fit in with the general air of luxury the house exuded.

After turning a key in the lock, he pushed the door open and swept out a hand, gesturing for me to precede him. "Welcome to Casa Gaines. We hope you enjoy your stay."

"We, huh?" I arched an eyebrow. "Is there another resident here I should be aware of?"

He chuckled. "*We* sounded better than just little old me. Anyway, so this is the entrance hall."

Lights flicked on and I finally got my first inside view of the main residence on the property. My jaw slackened as I tried to take it all in.

The floors were tiled with large, gleaming white squares that shone with the reflection of the warm yellow light inside. There had to be hundreds of lights in the ceiling that had all come on at once.

The entrance hall opened up to large living spaces, a dining room, and a short hallway that seemed to lead to the kitchen. Corridors led away from the main areas, the tiles giving way to plush-looking carpets in a pale gray color.

Although Taydom was a bachelor, his home was not furnished the way I might have expected it to be. It was warm and cozy, with area rugs that appeared to be Persian covering the tiles in the living room.

Comfortable-looking grey couches were arranged in front of the large flatscreen TV mounted on the wall. Dark wood made up his coffee table, bookshelves, dining-room table, and more.

The shelves were filled with books that had cracked spines, making them look like they'd actually been read. Another entire shelf was filled with vinyl records, and an old-style record player stood off to the side of it.

"Wow." I whistled below my breath. "You have a beautiful home, Taydom. I should have asked for this house when I was looking for a place to stay."

He laughed and tugged at my hand. "At least you know you're welcome anytime. Let me show you around."

"Yeah. Okay. Let me hear it then. Taydom Gaines in action."

"You got it." He cleared his throat and squared his shoulders, all traces of humor falling away from his expression. Once his transformation into professional Taydom was complete, he swept his hand out in an elegant motion but still hung onto mine with the other.

"So as you can see, this is the kind of house anyone would want to come home to. It's got enough space to fit the entire family without feeling cold or impersonal. It was designed by its former owner, who is a renowned architect. It's got every amenity you could possibly need, including a wine cellar, swimming pool, theater room, and the like."

"You have a theater room?" I asked, my voice strangely hollow in disbelief. "How did I not know that?"

He dropped the businesslike tone and laughed. "You never asked. I've also got a sauna if you're ever interested. The only rule is that you have to be naked to use it."

"I'm sure that rule has always existed and was by no means made up on the fly just then."

He shrugged and flashed me an innocent smile. "Absolutely. Everybody knows it's sauna best practice to be in the nude."

"Yeah, well, I mean obviously everybody knows all about sauna best practices." I rolled my eyes even though my lips curled into a smile. "We've all got them, so we're all studied up on how to use them."

"Of course." He squeezed my hand. "Do you want to see the rest of the place, or shall we go straight to the sauna?"

"Let's see the rest of the place." I might not know much about saunas or even all that much about pregnancy, but I was pretty sure a sauna was something to avoid. *That's if I really am pregnant.*

Just like that, my nerves skyrocketed again. Taydom must have felt me shiver because he gave me a strange look. "You okay?"

"I'm fine. It's just a little chilly in here." It wasn't. It was the perfect temperature actually, but whatever.

Taydom arched an eyebrow at me. "Are you sure you're not feverish?"

"I'll be fine." I plastered a wide smile on my face and dragged him with me in the direction of the corridor to our left. "I thought you were giving me a tour."

"I am, but promise me you'll tell me if you need to sit down or something." I could hear his concern in the sudden gravelly timber of his voice, but I waved it off.

"I will, but I'm fine. Let's go." I was surprised to find that the rest of his home was just as tastefully and warmly decorated. Every one of his bedrooms was fully furnished, beds made up as if he was expecting company to arrive at any given moment.

Four of the bedrooms had en suite bathrooms, leaving just one without its own. The master bedroom was about the size of my entire cottage and had a four-poster bed that could sleep a whole family.

By the time we were done with the tour, I was just as in love with his house as with my own. We ended in his kitchen, which I had seen before on the day I came to ask for his help with the cabinets, and he sat me down while he went to the fridge.

"What do you think?" he asked as he cracked it open. "Also, would you like a drink? I've got an excellent bottle of wine that I opened last night."

"I probably shouldn't have alcohol." I waved a hand when he frowned at me. "I took some medicine earlier and I'm not sure if having alcohol with it is a good idea."

"Right. Of course. Water okay? I think I've got some juice if you'd prefer that."

"Water's fine." I took a deep breath to calm my galloping heart, then nodded my thanks when he handed over an ice-cold glass of water to me. "So, uh, I wanted to talk to you about Illinois. Are you still planning on leaving tomorrow?"

He nodded. For a second, I saw a flash of nervousness in his eyes. "My pilot will be ready at eleven."

"If your offer is still on the table, I'd like to go with you. I've cleared it with everyone at school and I've been given the go ahead."

He blinked several times. Then his lips spread into a wide smile and he crossed the space between us in a few long strides before taking me in his arms. "The offer is definitely still on the table. I'd love for you to come with me."

"Great, then it's settled." I hugged him back and burrowed my face into his chest. "I'd better go get packed, but I'll see you in the morning."

"Yeah, sure." He held on to me for a minute longer before letting me go. "I'll see you in the morning, Elsie. Thank you for agreeing to come. You have no idea how much it means to me."

CHAPTER 30

TAYDOM

"When you said your pilot would be ready for us at eleven, I didn't think you literally meant you had your own jet." Elsie stared at the plane in front of us with a slack jaw, green eyes wide as she looked up at me.

I grinned and raised a shoulder. "Impressed? Have you flown private before? If you haven't, you'll soon understand why I bought a jet over another property."

"Oh, the choices you've had to make," she teased as she shot me a wink. "To answer your question, I haven't flown private. I haven't flown commercial, either."

"What?" My brows pulled together. "Are you saying this will be your first flight?"

"Yes," she said, sliding her hand into mine. "I guess I should thank you for bringing me with you. I'm sure I'm about to be spoiled for all future flights."

"You'll just have to keep flying with me." I hadn't planned to say that, but the words came out anyway. They were true, though.

Despite the lingering guilt over unintentionally dragging her into something that could make her feel used, I was excited about this trip.

Finding out that she'd never flown before was a bonus I hadn't expected.

Then again, I also hadn't expected to feel this way about getting to be the person she experienced a first with. I was feeling strangely proud. Proud, excited, and way too satisfied with myself.

It meant something to me to be the person responsible for exposing her to her first flight and to be the person who got to take it with her. Although on the other hand, I had learned that everything meant something when it was with her.

At some point during this week, I was hoping to find the right time to tell her. Our relationship had evolved over the last couple of months and I couldn't deny it anymore. I wanted her to know that I cared about her, and frankly, I needed to make sure that she knew I wasn't fucking anybody else. Hopefully, she would agree to do the same thing.

Stop fucking around about it, a snide voice chided at the back of my mind. *You want to ask her to be exclusive with you. Just do it.*

It was one I knew well and one that came from the part of my brain that was firmly and unashamedly honest with me. No matter how I tried to justify or reason certain things away, that part of me always cut through the bullshit. Just like it was doing now.

I wasn't sleeping with anybody else and I didn't want to. Considering that Elsie pretty much only ever left the property to go to class or to see Beth, I didn't think she was seeing anybody else either. Essentially, things would remain the same between us if we agreed to exclusivity. There would simply be more clarity.

That same snide voice inside snorted, but Elsie's laughter made me ignore it. She had her head tipped back as she shook it.

"I can't always and only fly with you. Why would you want that anyway? We're friends. We're not commandeer-your-plane friends."

"Why not?" I smirked as we walked toward the short staircase attached to the door. "Consider the plane yours to commandeer."

"In that case, can we change our flight path from Illinois to Spain?" she asked jokingly. "I've always wanted to see Malaga."

"Malaga, huh? Not Barcelona or Madrid?"

"Malaga," she insisted. "Not that I would mind seeing the other two either, but I really do want to go to Malaga someday."

I made a mental note of it but didn't say anything. Offering to take her to Spain once we were done in Illinois seemed like it could be a touch over the top. "I'm sure you will see it someday then."

"Yeah, me too." There was some emotion in her soft voice that I didn't recognize, but I was assuming it had something to do with her mother.

Earlier this morning, she had told me that she'd really been missing her while she hadn't been feeling well. It made sense, but the context in which she'd said it bothered me a little bit. It was almost like she'd said it to have a blanket excuse for getting emotional.

In the time I'd known her, she hadn't come across as very emotional at all, but there were certain subtle differences in her now. I'd noticed it last night, and it was still very much present this morning.

Whatever was going on with her, if there was something more than missing her mother, I was sure she would tell me when she was ready. In the meantime, I would just make sure I gave her whatever support I could.

"Are you kidding me?" she exclaimed as she reached the top of the stairs and peered into the cabin. Her head snapped to the side so she could look at me over her shoulder. "This is really yours?"

"It's really mine," I said as I climbed up the last step and stood beside her. "Impressed now?"

"You fucking know that I am. Anyone would be." Awe and disbelief dripped from her voice as her gaze tracked across the interior of the jet.

"Yeah, I guess you're right. It's a nice plane."

"You call that nice?" She pointed and then waved her hand around. "You call that nice? You have actual couches in here. And a TV. And a bar."

"There's also a full bathroom and a bedroom in the back."

Her smile became wider than I'd ever seen it and her lips parted. "I ask again, are you fucking kidding me?"

"Nope," I said cheerfully and slung my arm around her shoulders. "Let me show you."

The tour of the plane only took a few minutes. Ground staff for the airstrip had loaded in our luggage from my car, and just as I was leading Elsie to the bar, the pilot opened the cockpit door.

James had flown me around since I'd bought this unnecessarily ostentatious yet absolutely awesome toy last year. He had salt and pepper hair and a cap beneath his arm. "I've completed all the pre-flight checks, Mr. Gaines. If you're ready, I'll close the door and we can be off."

"We're ready. Thanks, James."

He nodded firmly and went ahead with sealing the door before disappearing into the cockpit. Elsie walked past the bar and tipped her head as she surveyed the seats. "Where do you want to sit?"

"We can't use the couches during takeoff and landing. Choose any of those seats." I pointed at the eight luxurious armchairs toward the front. "Also, we'll have to serve ourselves once we're in the air. There's a hostess on board, but she'll mostly be up at the front with James."

"I'm sure we can manage that." She nudged me with her elbow. "If you have any trouble getting your own drink, just ask me. I've been serving myself for years."

I rolled my eyes at her. "Smartass. Just choose a damn seat."

She walked up and down a few times before choosing a window seat in the row nearest to the couches. I took a seat beside her and buckled in.

Annie, the hostess and James's wife, came by to check on us, and a few minutes later, we were on our way.

To Illinois.

Where I would be introducing a girl who wasn't really my girlfriend to my parents.

Who thought she was, in fact, my girlfriend.

More than that, they thought she was the first girlfriend I was ever bringing home to meet them.

Fuck my life.

Elsie grabbed my hand when the wheels started rolling, her spine rigid as she closed her eyes. "I've heard this part is scary, but I didn't realize it would feel this strange. Please distract me. Tell me anything. Better yet, tell me what I'm in for when we get to your parents' place."

I chuckled but I also turned my palm over so it would be against hers and then stroked my thumb soothingly over her knuckles. "They're really old school. Conservative to a certain extent and obsessed with manners, but they're good people."

"Well, at least my mother taught me good manners," she mused as she gave me a smile. "At least I have that counting in my favor."

"As long as you use those manners she taught you, you'll be fine. I promise." I lifted our joined hands and pressed a kiss to the back of hers. "They're going to love you."

"We'll see." She took control of our hands then, kissed my knuckles, and turned in her seat to watch as we made our ascent. "Now that we're actually in the air, this feels a lot less scary."

"Good." I smiled as I leaned over her and pointed to a few things I thought might interest her.

The plane leveled out eventually and she beamed at me. "I made it through my first takeoff without screaming or peeing myself."

"Was that a possibility?"

She laughed. "I don't know. Maybe. I'm sure it's happened before."

"Probably." I shrugged. "For the record, thank you for not peeing on my leather seats."

"It was my pleasure." She grinned, but then I saw something that looked a hell of a lot like heat enter her eyes. "Speaking of which, what do we do now that we're in the air?"

"Whatever we want," I said, curious to know what she had in mind. "What would you like to do?"

She wiped the grin off her face and gave me a very exaggerated innocent look. Wide eyes, eyelashes batting, the works.

"Well, this is my first flight and I would like to remember it." She tilted her head slightly, gaze caught on mine as she batted those long lashes again. "I also think I might need to practice my manners before we get there."

"Yeah?"

"Yes." She let go of my hand, then held hers out to me. "May I please have your belt? I've thought of a wonderful way to make memories of my first flight, but you're wearing far too many clothes, and I'd love to help you out of them."

Fuck yes. It took me no time at all to get on board with this plan.

I arched a brow and reached down to undo the metal buckle. "That's so incredibly kind of you. Would you like my pants as well?"

"Oh, yes." More eyelash batting, but this time, she licked her lips as well. "If it's not too much trouble, could I ask you to accompany me to the bedroom? I would hate to scandalize the poor hostess should she walk in at the wrong time."

"I don't give a fuck about scandalizing her. I'll just tell them not to come in here, but if you want to go to the bedroom, we'll go there."

She pursed her lips as she glanced around the cabin. "Could you really make sure they don't come in?"

"Yes," I said without hesitation. I was already getting hard, loving everything about this. If she wanted to go hide away in the bedroom, that was fine by me, but I got the feeling she wanted to get down on her knees right here. I definitely wasn't about to complain about that.

Hitting a button on the console between our seats, I barked the order into the intercom for us not to be disturbed and looked up again to find Elsie staring at me.

"Is it done? That easy?"

"That easy," I said, my voice already getting rougher in anticipation. "You wanted my belt and my pants. Is there anything else I can give you?"

She nodded and beckoned at me to come closer. When I did, she brought her mouth to my ear and her lips brushed against my skin as she spoke. "You can give me your come and at least two orgasms."

I groaned. "I think you just blew my mind."

It was the greatest understatement that had ever been made, but fuck, I couldn't think straight. Not with my brain anyway.

I didn't know what had gotten into her since she hadn't talked dirty to me before, but fuck if I didn't like it. As with everything else about her, I liked it a whole fucking lot.

CHAPTER 31

ELSIE

Hormones and lust were funny things. One minute, I had been completely captivated by watching as the buildings below us grew smaller, and the next, I was so turned on I could barely think.

All it had taken was one trigger—just the one word *pleasure*—and I needed Taydom more than I'd ever needed anyone. My clit ached so badly it was all I could do not to reach beneath my dress to touch myself, and he hadn't done a single thing yet. Yet the overwhelming, all-encompassing need I felt prevented me from wondering or worrying about how strange it was that I'd gone from zero to ten thousand in less than two minutes.

My breathing grew heavier when I felt the muscles in Taydom's arms work as he reached for his belt again. He hadn't pulled away from me, but I could feel his movements. After placing the belt in my hands, he stood up from his seat and undid his pants, smirking as they dropped to his feet.

"I can give you everything you just asked for, but I think you forgot about something." His thumbs hooked into the elastic of his underwear. "But I'll give it to you anyway."

I had never just stared at him quite so openly, but I couldn't help

190

myself. He lifted the waistband away from his body before slowly pushing his boxer briefs down.

When his erection sprang free, I released a low moan. "Fuck. I want you in my mouth."

His nostrils flared with surprise, but thankfully, he didn't ask me why I was suddenly acting with such complete abandon. It was a good thing he didn't ask because I honestly had no idea where any of this was coming from.

Taydom looked down at me with barely disguised need and desperation in his eyes. His breathing was labored. He was staring at me like I was about to hand him some kind of award.

"Sit down," I said. My voice was soft, but he obviously heard me.

As he sat down, I slid out of my chair and dropped to my knees in front of him. He spread his legs to make space and I wasted no time.

It was like I was beside myself with need, being driven by it like it was an insatiable beast who insisted on having what it wanted right the fuck now.

Leaning forward, I licked his tip into my mouth and swirled my tongue around his head. He groaned and his hips thrust up like he couldn't help himself either. At least I wasn't alone in this insanity.

I worked him into my mouth slowly and used my hands to help me reach for the parts of him I couldn't fit in. His cock hit the back of my throat and his hands were suddenly in my hair. Not guiding or pushing, just holding me in position, fingers massaging my scalp.

I licked and sucked and moved my hand in conjunction with my mouth until he was moaning incomprehensible words. "Christ, baby. I'm too close. Stop, please stop."

I didn't listen to him. There was no way I was moving my lips off of him. I wanted to feel every drop of his come in my mouth and shooting down my throat.

What is wrong with me right now?

One final lick along the underside of his cock and he was groaning again before shooting his thick, hot come down my throat. Strangely, I didn't think I'd ever tasted anything better.

I'm even thinking like a pornstar now?

I still had no idea why, but I was also starting to wonder why I couldn't always be this free. At least when being intimate. I was enjoying the hell out of it and I had a feeling I was about to enjoy it even more.

"Holy shit," he grunted eventually. "That was fucking amazing. Come here."

Taydom pulled me to my feet, kissing me deeply as he guided me onto his lap. He didn't seem at all revolted or disgusted by the taste of himself on my lips, which turned me on even more. But I was done wondering why.

I couldn't concentrate anyway as he set my body on fire with his kisses. He slid his tongue against mine and heat pooled between my legs. As if they had a will of their own, my hips started grinding against him.

"Don't worry, baby," he murmured between kisses. "You made me come so hard, and I'm going to return the favor. Twice. Just like you asked."

He slid one hand along my thigh, stroking me slowly, building up an impossible pressure between my legs. His other hand pulled the top of my cotton sundress down to expose my breasts and immediately started rubbing my left nipple through my bra.

The hand on my thigh slid over the seam of my sex. The fact that I was still wearing my panties did nothing to cloud the stars I was already seeing behind my eyelids or the loud moan that escaped me.

He was breathing heavily against my chest, swallowing my sounds of pleasure and making little ones of his own. Just when I was about to start begging, he pushed my panties aside and made slow circles around my clit.

I moaned into his mouth again, almost unbearably sensitive to his touch today. My back arched, and our kiss broke, but it also drew Taydom's attention to my breasts. He sucked in a breath as he took a moment to stare at them, pupils dilated and mouth slightly open, before he put those talented lips to my aching nipples.

It didn't matter that I was still covered by the lace of my bra. His mouth was hot and wet and just fucking perfect. He alternated his free hand and mouth between them as his other hand slowly slid a finger inside me, still circling my clit with his thumb.

The pressure building in me was almost painful, but I was climbing towards a peak unlike anything before it.

Taydom kept stroking and circling and sucking, and before I knew it, my body splintered into a million different pieces as I found my release. He stilled once I started coming down, then smirked against my lips.

"That's one. You ready for two?"

I was panting, sated, but I nodded anyway. The beast was well and truly in control of me now, and that bitch really was insatiable.

"Good." He claimed my mouth with his again. "Let's go to the couches. It'll be more comfortable there."

My knees were weak, but I managed to wobble my way to the lounge area. Taydom guided me to a couch and motioned for me to have a seat. When he knelt in front of me, his pupils were still dilated, his eyes wide with lust, and he was looking at me like he wanted to devour me.

"Scoot to the edge for me, baby," he said as he gripped my knees and spread my legs open wide to make space for his broad shoulders.

My skin was on fire everywhere he touched me, every part of me suddenly aching for more. He tapped the side of my leg before snapping the elastic of my panties against my skin.

"Off," he growled, low and commanding.

I lifted my behind and he slid my panties down. Face to face with my exposed sex now, he drank me in with his eyes, moaning softly as he stroked my drenched core.

"God, babe. You're so fucking wet." He brought his glistening fingers to his lips and licked my juices off his fingertips. "So fucking sweet. I didn't have you pegged as someone who enjoys dirty talk so much, but it seems I was mistaken."

"Yep," I bit out. "I didn't know how much I liked it either."

It was difficult to focus on anything other than his fingers that were now playing with my clit, teasing my seam, and generally doing a fantastic job of driving me out of my mind.

"Good to know," he whispered before his mouth was on me. He licked slowly but hungrily along my seam. Up and down, sucking, darting his tongue into me before starting all over again. Letting out another low moan, he took my sensitive bundle of nerves into his mouth and sucked lightly before his tongue flicked against me.

It took him almost no time at all to reduce me to a trembling, moaning maniac again. I tried to buck my hips against him, but his strong hand kept me in place as he licked and sucked me until I saw nothing but fireworks.

Far too soon, the tension that had been building up inside me released in a glorious ball of light, my mind shattering in every different direction possible as I screamed his name. My fingers dug into his shoulders and my head dropped back against the couch.

He kept going, licking until he'd gotten every last drop before he crawled up over my body. Sliding a hand down to my thigh, he repositioned me until I was lying down. The tip of his cock rested against my entrance, positioned perfectly to slide into me.

Bringing his mouth to mine, he kissed me hard and passionately, twining his fingers around my own as he slid into me.

When he was all the way in, he stopped to let me adjust. Somehow, although it was far from the first time he'd been inside me, I felt fuller than ever before. Maybe it was just the two mind-blowing orgasms that had come before, but I felt more swollen than usual.

Taydom's muscles were taut, his eyes blazing with need. "You okay?"

"Yes," I breathed through clenched teeth. "But I need you to move. Now, okay?"

"Okay."

He finally started thrusting then. Slowly at first, but it was still the most incredible feeling ever.

Pleasure filled my body, taking over every inch of me. The entire world disappeared. The only thing that remained was the feeling of him inside me, his body on mine, breathing deeply and moaning into my ears, kissing my eyelids and my mouth as he whispered about how much he wanted me.

He rocked into me with a steady rhythm, with just the right amount of pressure, and miraculously, I felt the pressure building yet again. Almost painfully at this point. Luckily, I knew that he could and would release the knot he was building in me.

His breathing was ragged and I felt his muscles starting to shake as he drove into me more forcefully. He was nearly there and I was right there with him.

A final thrust and my world was shattering again into a million pieces. Gorgeous, brilliant white light exploded behind my eyelids and my toes curled as I came undone once more.

Taydom nipped at my bottom lip just before his eyes rolled back, muscled shoulders flexing and thighs quivering as he filled me up. I felt his orgasm pouring into me, cock twitching deep inside of me. And it was the most exquisite thing that I'd ever felt.

A low ding sounded in the cabin and he chuckled as he buried his head in my neck. "Your first flight and you never even got to feel like you were floating in the clouds."

"What do you mean?"

He propped himself up on an elbow and smiled down at me. "We're about to land, baby. The flight to Illinois isn't all that long."

"It's already over?" I croaked, my throat dry from all the panting and moaning. "Are you sure?"

"I'm sure." He dropped a kiss on my forehead. "We better get you cleaned up. That was the alarm to let us know the pilot is preparing for descent."

"Wow. Okay." I tried to sit up, but my limbs refused to cooperate.

Taydom chuckled as he withdrew from me, rolling over to stand up. "You relax for a few minutes. I'll get you cleaned up. Then we can get back to our seats."

I had barely managed to get my dress back on before he was buckling my seatbelt for me. Wispy white clouds welcomed me to Illinois before I spotted the farmland and towns below.

He took my hand again and held it until we touched the ground. Then he sighed and a grim smile spread on his lips. "Well, we're here. Let the Illinois adventure and mishaps begin."

CHAPTER 32

TAYDOM

Nerves coiled my stomach as we approached my hometown. My knuckles were white on the steering wheel, but I managed to smile at Elsie when we drove up to the small green sign announcing that we were entering Woodstock.

"This is it. The metropolis of Woodstock, Illinois." Greenery rose up beside the road and finally gave way to the familiar turn-of-the-century Victorian buildings that the town was famous for.

Elsie sat beside me in the rental car, her body turned to face outside. "This is beautiful. It's not what I was expecting at all."

"What were you expecting?" I glanced at her before turning my attention back to driving. "Dull and dreary?"

She laughed and I caught the movement of one shoulder lifting from the corner of my eye. "Maybe. I guess I just never expected a farming town to be so quaint and charming."

"We're listed on the Register of Historic Places. There may be a lot of farms around here, but there's a lot more to it than that."

Waving her hand to gesture at the green town square with the quintessential bandstand in the center of it, she turned to look at me. "Who would leave here? It doesn't look like a bad place to make a life."

"It's not," I agreed. It really wasn't. "It just wasn't for me. I might have grown up here, but I like the bright lights and the big city. I've always been drawn to it."

"This place must have a special place in your heart, though." Her green eyes filled with wonder as she flicked her gaze toward the window behind me. "It's like something out of a movie."

"It's been featured in several actually." Public parking areas surrounded the square, and I pulled into the first open spot I saw. "How about we take a look around and grab something to eat?"

Her brow creased. "Aren't you eager to get home?"

"A few more hours won't hurt anyone. They aren't expecting us until this evening anyway. During the day, they're all pretty busy. I figured this was a good time to show you around."

"Oh, okay." She sat up a little straighter and a smile tugged at the corners of her lips. "Yeah, I think I'd love to have a look around. I've never seen anything quite like this before."

"You ain't seen nothing yet." I shut the engine off and climbed out, then rounded the SUV to offer her my hand just as she was following me out.

She took it without question, winding her fingers around mine and holding on tight. "Lead the way then. I'm excited about this. Have I mentioned I've never experienced any place like this before?"

"You have." I smiled and took off down the paved sidewalk toward the shops situated around the square. "Wait until we start exploring. One thing I have to give to the town is the nostalgic atmosphere. It's unique to Woodstock if you ask me."

"Well, you're the only person I know around here. I guess I'll have to ask you." She let out a contented sigh as we meandered down the street underneath the canopy of the trees beside us.

Mottled sunlight shone through the leaves and created a blanket of shadows on the ground. We weren't quite at the shops yet, but I could already smell the leather polish from Mitch's handmade goods store and the lavender and jasmine wafting from Anne's artisan creations.

No matter how much I'd wanted to escape this place back in the day, it would always be home. The bad memories I had were more related to the farm than the town itself. Unlike my father, the town had also been willing to accept help from me on occasion. Though I'd asked to remain an anonymous donor, word had gotten out that several new community initiatives had been supported by me.

The grapevine around here worked fast and was in pristine working order. As a result, I'd grown even more famous around here than I had become once it became public knowledge that I'd made my first million.

Mitch was rearranging a display of leather purses in his window when he spotted me walking up. He blinked a few times as if he couldn't believe who he was looking at. Then his weathered face split into a wide grin.

"Taydom," he called, jogging out the door and holding his hand out to me. "How are you doing? I didn't know you were coming to town." He pumped my hand hard, then turned his smile on Elsie. "And who is this lovely young lady you've brought home with you?"

Inexplicable rage exploded out of some primal part of me to see another man looking her over with appreciation in his eyes. *Calm the fuck down, dude. Mitch is older than most of the buildings around here.*

As I got a grip on the sudden insanity that had taken me over, I realized it wasn't appreciation he was eyeing her with. It was curiosity. Which made sense, considering that Mitch played cards with my parents once a week and undoubtedly knew I was a committed bachelor.

"This is Elsie. She's a friend." I had to tread carefully.

Mitch was sure to mention to my parents that he'd run into me, perhaps before we even made it to the farm later. On the other hand, I couldn't go around introducing her as my girlfriend without having a discussion with her about it first.

As far as my family was concerned, she was my girlfriend. I wouldn't have to label the relationship in front of them. They would simply assume Elsie was the girlfriend I'd mentioned to them.

The rest of the town, however, was a different story. Regardless of my attempt to downplay the situation, Mitch gave me a knowing smile. "Friend, huh? Well, it's nice to meet you, Elsie. I'm Mitch."

He held his hand out to her and pumped it with as much enthusiasm as he had mine. "You must be quite the young lady to have caught the eye of our boy here."

"Nice to meet you, too, Mitch." Chuckling as she shook her head, she let go of his hand and stepped closer to my side. "I didn't realize your boy was such a local celebrity."

He raised his eyebrows at her, licking his lips in that way he had before divulging something juicy. Almost all the locals I knew had a tell when they were about to gossip, and this was Mitch's.

Time to step in.

"Come on, man. If I'd told her before we arrived, it would have sounded like I was bragging." I clapped a gentle hand down on his shoulder. "It was good seeing you, but we should get going. We've only just gotten here and I promised Elsie a tour before we head home."

"Of course, of course." He grinned and shot me a wink that was probably meant to be discreet but missed its mark completely. "Tell your mama I'm glad to see you've finally come to your senses. Have fun, kids."

I held back an eye roll and gave him a polite smile instead. "Sure thing, Mitch. See you around."

He gave us a wave and went back to his display, leaving Elsie to arch an eyebrow at me. "What was that all about?"

"Nothing." I waved it off. "He just likes to think he's got everyone all figured out. Let's go."

The farther we wandered into town, the more we encountered locals who were just as curious and nosy as Mitch had been. Elsie stopped asking about it after a while, but I knew she wasn't going to let it go.

Once we'd made it around the square and down a few of the streets leading off of it, I was starving. "You ready to stop for a bite to eat?"

She groaned and pressed a hand to her chest. "Yes, please. These heels are killing me and I passed the point of just hunger about fifteen minutes ago."

I frowned. "Why didn't you say anything?"

Amusement lit up her eyes. "It was too much fun watching you try to pretend that you're not some kind of local celebrity."

"I'm not a celebrity," I said, but I guessed the jig was up. "There are actually quite a few actual celebs who hail from here, but I'm not one of them. I'm just a local kid who made some money and didn't forget where he had come from once he had."

She chewed on her lip for a second. "Okay, I think I get it. You've given back to the community and that has made you some kind of hero?"

I shrugged. "Maybe. What I did wasn't heroic, though. This town gave me my roots and my childhood. The least I could do was remember them once I was able to."

Elsie took my hand again, dipping her head back to look into my eyes as she squeezed my fingers. "I'm starting to think the press may be wrong about you. You're not some rude, mysterious bad boy after all."

I lifted a hand to slide my finger under her chin and held her gaze as I pressed a soft kiss to her mouth. "Just don't tell anyone. You'll ruin my reputation."

"Your secret is safe with me." She smiled, but there was a flash of something in her expression I couldn't place. It was gone too fast to know for sure, but it had looked almost like a wince.

"Everything okay?" I asked, our faces still only inches apart.

"Yep, perfect," she said cheerfully, but when she took a step back, there was definitely something bugging her.

I figured it must have something to do with her mother. Maybe something I had said had reminded her of her mom, or maybe it was just being back in my hometown with me and knowing I was about to see mine.

Either way, I slung an arm over her shoulders and kept her close as we walked to a diner down the block. Elsie looped her fingers around mine dangling over her shoulder and half-rested her head against me.

To any outsider, we sure as hell would look like a lot more than friends. It hadn't been my intention. I'd simply wanted to offer her comfort, but I found myself liking the picture I knew we were making anyway.

My mood soured when we turned a corner and bumped into Sonny and Mel Williams, a couple who had been friends with my parents for years. Both of their mouths spread into mile-wide grins when they saw us, and I had to fight the urge to turn and run.

Elsie and I had been having a moment that was real, and now it was ruined. Sonny and Mel would be calling up my parents the second they left us to tell them what a cute couple we were, which meant that even this moment had now become part of the charade I'd accidentally gotten us into.

"Taytay!" Mel cried out and threw her arms around my neck. "Your mom told me you were coming, but I thought she said you were only getting in tonight."

"Yeah." I hugged her back and shook hands with Sonny. "We're heading on home later, but we wanted to explore a little and grab a bite to eat."

"That's understandable," Mel said to me, but her gaze was locked on Elsie. "You must be the special lady friend in our Taydom's life."

I cleared my throat. "Yes. This is Elsie."

"It's so good to meet you, darlin'." Mel gave her a hug too, which seemed to startle Elsie, but she patted her back and released her. "You're a pretty one. Oh, I bet you two are going to make the most adorable babies."

"Babies?" My heart skipped several beats. Shit. Of course, they would assume I was bringing a girl home I was that serious about. She was the first woman I was ever bringing home.

The question was how to get out of the situation without fucking it up on either side. I let out a good-natured chuckle. "We'll have to see about that."

Mel carried on for a few more minutes, also treating me like some kind of celebrity, before Sonny dragged her away. He mumbled his goodbyes and we waved after them.

I turned to face Elsie, mind racing as I tried to come up with a plausible way to explain that. Her face was as white as a sheet. "Shit, baby, what's wrong?"

"Nothing," she said absently, but her wide eyes and the lack of any color in her cheeks gave her away.

I went to stand in front of her, placing my hands gently on her shoulders and bending my knees to be at her eye level. "Bullshit. It's not nothing. Is it about what they said about babies? If it is, ignore them, babe. You know that generation. Everything is about babies to them."

"Yeah, I, uh," she stammered. "I know. I'm fine. I just need something to eat."

"Okay." I took a deep breath. I knew this was about more than hunger, but once again, I'd have to wait her out. Because once again, I wasn't telling her everything either.

Fuck, I'm getting sick of this.

This was the week. I was telling her everything while we were here and I was hoping she would do the same. If she didn't, it was fine.

My choice, however, was to come clean this week. If she needed more time, so be it. At least then, I wouldn't always have to be careful of pushing her for fear that she would push back.

"Let's go eat." I wound our fingers together again and we walked the last few yards to the diner in silence.

Elsie eventually relaxed again as we worked our way through our massive burgers, but that only lasted until we drove onto the farm. She was visibly tense as we rolled to a stop, with the gravel drive crunching under my tires.

Before I could reassure her again, though, my mother burst out of the front door and called my name. She also clapped her hands and sniffed before making her way down the rickety wooden stairs in front of the house.

It was showtime. I just had no idea how the hell to put the show on.

CHAPTER 33

ELSIE

Dogs barked and rushed off the wraparound porch winding around the farmhouse. Dusk was just starting to fall and the scene that greeted me looked like something out of a painting.

The house had two stories and seemed to be in need of some aesthetic repairs, but a warm glow emanated from the inside that made the place look like a real home. Towering trees surrounded it, but on both sides of the gravel driveway, there were only fields as far as the eye could see.

The fields and trees were dark, but with the sky painted in various shades of pink and orange, the darkness of the vast empty spaces didn't seem scary. In fact, it all seemed welcoming.

Everything and everyone here were nothing short of welcoming. Except for that one lady who had brought up having a baby with Taydom in the first minute that I'd met her.

Of course, given my current predicament, she might have been more correct than any of us at the moment. It had been a stark and very unexpected reminder of the secret I was possibly carrying.

I hadn't been prepared for it at all, and her words had hit me like a sucker punch to the gut. I had been able to tell that Taydom hadn't believed my excuse, but I would have my answer soon enough, and then he would understand. Whether the test came back positive or negative, he would know why the question had thrown me off.

A figure appeared in the doorway suddenly. The warm light from inside threw her face into the shadows but highlighted her silhouette enough for me to know that it was definitely a woman. Taydom's mom.

It had to be her. A wave of nausea rolled through me again, but this time, I was ninety-nine percent certain it was just nerves. I was about to meet the woman who had raised Taydom—and who could possibly be a grandmother right now without even knowing it.

The prospect of meeting her was daunting, to say the least. Taydom, on the other hand, suddenly didn't look nervous at all anymore.

All day, I'd had the feeling he was more anxious about this visit than he was trying to let on, but he couldn't hide it from me. I knew him too well by now. All the little nuances that gave him away were burned into my brain. It felt like I had known him forever and like all those little things were simply a part of my DNA.

When his mother started down the stairs, his entire demeanor changed. His shoulders came down, a radiant grin tugged at the corners of his full lips, and it was like his guard slipped away.

Turning to face me in the near darkness of the SUV, he planted a quick kiss on my lips. "Come on. Let's go say hi to Mom."

Yep. He's definitely excited about this. "Okay. Yeah. Let's go." I smoothed my dress out and hoped that most of the sweat that had been gathering on my palms was now on the fabric.

It turned out I needn't have worried about my palms. The woman had no interest in shaking my hand. She hugged Taydom like she hadn't seen him since he was a baby, then did the same with me.

"I'm so glad you two are finally here. I've been looking forward to this for too long." The words came spilling out of her. I detected the faintest hints of a midwestern accent, but I had gotten used to hearing it throughout the day.

"Yeah, Mom. I've missed you too." Taydom laughed and motioned toward me. "Mom, meet Elsie. Elsie, meet my mother, Gwen."

Gwen stepped back from us and landed in the pool of light streaming out from inside. It was the first time I could properly see what she looked like, and it immediately became clear who Taydom had gotten his coloring from.

Her skin was so tanned, she was almost golden, and long chocolate-brown hair tumbled in soft waves past her shoulders. Curious hazel eyes peered back at me, seemingly conducting the same onceover as me.

"I can't tell you how happy I am to meet you, Elsie," she gushed before drawing me into another hug. "You didn't tell me how pretty she was, Taydom. So pretty."

I felt my cheeks grow warm, especially when Taydom didn't respond. Gwen's body was soft as she gave me another impossibly hard squeeze, her shoulders only an inch or so above mine.

Guess the height comes from his father then.

She let me go, but I felt her eyes on me even as her lips kicked up into another smile. "Let's go get your things. Then we can get you settled."

"Riley and I can get them later, Mom." Taydom brushed a kiss to her cheek when he passed her on his way to the stairs, but she wouldn't budge.

"Nonsense. You get your own and I'll help Elsie with hers. Your brother's just gotten in from—" She cut herself off and shook her head. "The point is that he's enjoying a cold drink. Let the man sit for a minute."

"Funny, I don't remember ever hearing that from you before," he joked but started moving back toward the fancy black SUV he had rented. "But okay, if you insist."

Taydom ended up with both our bags, refusing to let me carry a thing. His mother shouldered my backpack, despite my protests for doing it myself, and she grumbled about how Taydom would never let her do anything.

They bantered as we made our way back up the driveway and to the house, while I tried not to get my heel stuck in the gravel. It had seemed like a good idea to put on heels, like it would help make a good impression on his parents.

Having now seen his mom's simple faded blue jeans and plaid button-down shirt, I was pretty sure heels weren't the way to go if I wanted to make a good impression. Even so, I was wearing them now, and making it into the house without faceplanting seemed vitally important in the whole making a good impression thing.

I listened to them as I carefully watched my step, and their banter put a smile on my face. It was easy to see how close they were, and I liked it.

Taydom groaned as we reached the top of the stairs. Then he abandoned the luggage to hug his mother again. "Roasted chicken and potato puffs? You're the best, Mom."

She chuckled, but his words had brought my attention to the smell hanging in the air, and I felt the onset of another wave of nausea. I drew in a deep breath, regretted it almost immediately, and pushed my hand to my stomach.

Dear God, please not now. I cannot get sick on their porch the first time I meet them.

"You okay out there, Elsie?" Gwen asked. "Come on in, sweetheart. Let's get you settled."

I nodded and forced a smile. I seemed to be doing a lot of that these days. "Yeah, I'm all good. I was just taking a moment to soak in the fact that we're finally here."

My answer obviously pleased her. She gave me a soft smile and ran her fingers through her dark hair while her eyes stayed on mine. "I can relate. Now come on in so we can introduce you to Riley and have a drink before dinner."

"Dinner?" I gave Taydom a pointed look. Sure, it had been a couple of hours since we'd had lunch, but I certainly hadn't expected to have to eat again today. My appetite really wasn't what it used to be.

"Of course," she said, exchanging a glance of her own with her son. "What did you do?"

"I might have taken her for a burger at The Station." He gave her the most adorable sheepish grin, and I nearly melted at the sight of it.

His mother didn't seem to think he was being cute at all. She swatted his shoulder and shook her head. "Well, I've made your favorite and you're going to eat." Her gaze swung to me, softening once again. "You don't have to eat anything if you're not hungry, honey. You can just sit with us if you'd like."

"Thank you." I remembered what he'd said about using manners and felt my cheeks turn beet red as I remembered what I'd used them for on the flight over here.

Taydom caught me red-cheeked and winked when his mother turned to lead us into the house, obviously knowing exactly what I was thinking about. Thinking about it made me acutely aware of the slight ache between my legs that had been left behind from his earlier antics, but before those thoughts could turn me on, Taydom grabbed my hand and led me inside.

"Stop it," he chided me, humor glinting in his dark eyes as he leaned down to speak near my ear. "If you keep thinking about it, I'm going to keep thinking about it. Since it won't do either of us any good right now, let's just agree to try to meet up later."

I arched a brow, but before I could ask what he meant by meeting up, his mother spoke up again. "Riley, honey? Your brother and Elsie have finally arrived."

"Coming," a rich, deep voice said from within the depths of the house.

It was only then that Taydom released me and caught up to his mother, leaving me with a minute to really take a look around the house. Everything in there had seen better days, but it was the homiest place I'd been in since I'd last been to Mom's house.

Faded and threadbare rugs covered pocked hardwood floors. The couches in the den looked lumpy and were covered in colorful throws that seemed to have been straightened just before we'd arrived.

A staircase with a smooth wooden banister led to the second story, and a blue carpet that was shiny with age covered the stairs them-selves. The area opened up to what I instantly knew was the heart of their home: the kitchen.

The scent of lemon, garlic, chicken, melting cheese, and a few other things was stronger in here, but my prayer seemed to have worked. No nausea threatened to knock me off my feet. Instead, the opposite happened. My stomach grumbled softly and I frowned at myself.

What the heck is going on with my body?

The disturbing thought was interrupted when a large figure rose from behind a long mahogany table in the kitchen. The man was as tall as Taydom, but he was broader and stockier. His muscles bulged, as opposed to Taydom's leaner build.

Since he was definitely too young to be his father and much too alike in appearance not to be related, I assumed this was the brother. He confirmed my suspicion a moment later when his glittering dark eyes widened in surprise.

"Elsie, huh? I gotta say, I wasn't convinced you existed. I'm mighty glad you do, though. I'm Riley. It's a real pleasure to meet you."

Taydom rolled his eyes. "Knock it off, Riley. I told you she existed."

"Yeah. Doesn't mean I believed you." He chuckled and pushed his chair back to give his brother a back-thumping hug and to shake my hand.

"It's a real pleasure to meet you, too," I said.

His palm was rough against mine and his grip firm. *Pretty sure even his calluses have calluses.*

Any woman who liked 'em rough, rugged, and hot would swoon over this guy. He moved with the same confidence his brother did, an almost cocky swagger. He looked a heck of a lot like Taydom, too.

Somehow though, he didn't do anything for me. I didn't even have the vaguest desire to check him out, no matter how good looking or alluring he was.

It had been becoming increasingly obvious to me that my feelings for Taydom ran so much deeper than I'd thought, but this just confirmed it once again. I'd tried justifying my incredible lack of interest in any other man by trying to convince myself that it was just because Taydom was one of the best-looking men I'd ever seen in my life.

Now here was a guy who was as close to his twin as I could get, and still nothing. *I'm in trouble. Big. Motherfucking. Trouble.*

But now wasn't the time to dwell on it.

Taydom motioned for me to take a seat at the table and Riley dropped back into his. He picked up his beer and went back to sipping it.

"Where's Dad?" Taydom asked after glancing down at the settings on the table. "Isn't he coming down for dinner?"

Gwen flashed him an apologetic smile and shook her head. "He's already turned in for the evening, baby. I'm sorry, but you know how he likes to rise before even the rooster does. You'll see him in the morning."

"Great," he muttered, then thanked his mom when she brought him a beer. "Is there anything I can help with?"

"Not a thing. You two just relax a bit. You've had a long day." She planted her hands on her hips and pointed at Riley. "Now you, on the other hand? I need something from. Pour your mama and Elsie here a glass of Chardonnay."

"I'm fine," I said instantly. "I've had a cold recently and I'm still taking the medication, so I can't have alcohol."

She nodded. "Good to know that you're responsible. Just the one glass of Chardonnay then, darlin'. What will you have?"

"Just some water," I replied.

"Got it," Riley said, getting to his feet once more and leaving the kitchen as Gwen disappeared to somewhere else.

"What did you mean earlier about trying to meet up?" I whispered to Taydom as I turned to face him.

He shrugged, but I saw an apology and was disappointed in the way he looked at me. "This is a three-bedroom house, which means there's only one free. I told you they were old school, so I'm taking the couch."

A laugh burst out of me. "Really?"

"Really." He smirked. "But I know where the creaky floorboards are. I can avoid them."

"No, don't." I leaned forward to give him a quick kiss before his family got back. "I like this. Besides, it's only a week."

The smirk turned into a pout as his eyes filled with disbelief. "Really?"

"Really." It was my turn to smirk. "Think about how much fun we'll have on the plane ride back."

If there even *was* a plane ride back together. The test results would probably come in tomorrow, and I had no idea what was going to happen with us after that.

CHAPTER 34

TAYDOM

The bitter scent of freshly ground coffee percolating roused me from my sleep. Covering a yawn with my hand as I stretched out on the couch, I opened my eyes to see my father filling his thermos at the kitchen counter.

His back was to me, a faded denim button-down shirt hanging loosely on his frame. I hadn't seen him for some time, but he sure had lost weight since the last time I'd been here.

Riley and I had inherited our dark hair from our mother. My father's used to be blond, but you wouldn't be able to tell anymore. It had turned completely silver, not a hint of gold remaining.

I was willing to bet that when he turned around, he was going to have deeper lines on his face as well. Clearing my throat as I sat up, I watched as he seemed to realize he wasn't alone. His shoulders came up, and I saw the scowl settling on his features when he pivoted and spotted me.

"What are you doing on the couch?" he asked gruffly. His dark eyes —my eyes—narrowed as he took me in. "Were you still asleep?"

"It's still dark out, so yes, I was. It's good to see you too, Dad." I dragged my hands through my hair and linked my fingers behind my neck. "How are you? I'm great. Thanks for asking."

He rolled his eyes at me and held up his mug. "Want some?"

"Sure." I walked toward him, hoping we would get a chance to talk before everyone else woke up, but he spun on his heel and called to me over his shoulder.

"Then get it your damn self. I have to get to work."

My fists clenched at my sides, but I took a deep breath to calm myself down. Getting into it with him first thing after we got here wouldn't do me any good. "Don't you want to meet Elsie before you go?"

"No. I'll be back later. Like I said, I have work to do." He said all this without turning back to look at me, and the screen door slammed shut behind him immediately after he'd said his last word.

I sighed. I couldn't even say he had surprised me with his less than warm welcome. Why I had even bothered getting up, I didn't know.

Unfortunately, I wasn't one of those people who fell asleep again easily. Since going back to bed wasn't an option, I took him up on his offer and got some coffee for my damn self.

The sky was still black as I settled at the kitchen table, taking a seat where I knew I'd be able to see it lighten when the sun rose. It was a while before that happened, but I didn't mind the quietness or the solitude.

Light footsteps padding into the kitchen made me turn my head from where the sun had just peeked out above the horizon. My mother's lips spread into a warm smile.

"You're up early."

"Yeah, well, I woke up when Dad made his coffee and couldn't go back to sleep." I held up the now empty mug to her. "I was just about to get a refill. You want one?"

"Sure. Thanks, honey." She walked up to the fridge and started pulling out ingredients for breakfast. "If you want to go grab a shower, use the main bathroom. I'm assuming your dad took off already?"

"Yep." My chair scraped lightly as I pushed it back. "Let me get you some coffee. Then I will take you up on your offer."

By the time I got back to the kitchen after getting cleaned up, Elsie was awake. She was already helping my mother with breakfast, flipping pancakes while Mom darted around doing a hundred things at once.

I folded my arms and leaned against the wall, just watching them together for a second. They'd hit it off pretty well last night and seemed to continue to do so this morning.

Elsie chuckled at something my mother said, her ponytail swinging from side to side between her shoulder blades. Dressed much more casually this morning, she had on a simple pair of jeans and a white T-shirt with flat leather sandals on her feet.

Her green eyes sparkled with laughter when she shifted and caught sight of me. "Good morning. How did the couch treat you?"

If my mother hadn't been in the kitchen with us, I might have responded by telling her how many times during the night I'd wished she was asleep beside me. As it was, however, I merely grinned and walked over to brush the softest of kisses against her cheek.

"It was fine, thanks. You sleep okay?"

"I did." She smiled up at me and I wished more than ever that we were alone. I wanted to kiss those lips properly so badly it hurt, but having my mother see it would just make it weird.

A sudden buzzing in her pocket had her stepping away from me. She dug her phone out and glanced down at the screen, then held the spatula out to me. "Could you take over for a minute? It's Beth. If I don't answer, she might send a rescue party after me."

"Sure." I took the utensil and propped my hip against the counter. "Make sure you tell her you came with me willingly. There's no need for her to send the cavalry after you."

She laughed but lifted her shoulders to give me a little shrug. "We'll see. If you mess up those beautiful pancakes, we may need a cavalry after all."

She winked at me as she lifted the phone to her ear, answered, and quickly disappeared out the back door. My mother didn't let the opportunity pass her by.

"Oh, honey, I like her. I'm so glad you brought her to meet us." The corners of her eyes crinkled on a huge grin as she came closer to take my hand, giving it a tight squeeze. "I should have known when you finally found someone, she would be a winner."

I tightened my fingers around hers and returned the grin, but inside, I was holding my breath. It was only a matter of time before she asked me if Elsie was *the one* and if I wanted my grandmother's ring. Hopefully, that time wasn't now.

Thankfully, Riley strode into the kitchen and broke up the moment. "Mornin'."

"Morning." I looked him up and down and realized that he hadn't been sleeping in. There was mud on his boots and sweat on his brow. "You been out already?"

He rolled his eyes at me and gave me a good-natured pat on the shoulder. "Of course I have. Do you want to come out with me later?"

"Sure. Yeah. Let me just check with Elsie and see what she wants to do."

"She thinks you should go help your brother out on the farm," Elsie said as she walked back into the kitchen. "I'll be perfectly fine here."

My mother clapped her hands to get our attention. "Now that's all sorted. Let's eat, shall we?"

We all took our seats after helping Mom move the feast they had prepared to the table. Then we dug in. The mood around the table was surprisingly light and jovial while we ate, and all too soon, our plates were empty, and Riley was chomping at the bit to get back to work.

"Have fun," Elsie whispered to me when I gave her a hug goodbye. "Don't worry about rushing back. I have some assignments to do and a book I've been trying to get to for ages."

"I'll have my phone on me. Call if you need anything." Reluctantly letting her go, I turned to my mother, smiling at me from the sink.

"Don't worry about her, sweetheart. I'll take good care of her." She waved her hand toward the back door. "Now go. You're burning daylight."

"Yes, ma'am." I gave her a mock salute and followed Riley outside.

My brother waited for me to catch up with him. "I'm happy you're here, man. Mom hasn't smiled this much in a long time."

We fell into stride beside one another as we headed out to find Dad. "How are they doing? Really doing, not just this bullshit about how everything is okay."

"Everything is not okay," he said bluntly. "Like I told you the other day, they're stressed, tired, and strapped. We've got no more leeway and nothing lined up to make it better."

I frowned, giving him a sidelong glance as our boots crunched the dirt beneath them. "What about Soki?"

The Asian company was the biggest client of most of the farms around here, but my mention of them made Riley tighten his jaw. "The entire industry has taken a hit, but it's because of companies like Soki. They just pulled out. No warning, nothing."

"Shit." I whistled between my teeth. It was no wonder things were so tense around here. Soki had been a big player in keeping our farm going. Without them and having had no time to prepare for it, things were about to get really bumpy. "What can I do to help?"

"Nothing." He blew out a breath. "Dad will tell you to come home and weather the storm with us. But at this point, doing it would be foolish. You're doing well. He shouldn't make you feel guilty about not wanting to give up a successful company for a failing farm."

I screwed my eyes shut as we walked, filling my lungs with the clean morning air to clear my head. "Failing farm? It's worse than I thought then."

Riley snorted. "Dude, it's so much worse than you can imagine. There are loans we took out—"

"It's about time you two got your lazy asses out here," our father barked when we neared him. He stood with his arms crossed and his feet planted a foot apart as he waited for us to approach. "Riley, it's time for you to stop gossiping and get back to work."

He flicked a disapproving glance at me. "I suppose you can help him while you're here. Unless you're too fancy for manual labor now."

"I came out with Riley so I could help. What do you need from me?" I half wished he'd just say he needed the money I'd come here to offer him, but I knew it wasn't even worth wasting a full wish on.

His dark eyes tracked Riley as he nodded and took off, then narrowed when he looked back at me. "Are you serious about wanting to help?"

"Yes. Dad, Riley told me about Sok—"

"I knew you were here for the wrong reasons," he spat at me. A vein throbbed on his forehead and his fingers curled into fists as he lowered his arms to his sides. "If you really want to help in a meaningful way, go find your brother. If I'm right, and I think I am, just take your little girlfriend and get the hell out of here. We don't have time to waste arguing about charity right now."

Steel hardened his tone and his eyes might as well have turned into flamethrowers as he glared at me. Then he spun around and stalked off. For the second time in one morning, my first time back home, I watched him march away from me.

Another heavy sigh fell from my lips as I gripped the back of my neck and tried to figure out my next move. Nothing I did made my father happy. It had always been that way. Now, even with the survival of the family farm on the line, he wouldn't so much as talk to me about it.

Maybe it was time I changed tactics. It was definitely something I had to consider if I couldn't get him to listen to reason very, very soon.

CHAPTER 35

ELSIE

Taydom and Riley let the screen door swing shut behind them, leaving me alone with Gwen. She wiped her hands with a dish-cloth and hung it neatly over the faucet.

"What do you say we finish cleaning up later? I'm in the mood for a walk. Would you like to join me?"

I nodded. "Sure. I'd like to see more of the farm."

"Let's go then." She smiled and led me to the entrance hall where she grabbed two faded ball caps from a stand. "Can't go out there without one of these if you don't want to look like you're a hundred years old when you reach my age."

"Thank you." I took the cap she held out to me. It was so well used that the Velcro barely cracked when I undid it to fit it to my head. How well-worn it was made it comfortable, though. I also had a feeling I was going to be grateful for it later.

Gwen twisted the doorknob and motioned me out ahead of her after she put her cap on. We started walking, and her hazel eyes were warm when she looked at me.

"Did he tell you that you're the first woman he's brought home to meet us?" she asked.

Had he? Honestly, my brain had been on the fritz since my

doctor's appointment and I really couldn't remember if he'd mentioned it. On the other hand, it wasn't like I was here as his girlfriend.

Despite how much we'd been touching and kissing and acting like we were together, technically, we were nothing more than friends. It felt like we were a lot more than that, though.

I had to choose my words carefully to answer her question. With the way we'd acted in front of her, it was natural for her to assume we were in a relationship. I didn't want her feeling like I had lied to her if I denied flat out that we were together. What made it a little trickier was that I didn't want Taydom to feel like I'd lied to his mother by saying that we were in a relationship either.

"I'm glad he brought me. I've been wondering about his family and it's great to get to meet you all." I breathed an internal sigh of relief. *There. No lies told.*

"It's great to get to meet you, too. We know so precious little about Taydom's life in Dallas. Don't get me wrong. I know the news people report on him and all that, but it doesn't seem right to read about him."

"I completely agree." Sometimes, I thought about how creepy it must be to have random strangers knowing so much about your life. Worse than that, women he'd never met speculated about the size of his dick on public forums. It was beyond weird. "He handles it well, though. In all the time I've known him, he's barely even mentioned it."

"He always has been very good at compartmentalizing. Knowing Taydom, he's so focused on his work that he's just gone and shoved all that other stuff into a box in the back of his mind."

I hummed my agreement and we lapsed into a comfortable silence for a few minutes as we continued strolling down the dirt path that led away from their house. The trees that surrounded us provided shade for now, but the air was thick with humidity and already hot.

"I've always loved taking walks in the morning," Gwen said finally, dipping her head but sending me a sly smile. "With three men in the house, it's been my secret escape for years. They've always worked hard, and they're not actually even inside the house all that often, but all that testosterone still gets suffocating sometimes."

"I can't even imagine that. Taydom is the only man I've really been in close contact with for an extended period of time for years. I honestly don't know how it would be to have three of them running around."

She chuckled. "I always hoped for a little girl to balance us out a bit, but it never happened."

I nearly stopped dead in my tracks. I felt comfortable with Gwen, and we'd hit it off last night pretty much instantly, but that was a very personal fact for her to have shared.

"I'm sorry," I said because I didn't have the first clue what else to say to that. "In our house, it was the opposite. It was only my mother and I. No men in sight."

"Was?" she asked, slowing down to put a hand on my forearm. "Where is she now?"

Unexpected tears burned the backs of my eyes and my throat tightened with emotion. I really hadn't thought we'd venture into territory as personal as this so soon, and I wasn't prepared for it, but something about Gwen reminded me of my mother. It made me want to confide in her, even though I'd barely known her for twelve hours.

"She passed away a few months ago."

A soft gasp drew my attention away from the leaves on the ground. Gwen's face was a mask of sadness and understanding. Before I knew it, she had wrapped me up in a hug.

"I'm so sorry, honey." She enveloped me in her arms and stroked my hair in that motherly way that just couldn't be replicated. "I've lost both my parents as well. It's just awful."

"Yeah." My voice cracked. "It really is. I didn't even get to say good-bye. It came out of nowhere."

"Oh, sweetheart." She hugged me tighter. "I wish I could tell you something that would make it hurt less, but there's nothing anyone can say that will do that. I can listen if you'd like to talk about her, though."

I sniffed and gave her a last squeeze before letting her go. "I think I would like to."

"Well, then." She gave me a sad smile and looped her arm through mine as we began to walk again. "Tell me about your mom, dear. Were you two close?"

I nodded and found myself glad she was holding me so close to her side. It was comforting in a way few things had been since I'd gotten that fateful call. "She was my best friend. It feels like my whole world turned upside down the day she died. I'm doing things that are so out of character for me, my brain doesn't seem to be functioning at full capacity. I don't know what I would have done if Taydom hadn't come into my life. Beth, my friend, and Taydom have been my rocks to lean on."

Her brows swept up. "Taydom, as in, my son, Taydom?"

"The one and only." I let out a deep breath. "He's meant so much to me these last few months. Thank you for raising him to have such a good heart."

"I'm surprised to hear all this." Her eyes widened and she waved her free hand. "I don't mean that I'm surprised to hear he has a good heart. He really does. What I am surprised to hear is that he's allowed you to see it. He doesn't let people in easily."

"So I've heard. He's never been that way with me, though."

She flexed her elbow to hold me tighter. "You must be very special to him."

"I don't know." I tugged the inside of my upper lip between my teeth. "I do know that he's very special to me."

There. I said it out loud.

A burst of energy ran through me at the words, sending my heart into a sprint. It was true, though. He was very special to me. I just had to figure out what to do about it.

After I receive that call later.

I couldn't believe I'd almost forgotten about the call, but I had. I nearly planted my face in my hands, but that might have raised some questions from Gwen.

Discreetly checking my back pocket to make sure I had my

phone on me, I did my best to focus on the conversation with Taydom's mother, even as I devised strategies about how I was going to get away from her if the call came while we were on our walk.

Gwen was so sweet to me for the rest of the morning. We walked for a long time before heading back to the house to get started on making lunch. I helped her make a chicken salad and freshly baked bread, but my pulse was racing, and I kept checking my phone to make sure I hadn't missed the call.

"I love that you're here, sweetheart," she said as she pulled the tray with the bread on it out of the oven and transferred it to a cooling rack. "I had to wait so long for my Taydom to bring a woman home to meet me, but now that he has, I'm glad it's you."

"Thank you." A soft, genuine smile touched the corners of my lips just as my phone started ringing. My heart jumped into my throat when I recognized the number for the health center. "Excuse me. I need to take this. It's school."

Technically, that wasn't a lie either. The student health center was at my school. It just wasn't schoolwork they were calling about.

Gwen nodded and carried on with the preparations for lunch, and I dashed out of the kitchen before answering. "Hello?"

Even with just that one word, even I could hear how breathless I sounded. I blamed it on my heart, which seemed to have taken up residence where my airways used to be.

"Hi, Elsie? It's Dr. April. I just got your results back. Can you talk?"

"Yes," I croaked out as I took the stairs two at a time. I needed to be in my room for this. *Taydom's old room. Whatever.* "What is it, April? What do the results say?"

I closed the door behind me and immediately leaned against it. Blood rushed in my ears, and my head suddenly felt warm and three times its size, but I still heard April's voice loud and clear.

"The test confirmed that you are pregnant."

My head landed on the wooden paneling of the door with a thump. "Are you sure?"

"Positive," she said gently. "I made them run it again, just in case.

Everything else came back negative. The pregnancy test came back positive three times."

"Three times." My knees went weak and I sank down to the floor. "There's no chance that it's a false positive?"

"No. Unless you have something in your system that is seriously messing with you, you're definitely pregnant."

"Okay," I whispered and closed my eyes as I brought my knees up to rest my head on them. "Thank you, April. I'll be in touch."

"No problem, Elsie. Let me know if you need anything. I'm here for you, okay?"

"Okay," I whispered again. "Bye, April."

I dropped my phone, not even sure if I'd disconnected the call before it clattered to the floor at my side. My breaths were coming in shallow pants and it felt like I had entered some parallel reality, like I'd detached from myself and was watching this happening to me without being me.

I'm pregnant. I'm pregnant. I'm pregnant.

Meanwhile downstairs, the father of my baby and his family were gathering to have a meal together. A meal I was expected to be at as well.

What the fuck do I do now?

CHAPTER 36

TAYDOM

"D on't worry about Dad," Riley said as we took off our boots at the kitchen door. "I know he snapped at you earlier, but it's not a big deal. He'll see soon enough that you *are* here for the right reasons, so don't worry about it."

Guilt twisted my gut. "Yeah, maybe. Thanks, bro. I should go check on Elsie."

I shoved the guilt down, but worry took its place. Elsie had begged out of lunch, claiming she wasn't feeling well and that she needed to lie down for a bit.

She hadn't even come down to tell me. I'd received a text from her when Riley and I had been on our way back to the house.

Mom told me they'd spoken about her mother that morning, though. She also said that maybe they shouldn't have walked so far while Elsie was recovering from a cold.

I'd gone up to check on her, but there hadn't been any answer to my knocks. While what my mom had said made sense, it just felt like there was more to it.

Elsie had looked fine this morning. One-hundred-percent healthy.

Mom had also told me that she'd received a call from school and that she hadn't seen her since. Concern over Elsie, Dad, and the farm had turned the day into a blur for me, and I was glad it was nearly over.

If Dad woke me up before the crack of dawn again tomorrow, I was rolling over without even opening my eyes and going the fuck back to sleep. But first, I had to find Elsie and make sure she was okay.

I checked my old room first, but she wasn't there. A few minutes later, I found her on the front porch. She was sitting in Mom's old rocking chair, her hands folded over her lower belly as she stared off into the distance.

She was so lost in thought that she didn't even notice me until I cleared my throat. "Hey, you okay?"

The chair rocked gently as she shifted to face me. There was something haunting in her usually bright green eyes. They were almost dull now, but she nodded. "I'm fine."

Before I could say anything else, she blurted out the last question I had been expecting. "Taydom, why am I really here? Your mom seems to think it's because I'm special to you."

"You *are* special to me." *Absolutely true.* "I wouldn't have brought you here otherwise."

She sighed, the sound so sad that it made my heart ache. "But that's not the only reason, is it?"

"No, it's not." It was truth time. I'd been wondering when I was going to get the opportunity to tell her, and here it was. She had given it to me on a silver fucking platter and I wasn't going to waste it.

I also didn't want to have this conversation while standing all the way on the other side of the porch. Crossing it in a few strides, I tried to come up with the right words and then sank down to my haunches in front of her.

"I wanted to bring you with me for all the reasons I mentioned to you before. All of those were true, but there's also something else."

She cocked her head, but those eyes remained dull. There wasn't so much as a spark of interest in them.

I brought my hands to her knees and rested them there. When she didn't push me away, I dragged in a deep breath and prayed she would understand. "The farm is in trouble. Big trouble. I saw an article about how the entire industry had taken a hit, but I hadn't known anything about it before that. My family didn't tell me."

Her brow furrowed. "Why not?"

"They don't want my help. Well, not financially anyway. My father still resents me for not staying and helping on the farm. It wouldn't have changed the current situation if I had, but he doesn't see it that way."

"What does that have to do with me?"

I dropped my chin and closed my eyes for a moment. "I needed a reason to come here other than wanting to offer them money. I told my mother there was someone I wanted to introduce her to."

Her brows rose, but she didn't respond immediately. After the pause, she licked her lips and nodded slowly. "Did you really want to introduce me to them?"

"Yes." Maybe it hadn't been about that when I'd first mentioned it, but things had changed. "There's no one I would rather have had here with me, Elsie. I—"

"I need to tell you something," she said suddenly, then swallowed a couple of times.

There was an urgency beneath the dull glaze in her eyes now, but my mother interrupted us before she could tell me whatever it was that was so important.

"Dinner's ready, kids. Come and get it while it's hot." She stood at the door and peeked out at us as she clapped her hands. "Double time. Let's go. It's getting cold."

"Can we have a minute?" I asked, but Elsie pushed my hands off her legs and stood up.

"It's fine," she said quietly. "We can talk later."

Without looking back, she disappeared into the house. My mother planted her hands on her hips and gave me a questioning look. When I shook my head, she sighed and went after my supposed girlfriend.

Once I was alone, I released a low groan and braced my hands against the wooden railing around the porch as I hung my head. *Christ. This trip is becoming a damn shit show.*

As it turned out, it only got worse from there.

When I walked into the kitchen, Elsie had already been introduced to my father and was conversing politely with him. He seemed okay while talking to her, but as soon as he saw me, his expression soured.

"You're still here?"

"Obviously." I was done backing down from him. I'd had the rest of the day to think about it after our confrontation earlier, and the polite approach wasn't getting me anywhere.

Whether he liked it or not, this was my family's farm as well. I had just as much right as anyone else to do whatever it took to keep it in business. "You don't have to be pissed that I'm here, Dad. Contrary to what you think, I really do want to help."

He dropped his fork on his plate with a loud clatter and banged his elbows down on the table as he glowered at me. "Why don't you start by owning up to why you are really here? As lovely as this young lady seems, you and I both know it's not about her."

"Fine," I exploded, throwing my arms out to my sides. "You want to know why I'm really here? I'm here to give you money. I came here because I want to help you save the farm. Is that really so bad?"

"We don't need your money." He pushed back from the table and stood up with so much force that his chair fell over. "I've told you time and time again, if you wanted to help, you could have stayed. You gave up your right to have any say over what happens with this damn farm the day you walked away from us."

"Jesus, Dad. I never walked away from you. I moved out and made a life for myself. You know, like kids usually do when they're all grown up. What I did wasn't a crime. It was the natural progression of life."

"Not when you're a farmer," he grunted. "That's not how it works around here."

Grabbing his plate off the table, he gave me one final glower and marched away. Again. It was all the man seemed to be able to do these days. Yell at me, then walk away. Like I didn't deserve a fucking minute of his time.

Riley sat back in his chair, sighing as he met my eyes. "I asked one fucking thing of you, Tay. One thing."

He didn't take off, but he didn't seem interested in speaking to me either. Elsie had watched the scene unfold with wide eyes, but she seemed surprised more than anything else.

My mother, however, looked like I'd just ripped her heart out with my bare hands. There was so much hurt in her expression that seeing it felt like a punch to the nads.

"So Elsie isn't your girlfriend?" she asked slowly, her gaze darting from mine to Elsie's and back again. "Are you even in any kind of relationship?"

"No," I said without thinking. She wasn't my girlfriend, but it was only when I saw the look that suddenly settled on Elsie's face that I realized how that had sounded. "I mean—"

"I think I've heard enough." My mother pushed her chair back with much more grace than my father had. She left her plate behind and went off toward their bedroom after him.

"Fuck, dude." Riley shook his head at me. "I warned you about this. I fucking knew you were going to fuck things up even further. Mom was— never mind. You don't even deserve to fucking know."

"You trying to set a new record for how many times a person can say *fuck* in one sentence?" I arched a brow, knowing I was being a dick but unable to stop myself.

They were all being ridiculous, acting like I'd committed some kind of heinous crime when in reality, all I'd done was move out and get a job of my own. It was something parents of freeloaders all over the world wished for, yet when I'd done it, my entire family had turned against me.

As if to prove my point, Riley flipped me off and went his own way as well.

Elsie slumped in her chair and I let out a sigh, shaking my head. "Can you believe them?"

"I'm tired," she said, standing up from the table. "I'm going to bed, Taydom. Good night."

"Elsie. Wait." I still had to fix things with her, to explain that I hadn't meant my denial of our relationship in the way it had come out.

She shook her head, yanking her arm up when I tried to reach for her hand. "No, I'm not waiting. I'm tired and going to bed. Good night, Taydom."

CHAPTER 37

ELSIE

What the hell was that?

I was still reeling when I collapsed in the middle of Taydom's double bed. Flipping onto my back, I folded my hands over my stomach and stared at the beams in the ceiling.

That showdown had shocked the living daylights out of me. One minute, everything was fine, and the next, it was like someone had lit a match and tossed it into a gas tank.

Crazy shit.

Crazy shit that I had been embarrassed to be in the middle of. Taydom's family seemed like nice people. I had genuinely gotten along with his mother today, and now she would think I was some kind of liar who had been in on a plot to deceive her.

I wasn't a liar. I didn't play games or distort the truth. Well, not usually anyway.

With the secret I was keeping, I supposed I couldn't get up on too high of a horse. The difference was that I'd only been sure for a few hours that there was a secret I had been keeping.

Taydom had planned to lie to his parents. He'd invited me here intending to use me to deceive them, to give him an excuse to come here.

I could understand that he wanted to help them and that he was in an impossible situation of being able to help but not being allowed to. What I couldn't understand was why he hadn't just told me from the start.

Because then you wouldn't have come, a nagging voice said in the back of my mind. I shut it up fast. Maybe I wouldn't have agreed to come if I'd known, but maybe I would have. If Taydom had been honest with me about what was going on, I liked to think I would have still agreed to come. If only so I could help him out for a change.

Arguing hypotheticals with myself would not get me anywhere, though. I had real problems to solve.

It had become abundantly clear to me downstairs that I shouldn't be here. Taydom might have been honest when he'd told me he'd wanted to introduce me to his family anyway, but I highly doubted that they wanted me around after that.

Moreover, he had to focus on his family while I had to focus on mine. My fingers twitched on my stomach. Somewhere below the spot where my hand kept absently going on my belly, there was a little human growing.

A little human who was counting on me and for whom I was wholly responsible. The shock of that revelation hadn't worn off yet, but after my initial meltdown, I had decided to take it one step at a time.

I had thought the first step would be telling Taydom about the life we had created, and I had been about to when his mother had interrupted us. Now it felt like step one might be something different.

Regardless of what happened here, Taydom and I would eventually go back to Dallas. Hopefully, he would only return after he sorted out what was happening with his family. But I wasn't convinced that hanging around for the rest of the week was a good idea.

For one, I would be a constant reminder of his deception. Every time they saw me, they would think about the lie he had told.

Maybe it would be for the best if I left. His family might be pissed at him, but maybe after a few days alone and with space to think and breathe, they would calm down enough to let him explain himself.

Unfortunately, going back to Dallas by myself wasn't without its own challenges. Especially since I was ninety-nine percent sure that if I left, Taydom would insist on coming with me.

I couldn't let him do that.

But staying wasn't something I felt like I could do either. For his good, for their good, and for my own. Giving everyone some space right now felt like the best thing to do.

How to do it would be tricky to figure out but not impossible. Rolling to my side, I snatched my phone up and opened a ride share app. I wasn't entirely certain if they had those kinds of services around here, but the app opened and informed me that there was, in fact, a car available.

It was thirty minutes away, but it was good to know that I had the option. The second thing I had to do was see if there were any flights available to take me home.

A quick check online informed me that getting a flight wouldn't be a problem either. Booking at the last minute was a little pricey, but this was an emergency. Plus, it wasn't so pricey that it would leave an unrecoverable dent in my savings. *Thank God his parents live in Illinois.*

If they had lived farther away, well, going home early might not have been an option. Satisfied that it was a viable option if that was what I decided on doing, I closed my browser and the ride share app and just stared at my phone for a minute.

It should have been easy to order the ride, book my flight, and just leave this mess behind, but it wasn't. While I was convinced it was for the best for me to leave, I just couldn't seem to get myself to pull the trigger.

There was a layer to this whole thing they didn't know about yet. The baby. I had to consider what effect my sudden disappearance would have on how they felt about the baby going forward.

Sure, it was up to Taydom whether he or his family would play any role in this baby's life, but I couldn't discount the fact that my actions now could have consequences for him or her in the future.

Blowing out a breath, I opened my contacts and scrolled to Beth's number. I wouldn't tell her or anyone else about the pregnancy before I told Taydom, but I needed her advice.

She answered on the first ring. "Hey, I was just about to call you. How did your first whole day of farm life go?"

"Not so good." I sighed and rolled to my back, watching clouds drift lazily in front of the crescent moon. It wasn't completely dark out yet, but the moon had risen, and the sky was slowly darkening. "It turns out that Taydom had ulterior motives when he brought me here."

"What the hell?" she asked, her voice tense. "What ulterior motives? What did he do?"

I quickly explained the highlights to her. "Long story short, he used me as an excuse to come home. The farm is in trouble, and he wants to help them, but they don't want to be helped."

"He used you?" She was fuming now, and for a second, I was glad there were so many miles between her and Taydom. "Why did he need you as an excuse to visit his own family?"

"It's complicated, and I don't want to betray his trust by saying too much, but he needed a reason to come, and he told them we were in a relationship."

"Aren't you?" she asked after pausing for a beat. "I know you keep saying you're just friends and all that, but it seems to have gone well past that point."

"It has," I admitted, my voice small. "We haven't talked about it outright or anything like that, but I also feel like things have changed. I guess we'll have to tackle that once he's done here. I don't want to add more to his plate right now."

"It's that bad?"

I nodded, even though I knew she couldn't see me. "It is. They had a huge fight about it around the dinner table, and everyone stalked off and went their own ways."

"Wow." She whistled under her breath. "They've had dinner already? Isn't it way too early for that?"

I laughed, glad that she'd found a way to lighten the mood a little.

"That's hardly the issue, but yes, we have had dinner. Everything happens much earlier here."

"I've heard farmers get up early," she said, then hesitated again. "What are you going to do?"

"I don't know. That's why I'm calling you. I was hoping you had some advice for me." I froze when I heard a creak outside the door.

I listened for more sounds, but all I heard was Beth's voice. "I can do that. What are your options?"

"Staying or going home early." I kept my voice low, just in case there was someone outside.

"Easy," Beth said cheerfully. "Leave. This isn't your fight, and family fights are not something outsiders should get involved in. Families are bound together, so no matter how much they fight, eventually they'll end up at least trying to sort through their shit. It's usually the outside people who get involved, no matter how well intentioned they are, that end up being iced out."

"True." I'd once read somewhere that people should never get involved in business with family or in family business. What Beth said had reminded me of that. "Do I tell Taydom I'm leaving?"

"Probably not. Unless you think he might want to leave with you."

"I don't think he can or that he should. From what little I understand or have been told about this situation, it's serious. He came here for a reason and I think he needs to stay."

"Then don't tell him," she said as if it was that simple. "Pack your stuff, get a cab, and come home. Text me your flight details and I'll pick you up."

"No, that's unnecessary. If I catch a red eye, I'll get in at some God-forsaken time. I'll just take a cab home. Don't worry about it."

She sighed heavily. "I don't give a damn what time it is. Just text me your flight details."

"Okay," I said. "I'll text them to you so someone has them, but I'm still taking a cab."

"We'll see." Beth spent several more minutes making sure I was okay before hanging up.

Once she ended the call, I had made my decision. Getting up off the bed was easier now than it had been when I'd left the room earlier to speak to Taydom.

Talking to Beth had lifted a weight off my shoulders, and I was now determined to do everything that needed to be done the right way. This wasn't the time to tell Taydom about the pregnancy. Once everything here was sorted out and he came back to Dallas, telling him would be the first thing on my list of priorities.

For now, he needed to help the family who had raised him. I would take care of the family we had created for the time being. The baby and I would be okay. Hopefully, his family would be too.

Moving quietly around the room, I gathered all my things and packed my bag. I called the cab, but if I was being honest with myself, I would have rather walked all the way to the airport than to stay in this house for another night.

It was like I could feel the tension coming off the walls of the place. It wasn't healthy, and as Beth had said, it wasn't my fight or my tension. No one liked interlopers in their business.

Once my bags were packed, I flicked the light in the room off and hoped they would think I'd gone to bed. I sneaked down the corridor with my bags and took a peek down the staircase before descending it.

Voices were going at it again in the kitchen, but I didn't bother to stop and listen to what they were arguing about now. Instead, I took it as a sign that I really shouldn't be here and made a beeline for the front door.

I moved as fast and as quietly as I could, only slowing down to open and shut the door carefully. Muffled voices still carried from inside, but they faded as I lugged my stuff down the long drive.

So far, so good. I breathed out a sigh of relief when I didn't hear the telltale crunch of gravel showing there was someone behind me. The only sounds in the warm night air were my own shoes and bag on the ground and my breathing.

When I finally reached the road, I sat down on my suitcase and let the reality of the day wash over me. There were still so many things I didn't understand and so many things I wished I could talk to Taydom about.

I was still reeling, but now that I was out of the house and on my way home, there was one thought I couldn't get past. Taydom had lied to his mother about me. The same mother he claimed to be so close to.

I'd told him how much I was missing my own mom and how I would do anything to speak to her again, and the whole time, he'd been lying to his. I couldn't believe he would do that, and I didn't know how I would be able to fully trust him again after this.

CHAPTER 38

TAYDOM

My heart slammed to a stop when I opened my bedroom door to find it empty. "Elsie?"

Nothing but silence answered me. I moved farther into the room, but in the ambient light of the moon shining in, I had made out that the bed was empty even from the doorway.

Turning in a slow circle in the darkness, I soon figured out that there wasn't anyone in here. My feet were racing out before my brain had time to catch up. I checked the bathroom and then the kitchen, wondering if maybe she'd gotten hungry or wasn't feeling well.

There was no one there, so I checked outside next. Again, no one.

The creak of the kitchen door had me racing back there, but it was only Riley. He frowned when he saw me, holding up both hands. "Whoa, there. What's going on? Why are you so pale?"

"It's Elsie. I can't find her."

His head jerked back, and his eyebrows rose. "What do you mean you can't find her? She has to be here somewhere. Unless you had a fight with her, too?"

"I didn't. I…" I rubbed my eyes with the heels of my hands and heard blood pounding in my ears. "I didn't have a fight with her necessarily. It was more like the other fight just bled into our relation-ship as well."

"Have you seen her since? It's been almost two hours."

"No. I went up to apologize to her, but then I figured I'd better walk it off first. I was still halfway out of my fucking mind when I went up there the first time. Took a walk, then I went back, and she wasn't there."

"I saw Mom and Dad out there as well," Riley said, still frowning. "If we were all out walking, maybe she is too?"

I shook my head, my stomach twisting at my words. "The room is empty. None of her stuff is in there, either."

"Fuck." Riley scrubbed his hands over his jaw. "Okay, we need to find her then. Does she know anyone around here?"

"No." I ground my teeth together and took in several deep gulps of air. The emotions flying through me were making me feel too volatile, too uncertain.

Blood continued to rush in my ears, and the icy tentacles of fear were winding themselves around every one of my organs. I doubted there was any blood left in my cheeks and I felt sick to my stomach.

I was also vaguely aware that my hands were shaking, but that was the least of my worries. "She doesn't know anyone in the area, Riley. Where the fuck is she?"

"Language, Taydom," my mother's voice chided from the kitchen door. She stomped to clean her boots. Then her brows drew together when she saw my expression. "Where is who? Elsie?"

"Yes," I said and told her what I'd just told Riley. When my father appeared behind my mother, I scowled at him. "This is all your fault. Now she's gone and I don't have the first fucking idea where to start looking for her."

"First, there have been enough F-bombs dropped in this household tonight. I will not tolerate any more." My mother crossed her arms as she entered the kitchen and walked right up to me. "Second, don't blame your father. This is no one's fault and everyone's fault all at the same time."

"You can't really—"

She slashed a hand through the air. "I said enough. Listen to me, Taydom. Blaming your father will not help us find her, nor is it going to help us talk through our own situation."

"Talk through it?" Riley asked incredulously as he folded his own arms and narrowed his eyes at me. "There is no talking through this. Neither of them will—"

My mother turned to face him. "Keep quiet and sit down. Both of you."

Her tone brooked no argument, and knowing her as well as I did, I knew the fastest way to getting out of here to find Elsie was by listening. Riley and I both yanked chairs out and sat down, then watched as my mother and father did the same.

Mom always had been the voice of reason in our household, but it surprised me my father was going along with her on this. That wasn't something I'd seen before.

She set her hands down on the table and glanced at my father. "Before any of you say anything, I want you to listen to me. There's a girl out there that we need to find. But our actions drove her away in the first place. If we have any hope of finding her and convincing her to come back, we can't allow another argument like the one earlier to take place."

"But, Mom," I protested, my leg bouncing. "She's out there alone. I need to get to her."

"She's a smart girl." My mom leveled me with a look. "She'll be fine. If you chase after her without clearing anything up here, I will hazard a guess she's just going to order you back. I've only known her for a little over a day, but she's strong, and she's gotten used to dealing with things on her own since her mother's passing."

Riley objected this time. "But, Mom."

Mom turned that silencing look on him. "Our problems drove her away. No doubt about it. So we will sit here and talk for a little while. Then we'll all go out and look for her, okay?"

My chest was tight, and my heart was thumping, but something inside me knew my mother was right. "Okay."

"Fine," Riley spat.

"Good," my father said. His head was hanging, but then he lifted it to look into my eyes. For the first time, he allowed me to see the anguish in his expression, the fear and the exhaustion. "I need to say some things and I don't want either of you to interrupt me."

He waited for us to nod before continuing. "You broke my heart when you left us, Taydom."

I opened my mouth to argue, but the look in his eyes held me back. There was a rawness there that was almost painful to see.

"I knew you weren't going to stick around." He sighed. "I always knew you weren't going to make the farm your life. I just couldn't fathom you actually giving it up. The thought never crossed my mind to do it and I know it never crossed Riley's either."

My brother nodded but didn't say anything.

"Farming is in our blood and it's taken me a long time to understand that it's not the same for you," my dad said. "What you said earlier about it being natural for kids to grow up and leave is true. Don't think I don't know or understand that. I do. It just hasn't been the way of life for our family."

Again, I was tempted to speak up for myself. But then he surprised the fuck out of me when he sighed and said the last thing I'd ever expected to hear him say. "I'm sorry, Taydom. I should never have treated you the way I did, especially not the way I did after you left."

My jaw dropped, and so did Riley's, but my mother had obviously known what he was going to say. She reached out and took his hand, her eyes misty.

Dad turned his hand to wind his fingers around hers. "It's something your mom and I have been going around and around on for a long time, but this visit has opened my eyes. Truth is, right now, I'm glad you got out. The fact that you would go to such lengths to get us —to get me—to listen to you speaks volumes. I don't approve of you using that girl in your scheme, but doing something like that is so out of character for you that your mother has pointed out to me how much it must mean to you to help us."

"It does," I said. "It means everything."

He nodded. "I thought so, but don't think you're entirely right. It means a lot to you, but not everything. It doesn't take a rocket scientist to see that Elsie means something to you, too."

A lump appeared in my throat, but I managed to force out words around it. "She does."

"She's not your girlfriend, but you want her to be, don't you?" my mother asked, her voice gentle as she brought her gaze to mine.

"Yeah." I cleared my throat to get rid of that stupid fucking lump. "I love her, Mom. I love her and now I've screwed it up."

A radiant smile spread on Mom's face even as tears started leaking out of her eyes. "I knew it couldn't all have been an act. She loves you, too, you know?"

I blinked. "You think?"

She shook her head. "I don't think. I know. I've kept a very close eye on both of you since you arrived, and there's no doubt about it."

My heart nearly exploded at hearing her words, but there was a more pressing question than to ask my mom how she could be so sure. "What do we do now?"

"Now," she smiled and released my dad's hand, "we hug it out and then we go get her."

"How do we find her?"

She rolled her eyes at me. "She's at the airport. A girl like that isn't wandering around in the streets like some damsel in distress, hoping you're going to come rescue her. She would have taken decisive action. I'm willing to bet she called a cab and is on her way to the airport as we speak."

"What if you're wrong?" My heart was pounding again. "I know she's not a damsel in distress, but what if she's not at the airport?"

"If she's not there now, she'll be there tomorrow morning. On the way to the airport, you can check the commercial flights. If there's still a flight out tonight, that's the plane she'll be on. If not, we'll start checking the hotels near the airport. We'll find her."

"What about the farm?" Riley asked and held up a hand when Mom turned to glare at him. "What? You said we had to sort out our own shit before we go get her, so what does this mean for us?"

Dad cleared his throat. "It means that when we get back here, whenever that might be, we're going to sit down together and figure out how to save this place."

"If it means accepting help from him?" He inclined his head toward me.

"Then that's what we'll do." Dad released a deep breath and gave me a firm nod. "We won't take any handouts, but we can work out the terms later."

"Works for me." It was more than I'd ever hoped to hear from him. More than I could have dreamed of actually. "Let's go get my girl."

Mom, Dad, Riley, and I all piled into Mom's minivan. Why she still had the thing, I didn't know, but it sure came in handy right now.

I got behind the wheel and broke the speed limit all the way to the airport. Mom, Dad, and Riley all competed over who could give me the loudest advice on how to win her back. Then Riley jumped behind the wheel when we screeched to a stop outside the departures terminal.

I ran into the airport and immediately started scanning the relatively quiet space for her. It wasn't as easy to find someone in an airport as movies made it seem, but I managed it eventually.

Elsie stood in front of one of the ticketing booths, her bag standing next to her with the handle extended. She was just pulling a card out of her wallet when she saw me racing up to her.

"Elsie! Don't do it. Don't buy the ticket."

Several people stopped to stare at me, and a security guard left his post to approach me. I ignored all of them, even the people who had taken out their phones and seemed to be recording me.

I didn't give a fuck about any of them.

The only person I cared about was Elsie. She was the only one I could focus on, like my vision had narrowed to include only the raven-haired, green-eyed girl who had turned now and was looking at me as if she wasn't sure I was really there or not.

"I'm here, Elsie. I'm here and I'm sorry. Please don't buy that plane ticket." I held my breath and waited for her to say something, anything, as I prayed my apology wasn't too little, too late.

241

Now that I'd finally admitted to my family and myself that I loved her, I'd realized just how very true it was. What I felt for her was unlike anything I'd ever felt before.

I couldn't lose her, especially not without even telling her how I felt. I had no idea how to go about doing it, but it was now or never.

CHAPTER 39

ELSIE

U nless I'd somehow gotten drugged somewhere between the airport and Taydom's parents' house, the man himself was running toward me. There were so many questions flying through my brain, I couldn't begin to process them all.

There was a tall, dark, and handsome billionaire racing through an airport trying to stop a girl from buying a plane ticket. I'd seen this movie before. Several of them actually. I just never in a million years thought I'd ever live such a moment.

Security guards straightened and moved forward a little, but they didn't seem alarmed at all. It was almost like they really had seen this happening before.

Huh? I frowned as I tried to make sense of the scene I found myself living. *How the hell is this possible?*

"I'm so sorry," Taydom said again. The edge of desperation in his voice yanked me out of my thoughts and I came to, with him standing in front of me.

There was so much emotion burning in his dark eyes that my knees nearly buckled. His usually tidy hair was standing up all over the place, like he'd been running his hands through it for hours.

"I never meant for you to feel like I used you," he said, his voice rough. "Honestly, I didn't even think about it that way until Drew mentioned that was what it might feel like to you."

"Andrew?" I frowned. "He knew about all this?"

He nodded. "Yeah. I mentioned it to him that my parents were in trouble and one thing led to another from there. It was stupid not to tell you, but I was afraid of how you would react. I promise I never meant to hurt you."

"You might not have meant to, but you did."

"Yeah, I did." He reached for my hands, and when I didn't move them away, he took them gently and stroked my knuckles with his fingertips. "I'm so, so sorry. I should have just come clean as soon as I realized there was another angle to what my plan might look like."

"Why didn't you?" It was something I hadn't been able to figure out. "Why wouldn't you just tell me you needed help and why?"

"Because I'm an idiot." He managed a lopsided smile, but it melted off when his gaze caught on mine. "Look, I might have lied to you about why we were here, but I'm not lying to you about any of this. I really did want to introduce you to my parents. I love you, Elsie. I know we haven't talked about what we are to each other and you don't need to say it back, but I love you."

"You love me?" My chin dropped, along with my heart.

It was funny. Or it would have been if the secret I was holding on to wasn't about to blow us out of the fucking water. "Taydom, I—"

"You don't need to say it. Really. I just wanted you to know that I love you. If you want to leave right now, we can. I'll come with you, or you can come back to the farm with me, but just please don't leave me."

"Leave you?" I closed my eyes and took a deep breath. Maybe this wasn't exactly the right time and place to drop the bomb I was carrying inside. "I wasn't leaving you, Taydom. Well, okay, I mean I was physically leaving you to sort out the stuff with your family, but I wasn't calling things off between us."

"You're not?"

"No." I looped my fingers between his and squeezed. "I would have told you if I was leaving you, even if we never talked about what was going on between us. I wouldn't just ghost you."

Warmth flooded his eyes, softening the tension around the corners as he took a step closer to me. "I've sorted things out with my family. Mostly anyway. If you want to go home, I'll call my pilot right now and we'll go."

"You've sorted things out with them?" I twisted my arm without letting go of his hands and glanced down at my watch. "I've barely been gone for three hours. When did you have time to sort things out with them?"

"Mom sat us down and set us straight. I think she's been working on my father for a while, but none of us knew about it."

"Have they accepted your help then?" I closed the last remaining inches between us and tipped my head back to keep looking into his eyes.

He sighed and lifted a shoulder in a small shrug. "It looks like they're going to. We were going to work out the details when we got back to the farm, but if you want to leave, I can work it out with them by phone."

"No," I said firmly. "This is what you've come here to do. You should do it. I'll be at home when you're ready. Then we can talk."

"No." His voice was just as firm as mine had been. "I love you and I'm not letting you go. I know we have a lot to talk about and I'm not waiting another week. I should have talked to you about all this weeks ago. I don't want to waste more time."

"Taydom," I whispered, releasing one of his hands to rest mine softly on the sharp stubble on his jaw. "There's something I need to talk to you about that I don't think we should talk about at your parents' house. It's important for you to finish what you started here. I can wait. A week isn't going to kill me."

A determined gleam came into his eyes. "Maybe not, but there's a decent possibility it would kill me. I don't think my heart could take it to be separated from you right now. If you need to talk about something that you're not comfortable doing at my parents' place, let's get a hotel. Give me a minute. I'll say goodbye and tell them we might see them tomorrow."

"Say goodbye?" My heart fluttered in my chest. "They're here?"

A slow smirk spread on his lips. "Yes. They're all here. Even my dad. I told them I loved you and they insisted on coming."

My eyes widened as I tore them away from Taydom's. I quickly found his parents and brother lingering next to a pillar behind him. They were far enough away not to hear what we were saying, but they certainly had an unimpeded view.

Gwen had both her hands in front of her mouth, her head resting on her husband's shoulder as she blinked back tears. Riley's brows were high and his hands were shoved in the pockets of his jeans, his expression a perfect mix between keen interest and fake boredom. I nearly laughed at the sight of it.

"What are they going to think if you tell them we're going to a hotel?"

The smirk grew wider before it melted into a hopeful smile. "I don't really care. Is that a yes?"

I couldn't resist him. Not when he was looking at me like that and not when I had something so important to tell him. "Yes. Let's go."

He took my hand and gripped it like he was afraid I would take off again. He held me close to his side as we went to say our goodbyes to his family. Taydom pulled out his phone while I hugged his mother.

When they turned and walked back to the doors, Taydom led me off in the opposite direction. He tucked me in under one arm and used the other for my bags.

"I got us a room at a hotel just across the street. There's a bridge connecting it to the terminal. If you want your own room, just tell me and it's yours."

"One is fine." *For now.* When I told him, he might feel differently about it.

I was thankful that the hotel was so close by. It meant that if I had to, I could come right back and hop on the first flight out in the morning.

We were silent as we checked in, but Taydom didn't let go of me once. The room he had booked was huge, the carpet thick and plush and the twinkling lights of the city illuminating it through a bank of windows on one side.

After closing the door behind him, he parked my bags next to it and crossed the room. A lamp came on as he flipped the switch and bathed the room in a warm glow.

Without saying anything, he went to sit on the edge of the bed and patted the spot beside him. I walked over to him and he took my hands in his again as soon as I sat down. "What did you need to talk to me about?"

His eyes were these warm, dark pools of emotion that were unwavering on mine. Knowing that what I was about to say might mean he would never look at me like that again nearly broke me.

My throat suddenly felt tight, and I was struggling to draw enough oxygen into my lungs, but I sat up straighter and forced myself to be as honest with him as he had been with me.

"Before I tell you what I need to, I want you to know that I love you, too." My voice came out past the coils constricting it, but it was barely above a whisper.

Taydom started to smile, but I shook my head, and a deep frown formed between his brows. "I'm not allowed to be happy that you love me?"

"You are, but you might want to hang on a minute. Please know that what I'm about to say doesn't negate the fact that I love you, nor is it what caused me to love you. I've been in love with you for a while now. I just didn't know how to tell you."

"Okay." His frown deepened and concern tightened his jaw. "You're starting to scare me, babe. What is it? What's going on?"

"I went to the doctor the other day because I wasn't feeling well." I kept my eyes on his. "She called me back today. The results of my blood test came in and I'm pregnant."

It felt like the entire world came to a standstill as soon as the words left my mouth. I couldn't move. I couldn't breathe. All I could do was sit there and watch as Taydom worked through what I had just told him.

At first, his expression was completely blank. Then his jaw slackened and his eyes widened. He blinked rapidly and swallowed a few times before focusing on me again. "You're sure?"

His voice was as low as mine, but I'd heard him just fine. "A doctor I know ran the tests. I'm sure."

After a few more seconds of utterly stunned silence, his mouth spread into a wide smile. "Elsie, baby, I..."

"You're smiling?" A spark of hope lit my heart on fire.

"Of course, I'm smiling." He opened his arms and pulled me into them. "This is the best news ever."

"It is?" I pulled back enough to look into his eyes again. "You're not angry or disappointed or shocked?"

"I'm surprised as fuck, but I'm not angry, and I'm definitely not disappointed." He lifted my hands and peppered the backs of them in soft kisses while he spoke. "This is more than I ever could have asked for. I found you, I love you, you love me no matter how big an idiot I've been, and now we get to have a baby. I never thought any of this would happen for me."

"But you wanted it to?" I asked cautiously, afraid to let myself believe that maybe, just maybe, I wasn't going to be alone in this. "When we talked, you said—"

He cut me off by bringing his finger to my lips. "I never said I didn't want it. I want it, baby. I just never wanted it with anyone but you. I'm sorry I was such an asshole, and I'm sorry you felt like you couldn't tell me before, but I love you, Elsie. There's nothing I want more than to make a life and a family with you."

"I'm still angry with you," I murmured as I brought my hands up to rest them on the nape of his neck. "Promise me you'll never lie to me again?"

"I promise." He kissed my eyelids and the tip of my nose. "It was a mistake. I can't promise I'll never make another one, but I do promise it won't be that one. It never even occurred to me that it might look or feel like I was using you because it was the very last thing I intended to do."

I nodded slowly. "You embarrassed me today. Do your parents know I wasn't in on it?"

"Absolutely. I told them everything on the way to the airport. Neither of us fooled my mom anyway. I think it came as a shock for her to hear we weren't really together because she said she could see from a mile away how in love we were with each other."

A smile tugged at the corners of my lips. "Now that I think about it, we have been overly affectionate."

"Exactly." He planted a chaste kiss on my mouth. "Riley said even he was confused when I told them we weren't in a relationship."

"Did you really get things straightened out with your father?"

There was a flash of sadness in his eyes, but he nodded. "I don't think he'll ever fully understand why I didn't join the family business or where he went wrong with me not having farming in my blood, but at least he accepts it now."

"That's great." Tears blurred my vision. I blinked them away, not wanting to miss a second of the earnestness and vulnerability he was showing me right now. "So what now?"

"Now, if it's okay with you, we're going to have makeup sex. Then we're going to make love, and after that, I'm going to hold you all night. In the morning, we'll go back to the farm to get my stuff and clear up some logistics with my dad, and after that, it's up to you. We can stay here. We can go back. Wherever you are is the only place I want to be."

"I can live with that." I pulled him closer and kissed him until we were both breathless and wanting.

The all-consuming need for him made more sense now. I'd read that pregnancy hormones could do this to a person, but holy smokes, I hadn't really gotten it until I got it. I got it completely now, though.

Thankfully, Taydom was more than up to the task. He made love to me for hours before we finally fell to the mattress, sated, sweaty, and exhausted.

As he murmured sweet nothings into my ear, his breath ghosting across my heated skin, I felt that sense of being home again. No matter what had happened between us, it had only brought us closer together.

I had a feeling that it wouldn't matter what we faced in the future. We knew each other's hearts and that would get us through. With thoughts of Taydom's big, beautiful, and surprisingly soft heart swirling through my head, I finally drifted off to sleep and dreamed about how amazing it was that I was going to get to see him being a father.

EPILOGUE

Taydom

"I can't believe it's been six months already," my mother exclaimed as she hugged Elsie, then pulled away to place her hands on the baby bump. "Hello, sweet little grandson in there. Granny can't wait to meet you."

"Mommy can't either." Elsie grimaced as she sank back onto the couch she had vacated to greet my parents. "If he keeps growing at the rate he is now, I'm not going to be able to move by the time he comes."

I dropped a kiss on top of her head as I walked behind her. "It's only another few days, babe. Besides, you don't have to move. I'll just roll you to the hospital when the time comes."

"Taydom," my mother scolded, swatting me on the shoulder when I opened my arms to hug her. "I know you're only joking, but that's just not something you say to a pregnant woman."

"Tell him, Gwen," Elsie cheered while trying to tuck one leg beneath her. "He's been impossible."

"If by impossible, you mean the most loving, caring, helpful father-to-be in the world, then I agree." I turned to wink at her, then held out my hand to shake my dad's.

He shot me a wry smile before he took it. "It's best to listen to your mother on this one, boy. Trust me. I went through it twice and I learned a thing or two about the appropriateness of certain comments, regardless of how true they might be."

Mom did her best to glare at him but broke down laughing as she sat down next to Elsie. "Men, huh? Can't live with them, can't live without them. Will you two go get us something to drink? I'm parched. We've been traveling all day."

"We left home three and a half hours ago, Mom," Riley said, rolling his eyes at her. "You flew here on Taydom's cushy jet and he had a driver pick us up at home. You can't be that parched."

"Don't think just because we're in the big city now that you can get sassy with me," she retorted. "You've also just nominated yourself to be our personal errand boy for the weekend. Go on. Shoo. Two cranberry juices, please."

"You're the best." Elsie smiled at my mom. The two of them had become as thick as thieves after the mishap in Illinois all those months ago.

They video chatted at least once a week and texted almost every day. There was nothing Mom didn't know about Elsie at this point. She'd even had her on video call for one of our appointments at the doctor.

There had been tears. Lots of them. And not only from the women. Seeing my mom and my girl cooing over my baby with his heartbeat coming strong over the ultrasound machine, I might have shed a few tears myself.

Not that I would ever admit it.

Dad followed Riley and me out of the house to the bar in the entertainment area. "When are you flying out again?"

My brother sighed. "Later this afternoon, Dad. You know this. We've been through it twenty times and that's just counting this morning."

"I know," my dad replied gruffly. "Don't take that tone with me. It's been three fucking decades since I've been away from the farm for a couple of weeks."

"You wanted to come with Mom." Riley's exasperation came off him in waves. "If you don't trust me to be in charge, why don't you leave me here and you go back to Illinois?"

Indignation flashed in his eyes, and his nostrils flared. "I'm here for my grandson's birth. I'm not going back. I'm just making sure you're on top of things."

I clapped my brother's shoulder. "Thanks for coming out with them. I know you're only going to be here for a few hours, but it means a lot that you came."

"What are you talking about? I wouldn't miss this for the world." He grinned and wagged his eyebrows at me. "You nervous?"

"Like a fucking cat that hears the bath running." I ducked down to grab the juice out of the bar fridge and filled two glasses before looking at my dad. "You got it, right?"

His weathered face lit up with a smirk, and his dark eyes shone. "Of course, I've got it. You want to see it?"

"Uh, yes? I'm planning on giving it to her in a few minutes. I have to see it and have it on me before I can give it to her." I wiped sweat from my brow with the back of my hand. "Please don't make this any more stressful than it already is."

"You're stressed about giving it to her now? It's a bit late for that, isn't it? You should have been stressed about giving it to her nine months ago."

"My brother, the fucking comedian," I growled while Dad gave Riley a glare that would have made many other men shake in their boots.

Riley just shrugged. "What? It's true. Both of you know pretty damn well how babies are made. If you can make the actual babies, why can't I joke about it?"

"Because it's inappropriate," Dad said, but I didn't miss the small upward tilt of his lips. When he dipped his hand into his pocket, I had to breathe deeply to keep from passing out.

"There you go." He pulled out a shiny black velvet box and handed it over. "Grandma Betty's engagement ring. Resized and cleaned by Mr. Harold's grandson himself. He said to tell you that his grandfather would have been proud you're keeping the ring he made for your grandmother in the family. Said he thought you'd go to one of those fancy stores to buy a new one."

"I thought about it, but I think this will mean more to both of us." I took the box from him, then pulled him in for a back-thumping hug that he only tolerated for all of three seconds. "Thanks for taking care of it for me, Dad."

"You're welcome." He stepped back and jerked his head at the house as he tucked his thumbs into his belt buckle. "Well, you going to make us wait all day or go in there and do what needs to be done?"

I tightened my grip on the box, then flipped it open to reveal the ring I hoped would live on Elsie's finger from here on out.

The gold band was wide and shone like they had polished it to within an inch of its life. In the center was a diamond that reflected rainbows onto the ceiling in the early afternoon light.

Two smaller diamonds sat on either side of the brilliant-cut center stone. It was classic, simple, and beautiful, which was exactly what Elsie had told me she'd always dreamed of in an engagement ring.

She just didn't know about this one. My mother had mentioned my grandmother's ring to her a few times, but they were expecting the baby to be born before I popped the question. Which was why I'd enlisted Dad's and Riley's help.

My parents had wanted to come once the baby was born, but it hadn't been difficult to convince my mother they should come a few days earlier. Elsie had been excited about my mom being at the hospital for the birth. Not necessarily in the room, obviously, but just there.

Since they had become so close, she claimed it was the closest she could come to having her own mother there. I knew it was something she desperately wanted, so I made it happen for her.

There was another reason I'd asked them to come earlier, though, and I was holding it in the palm of my hand. Dad would never have sent the ring via courier, and I'd been too busy getting things set up at work so I could take some time off after the baby came to fetch it from them.

So here they were. My family and the ring were finally all under one roof.

The cottage Elsie had moved into almost a year ago finally had inhabitants again. Well, it would for a few weeks while my parents were here.

After we'd gotten back from Illinois, I'd moved her in with me. It hadn't been that big of a leap for either of us to make, and it had actually gone pretty smoothly.

I had turned the guestroom closest to the master bedroom into a nursery with robin's egg blue walls and puffy clouds painted on them. Airplanes hung from the ceiling and there was one mounted above the changing station.

Elsie and I had finished packing the diaper caddy and a whole bunch of other goods I was going to get intimately familiar with just this morning. Everything was ready, and now that my parents were here, there was only one thing left to do before we were one-hundred-percent ready.

Riley grinned at me. "Go get her, bro. I hope she says yes by the way. It will be super awkward for us to be here if she doesn't."

Wonder above wonder, it was my father who raised his middle finger the fastest. "Don't be jealous, Riley. If you'd pull your head out of your ass, you could be next."

"Fat chance," Riley mumbled. "I like Elsie, though. I don't mind you getting married if it's her you're getting married to."

"Gee, thanks." I flipped him off too, but it was halfhearted.

My father's hand came down on my shoulder, and he squeezed it. "Go ask her. We'll be right here getting things set up. Just send your mom out here if you don't want an audience."

"Thanks." I licked my dry lips and downed half of Elsie's juice before I topped it off again. "Here goes nothing. Wish me luck."

"Luck," both of them said.

Then I walked away. By the time I got back to the living room with their juices, I was practically hyperventilating. I handed my mom's over first. "Dad needs to talk to you about something. They're out back."

"Okay." She frowned. "Is everything okay?"

"Perfect," I said. "We'll be out in a minute."

Her eyes narrowed. Then suddenly, she beamed at me. It was like she'd seen the outline of the ring box in my pocket or maybe—and this was the more likely scenario—my father and brother hadn't been able to pull one over on her.

I hadn't wanted to leave her out of the process, but I'd wanted it to be a surprise. Besides, it wasn't like there had really been a process. My father had gotten the ring out of their safe and taken it to Mr. Harold's store. Riley had picked it up again a few days later and gave it back to Dad, who had put it back in the safe until this morning.

There were tears in my mother's eyes as she blew me a kiss and winked at me before leaving the room. But Elsie didn't see her. She was looking at me with her head tilted and her eyes narrowed in suspicion.

"What's going on this time?"

"What do you mean?" I asked innocently, pretending there wasn't a ring burning a fucking hole in my pocket right then.

She crossed her arms under her deliciously swollen breasts, smacking me when she noticed my gaze had dropped. "I mean that I know that look, and the other one. You're up to something, and no, we're not ducking out for a quickie. Your parents just arrived."

"I know, but we can make it real quick." I smirked at her and bent over to kiss her, but she shook her head and only allowed a small kiss before she arched a questioning brow at me.

I lifted my hands out to my sides. "Okay, fine. If you insist on knowing what I'm up to, please come with me."

"Come with you where?"

"Just come with me. I promise it's not far." It wasn't, but I knew it would feel that way to her. I held out my hand and breathed an internal sigh of relief when she took it.

"You know walking can induce labor, right?" She groaned as she stood up, immediately bringing her hand to her left side. "The baby and one of my ribs are having a fight. My rib is losing, in case you were wondering."

"I'm sorry, baby." I pressed a kiss against her temple as we walked to the front door. "He'll be here soon at least."

"Yeah, I know." She smiled as she melted into my side and wound an arm around my waist. "Where are we going?"

"Just outside for a second." I opened the door, and once we were out, I slung my arm over her shoulders again.

Elsie shielded her eyes from the sun with the hand not around my body, leaning back a bit to glance up at me. "Why exactly are we going outside?"

"You'll see." I led her to the driveway. More specifically, to the first bend in it. It was where I had first heard her gasp when she saw the cottage.

When we stopped there, she frowned up at me. "What are we doing, babe?"

"Give or take a month or two, about a year ago, I drove up this very driveway with a girl I had met recently on my mind. Try as I might, I couldn't stop thinking about her. I knew she was looking for a place to stay, and despite how crazy it seemed, when I came home, I wondered if she wouldn't enjoy living here. With me."

"You'd better be talking about me," she teased and put her hands on her hips as she peered up at me. "Why the trip down memory lane, love?"

"Because of exactly that. I love you. I knew you were different from the moment I met you, and I'm pretty sure my love for you was always there. It was just waiting for you to come along, and then it was waiting for my stupid brain to catch up."

"Your brain isn't stupid," she said and smiled at me. "It might have had that one lapse in judgment, but we've moved past that."

"Yeah, I know we have, but it was still stupid to have gotten you involved." I ran one hand through my hair and stuck the other into my pocket, pulling out the ring before lowering myself down onto one knee.

Elsie sucked in a sharp breath but didn't interrupt me again.

"I was so happy when you agreed to take this place. It didn't make any sense to me at the time, but now I know it was because my soul recognized yours as its mate. I want us to be a family, Elsie. Will you marry me?"

Tears glistened in her eyes, and when I popped open the box, her hands flew to her mouth. "Taydom, that's absolutely beautiful."

I straightened up and wound my arms around her waist, her hard belly pressed up against me. "It was my grandmother's. What do you say? Want to wear it for, say, the rest of your life?"

"Yes." She gave me the biggest, most gorgeous smile before going up on her toes and looping her arms around my neck. "I'd love to, baby. I love you so much."

My family must have sneaked around the corner of the house from the entertainment area because as I was sliding the ring onto Elsie finger, loud cheering and whooping started. When I jerked my head around to see what was happening, all three of them plus Andrew and Beth—who I had no idea how or when they had gotten in—came running at us.

Riley winked at me. So I had a good idea he'd had something to do with ensuring that our best friends were here for this. When he gave me a hug to congratulate me, he confirmed it. "I thought she might want her friend here, and since Drew has been there for you when I couldn't, I figured he should be here too."

"Thanks, bro." I pulled away from him to see Mom, Beth, and Elsie in a group hug. Unable to resist, I went to join them, then felt Andrew and Riley close ranks at my sides.

When another pair of arms surrounded mine, I turned my head to see even my father had joined in on the hug. At the question in my eyes, he simply shrugged.

"What? If this is the beginning of a happily ever after, I want to be in on it this time."

"It's not an *if*." I winked at him and planted a kiss on Elsie's cheek. "It *is* the beginning of a happily ever after."

Elsie turned in the center of everyone's arms to seek mine out. When I drew her up against me, her eyes went wide. "I hate to break up this moment, but I'm pretty sure the happily ever after is about to start right now."

Panic hit my gut, but I jumped into action the next second. "It's okay, baby. We're prepared for this."

Throwing an arm into the air, I waved it in a circular motion and made eye contact with my brother and best friend. "Pack it all in, boys. We're continuing this party at the hospital. There's going to be one extra guest joining us.

Elsie grinned at me. Then her face contorted as she grabbed my arm. "You're going to have to bring the car around. The part of the happily ever after who's been growing inside me has decided he's tired of waiting. He's not missing this party, even if it means he has to come out right now."

"I'm on it." I smacked another kiss on her temple. "I've got you, baby. Always. Forever."

It was only a little over an hour later when Cooper James Gaines came kicking and screaming into the world. I lost my heart to the little guy the first time I held him in my arms, and as I watched Elsie cradling him, I knew that our happily ever after was off to the best start it could have gotten.

The End.

ABOUT THE AUTHOR

Hey there. I'm Weston.

Have we met? No? Well, it's time to end that tragedy.

I'm a former firefighter/EMS guy who's picked up the proverbial pen and started writing bad boy romance stories. I co-write with my sister, Ali Parker, but live in Texas with my wife, my two little boys, a dog, and a turtle.

Yep. A turtle. You read that right. Don't be jealous.

You're going to find Billionaires, Bad Boys, Military Guys, and loads of sexiness. Something for everyone hopefully.

Fake It For Me

My Holiday Reunion

Take It Down A Notch

Show Me What You Got

Heartbreaker

Made in the USA
Middletown, DE
22 May 2020